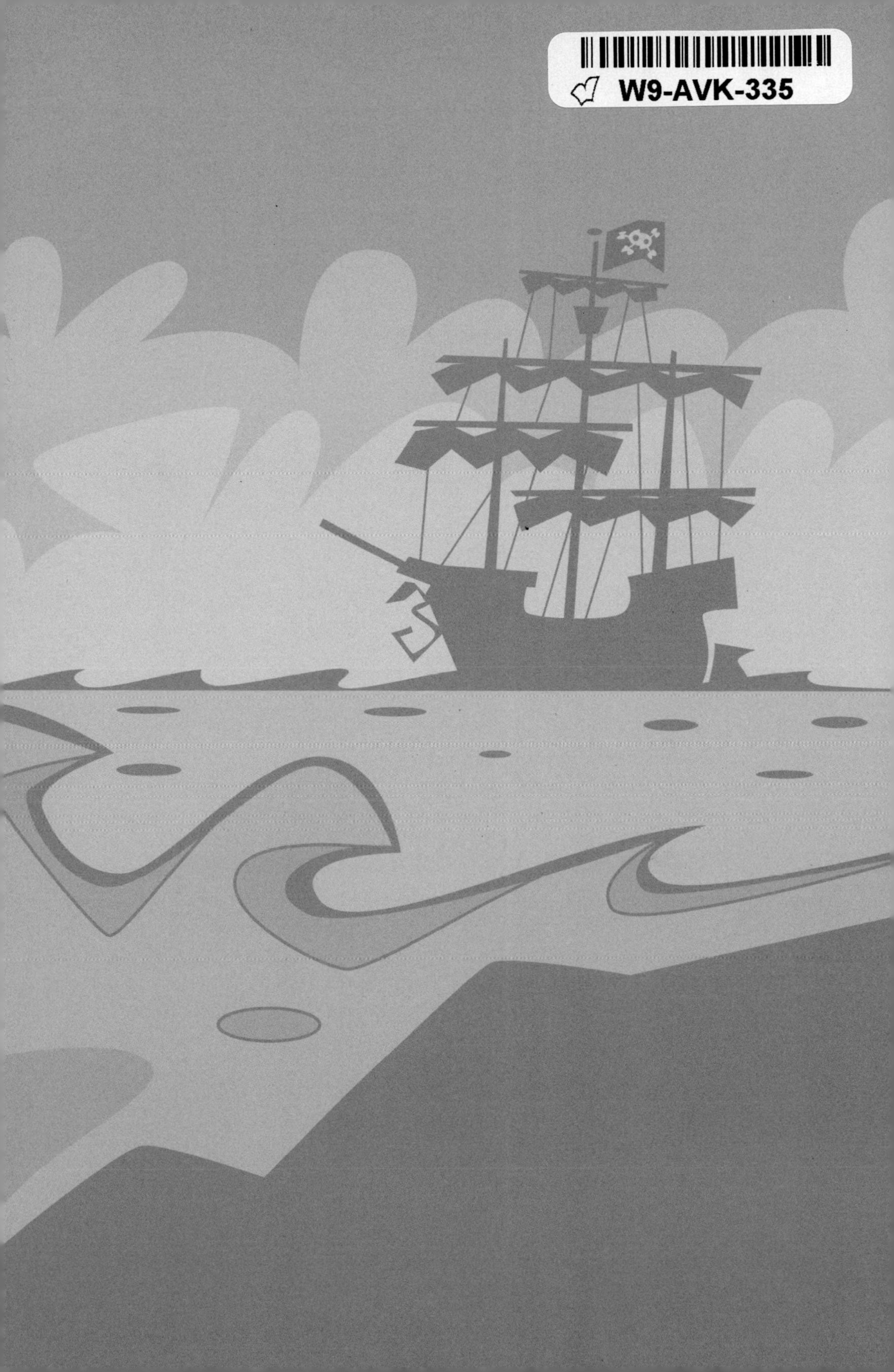

HORRENDO'S
CURSE

ANNA FIENBERG

ART BY
RÉMY SIMARD

ADAPTED BY ALISON KOOISTRA

 annick press
toronto + new york + vancouver

FOR STEFANO WITH LOVE—A.F.
TO BENOIT C.—R.S.

Graphic novel adaptation by Alison Kooistra
Based on the novel *Horrendo's Curse*, © 2002 Anna Fienberg
Cover design by Natalie Olsen, Kisscut Design

Annick Press Ltd.

We acknowledge the support of the Canada Council for the Arts, the Ontario Arts Council, and the Government of Canada through the Canada Book Fund (CBF) for our publishing activities.

ONTARIO ARTS COUNCIL
CONSEIL DES ARTS DE L'ONTARIO
50 YEARS OF ONTARIO GOVERNMENT SUPPORT OF THE ARTS
50 ANS DE SOUTIEN DU GOUVERNEMENT DE L'ONTARIO AUX ARTS

Cataloging in Publication

Kooistra, Alison, 1979-
     Horrendo's curse : the graphic novel / Anna Fienberg ; art
by Rémy Simard ; adapted by Alison Kooistra.

Also issued in electronic format.
ISBN 978-1-55451-549-3 (bound).—ISBN 978-1-55451-548-6 (pbk.)

     1. Fienberg, Anna. Horrendo's curse. 2. Graphic novels.
I. Simard, Rémy II. Title.

PN6733.K65H67 2013   j741.5'971   C2013-901251-6

Printed in China

Published in the U.S.A.
by Annick Press (U.S.) Ltd.

Distributed in Canada by
Firefly Books Ltd.
50 Staples Avenue, Unit 1
Richmond Hill, ON
L4B 0A7

Distributed in the U.S.A. by
Firefly Books (U.S.) Inc.
P.O. Box 1338
Ellicott Station
Buffalo, NY 14205

Visit us at: **www.annickpress.com**
Visit Rémy Simard at: **www.remysimard.com**

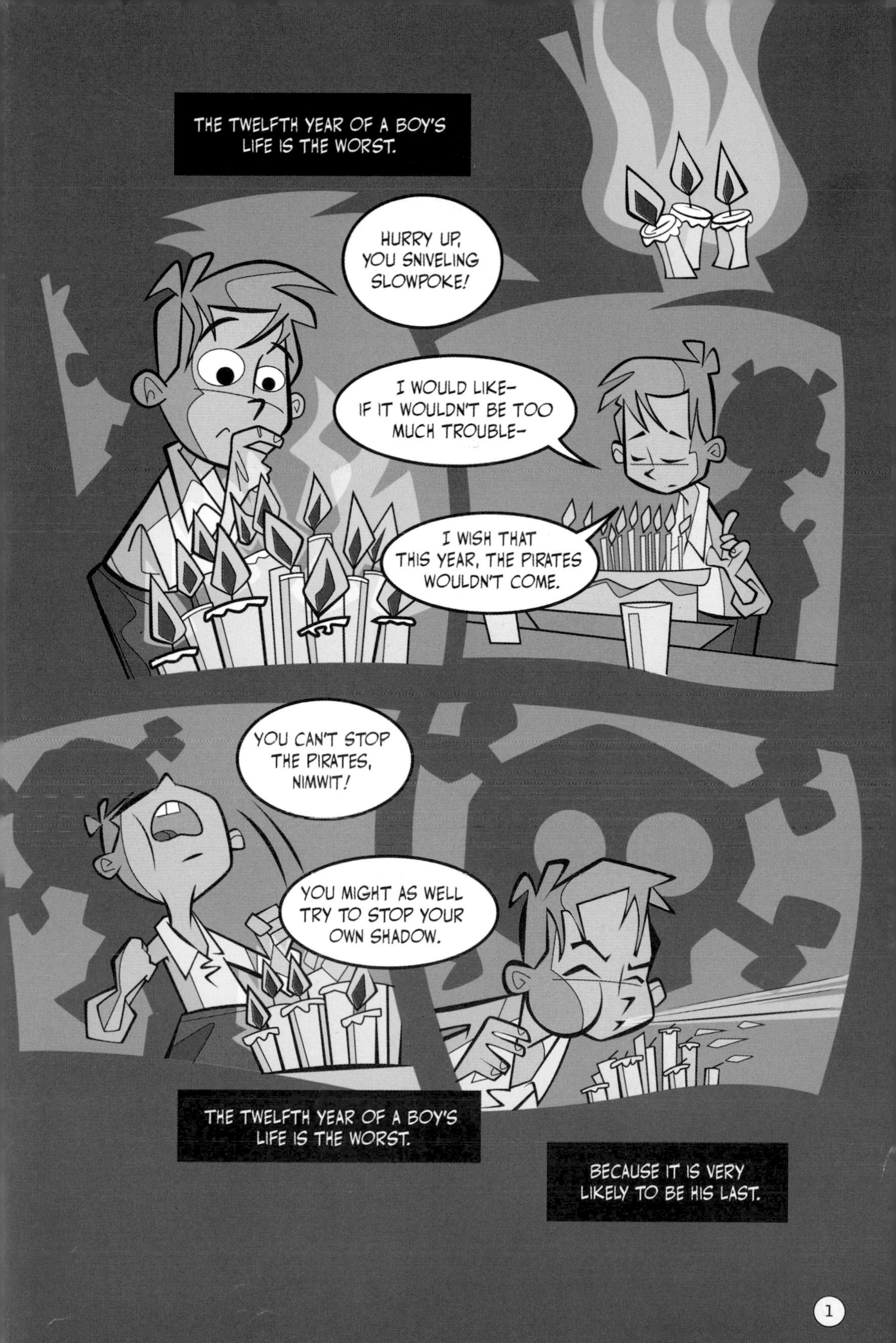
THE TWELFTH YEAR OF A BOY'S LIFE IS THE WORST.
HURRY UP, YOU SNIVELING SLOWPOKE!
I WOULD LIKE– IF IT WOULDN'T BE TOO MUCH TROUBLE–
I WISH THAT THIS YEAR, THE PIRATES WOULDN'T COME.
YOU CAN'T STOP THE PIRATES, NIMWIT!
YOU MIGHT AS WELL TRY TO STOP YOUR OWN SHADOW.
THE TWELFTH YEAR OF A BOY'S LIFE IS THE WORST.
BECAUSE IT IS VERY LIKELY TO BE HIS LAST.

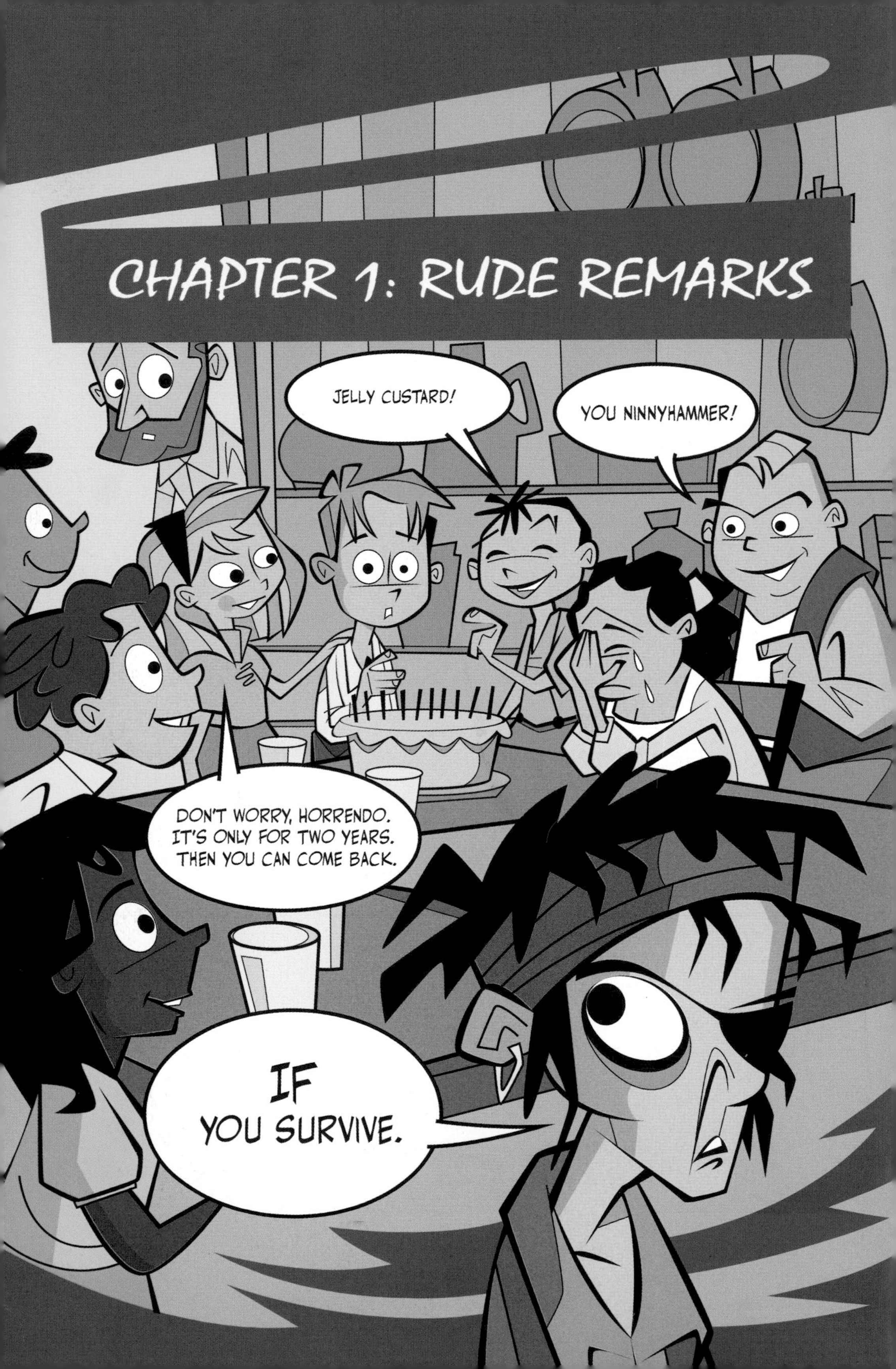
CHAPTER 1: RUDE REMARKS
JELLY CUSTARD!
YOU NINNYHAMMER!
DON'T WORRY, HORRENDO. IT'S ONLY FOR TWO YEARS. THEN YOU CAN COME BACK.
IF YOU SURVIVE.

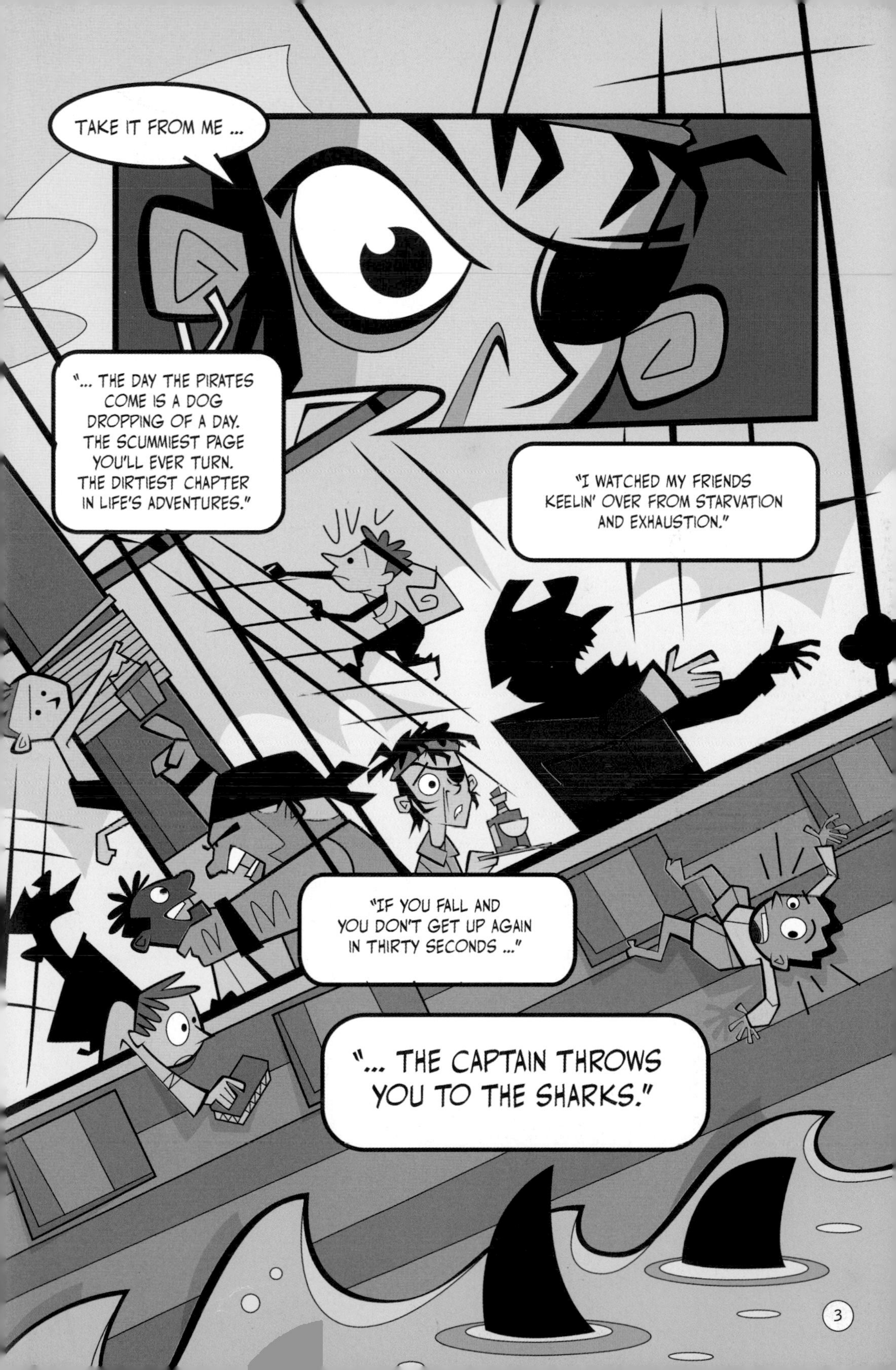

TAKE IT FROM ME ...
"... THE DAY THE PIRATES COME IS A DOG DROPPING OF A DAY. THE SCUMMIEST PAGE YOU'LL EVER TURN. THE DIRTIEST CHAPTER IN LIFE'S ADVENTURES."
"I WATCHED MY FRIENDS KEELIN' OVER FROM STARVATION AND EXHAUSTION."
"IF YOU FALL AND YOU DON'T GET UP AGAIN IN THIRTY SECONDS ..."
"... THE CAPTAIN THROWS YOU TO THE SHARKS."

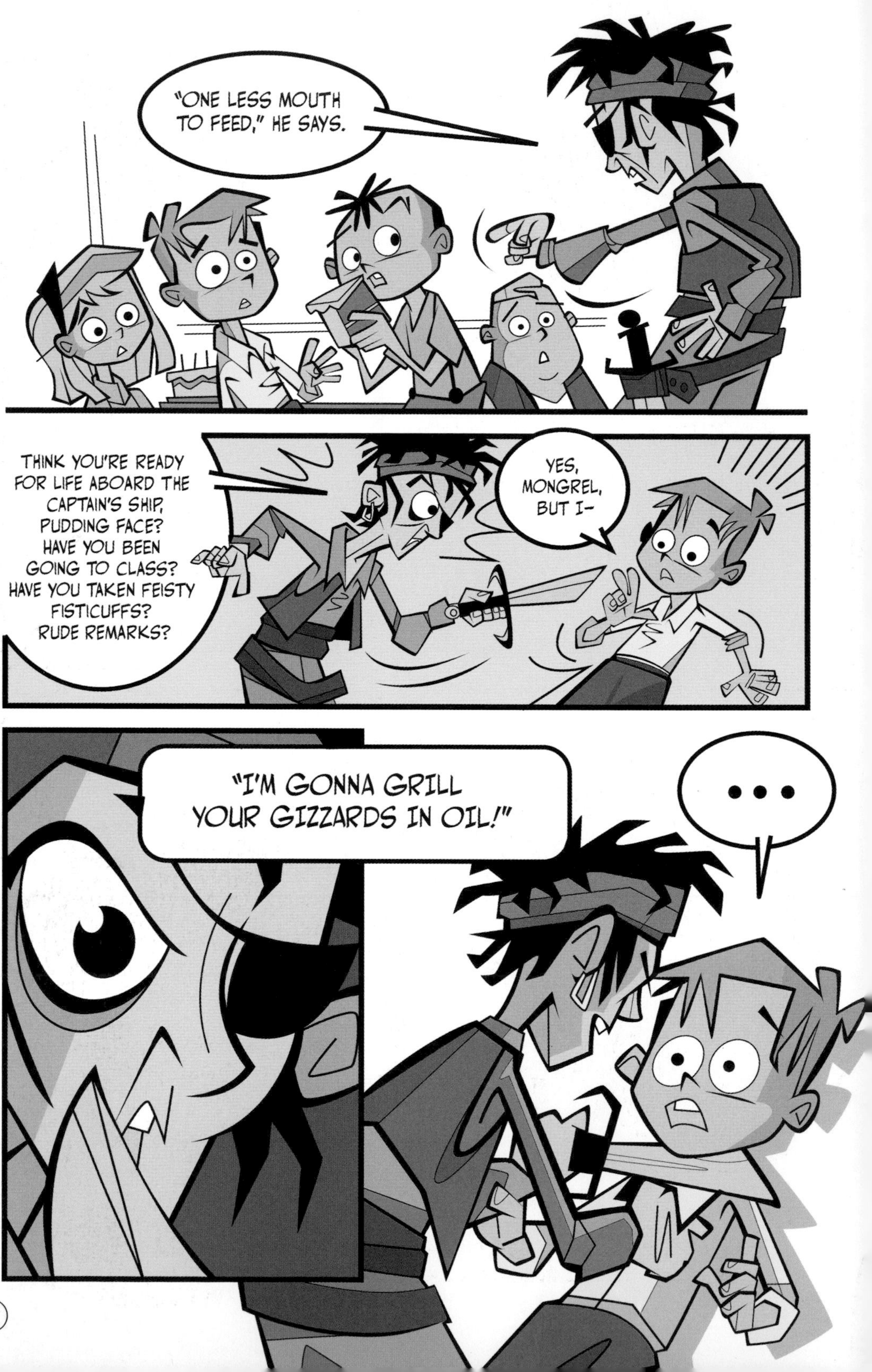
"ONE LESS MOUTH TO FEED," HE SAYS.
THINK YOU'RE READY FOR LIFE ABOARD THE CAPTAIN'S SHIP, PUDDING FACE? HAVE YOU BEEN GOING TO CLASS? HAVE YOU TAKEN FEISTY FISTICUFFS? RUDE REMARKS?
YES, MONGREL, BUT I–
"I'M GONNA GRILL YOUR GIZZARDS IN OIL!"
...

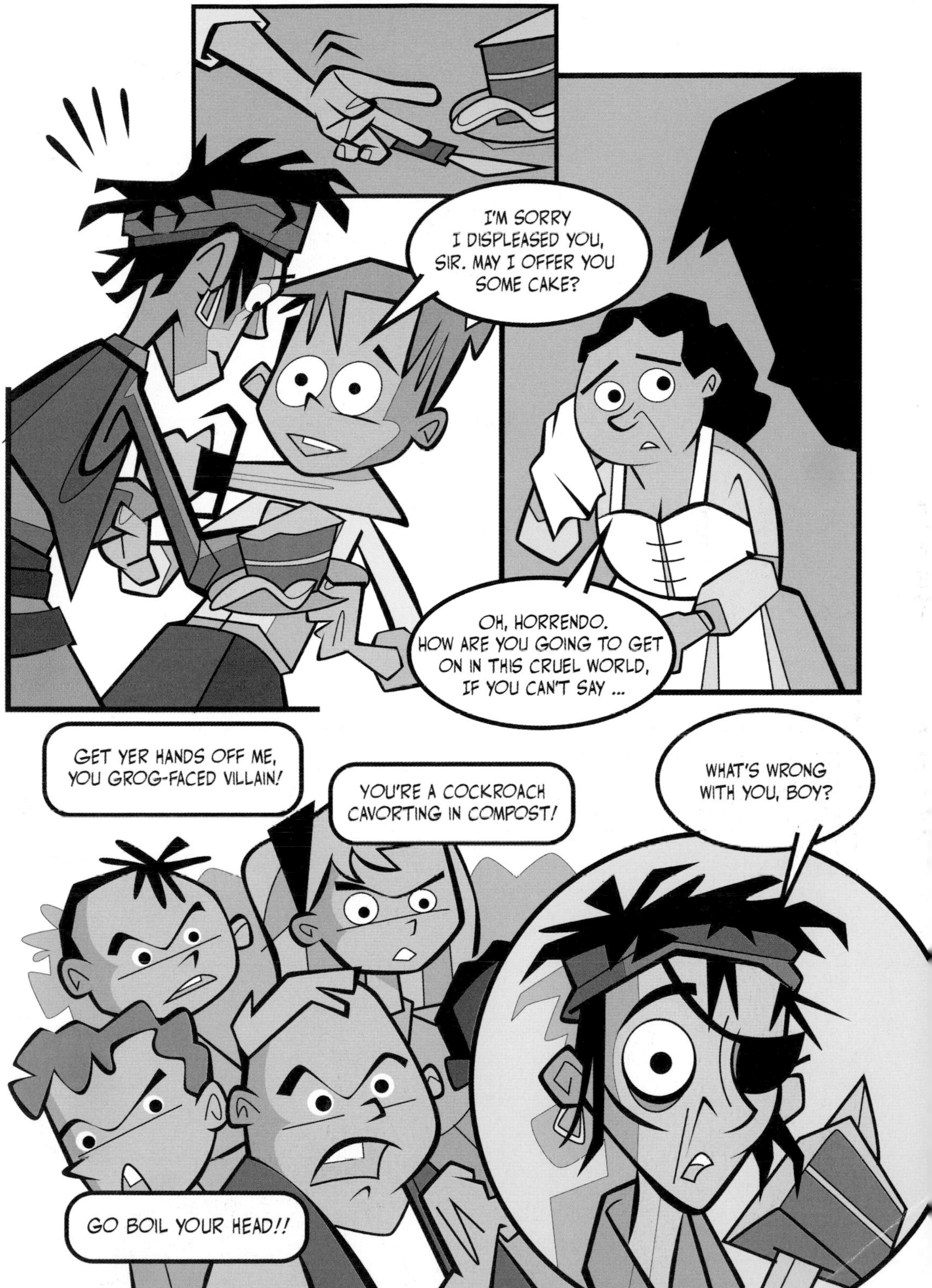
I'M SORRY I DISPLEASED YOU, SIR. MAY I OFFER YOU SOME CAKE?
OH, HORRENDO. HOW ARE YOU GOING TO GET ON IN THIS CRUEL WORLD, IF YOU CAN'T SAY ...
GET YER HANDS OFF ME, YOU GROG-FACED VILLAIN!
YOU'RE A COCKROACH CAVORTING IN COMPOST!
WHAT'S WRONG WITH YOU, BOY?
GO BOIL YOUR HEAD!!

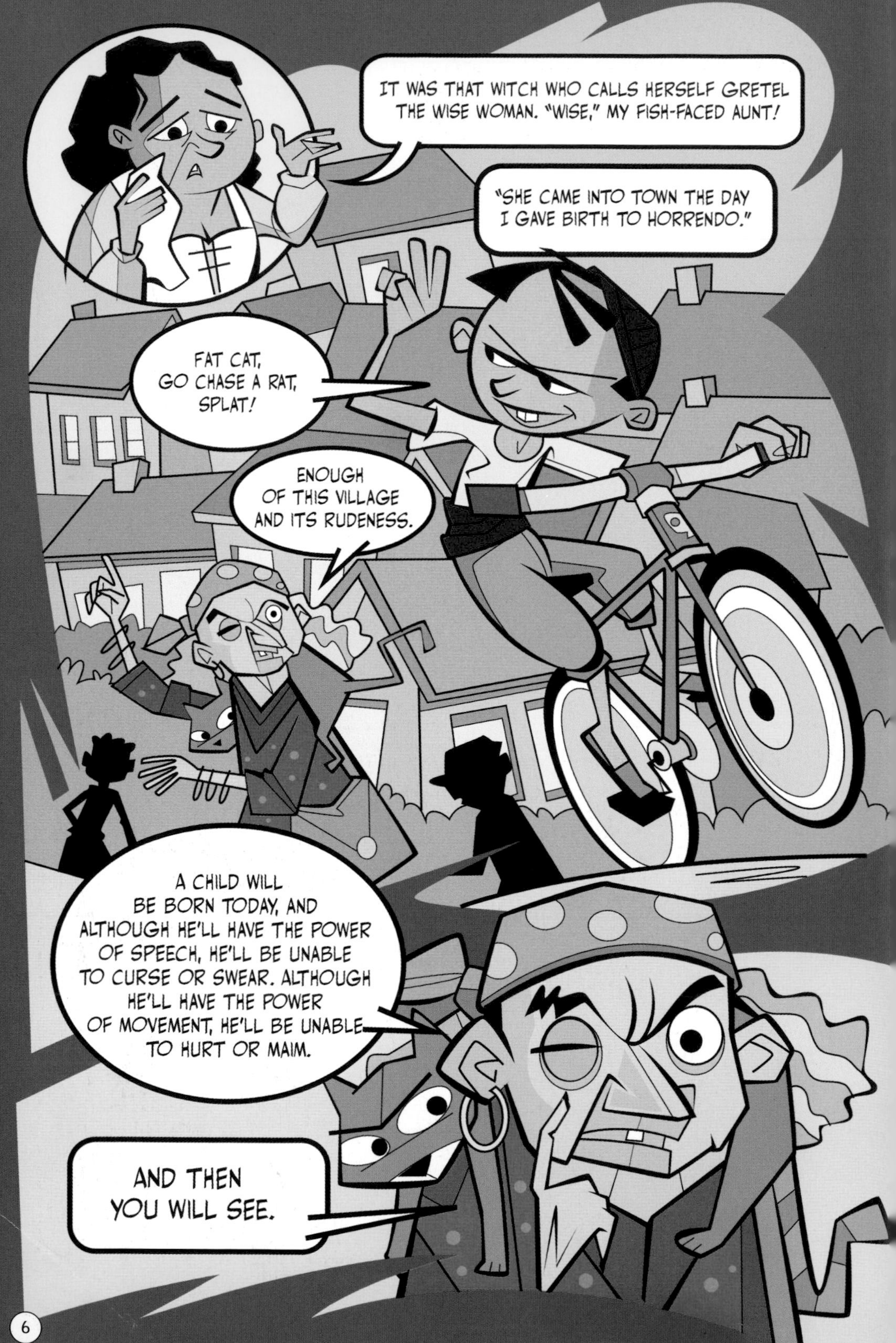
IT WAS THAT WITCH WHO CALLS HERSELF GRETEL THE WISE WOMAN. "WISE," MY FISH-FACED AUNT!
"SHE CAME INTO TOWN THE DAY I GAVE BIRTH TO HORRENDO."
FAT CAT, GO CHASE A RAT, SPLAT!
ENOUGH OF THIS VILLAGE AND ITS RUDENESS.
A CHILD WILL BE BORN TODAY, AND ALTHOUGH HE'LL HAVE THE POWER OF SPEECH, HE'LL BE UNABLE TO CURSE OR SWEAR. ALTHOUGH HE'LL HAVE THE POWER OF MOVEMENT, HE'LL BE UNABLE TO HURT OR MAIM.
AND THEN YOU WILL SEE.

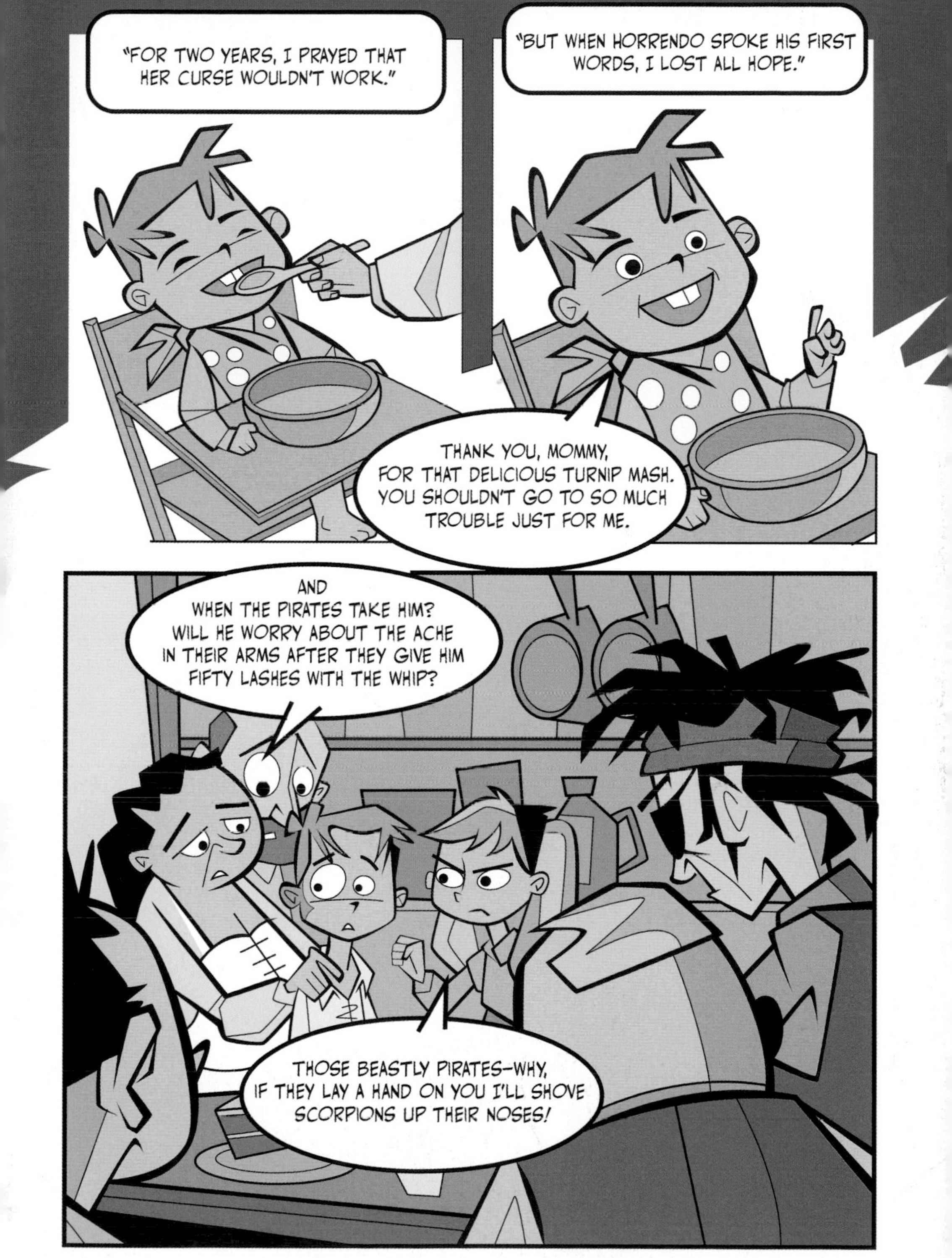
"FOR TWO YEARS, I PRAYED THAT HER CURSE WOULDN'T WORK."
"BUT WHEN HORRENDO SPOKE HIS FIRST WORDS, I LOST ALL HOPE."
THANK YOU, MOMMY, FOR THAT DELICIOUS TURNIP MASH. YOU SHOULDN'T GO TO SO MUCH TROUBLE JUST FOR ME.
AND WHEN THE PIRATES TAKE HIM? WILL HE WORRY ABOUT THE ACHE IN THEIR ARMS AFTER THEY GIVE HIM FIFTY LASHES WITH THE WHIP?
THOSE BEASTLY PIRATES—WHY, IF THEY LAY A HAND ON YOU I'LL SHOVE SCORPIONS UP THEIR NOSES!

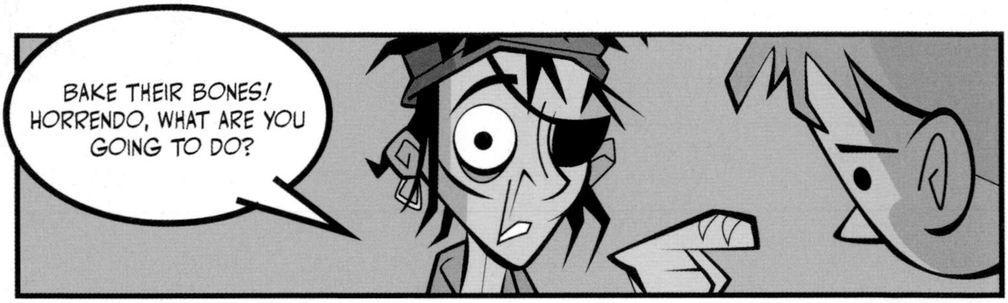
BAKE THEIR BONES! HORRENDO, WHAT ARE YOU GOING TO DO?

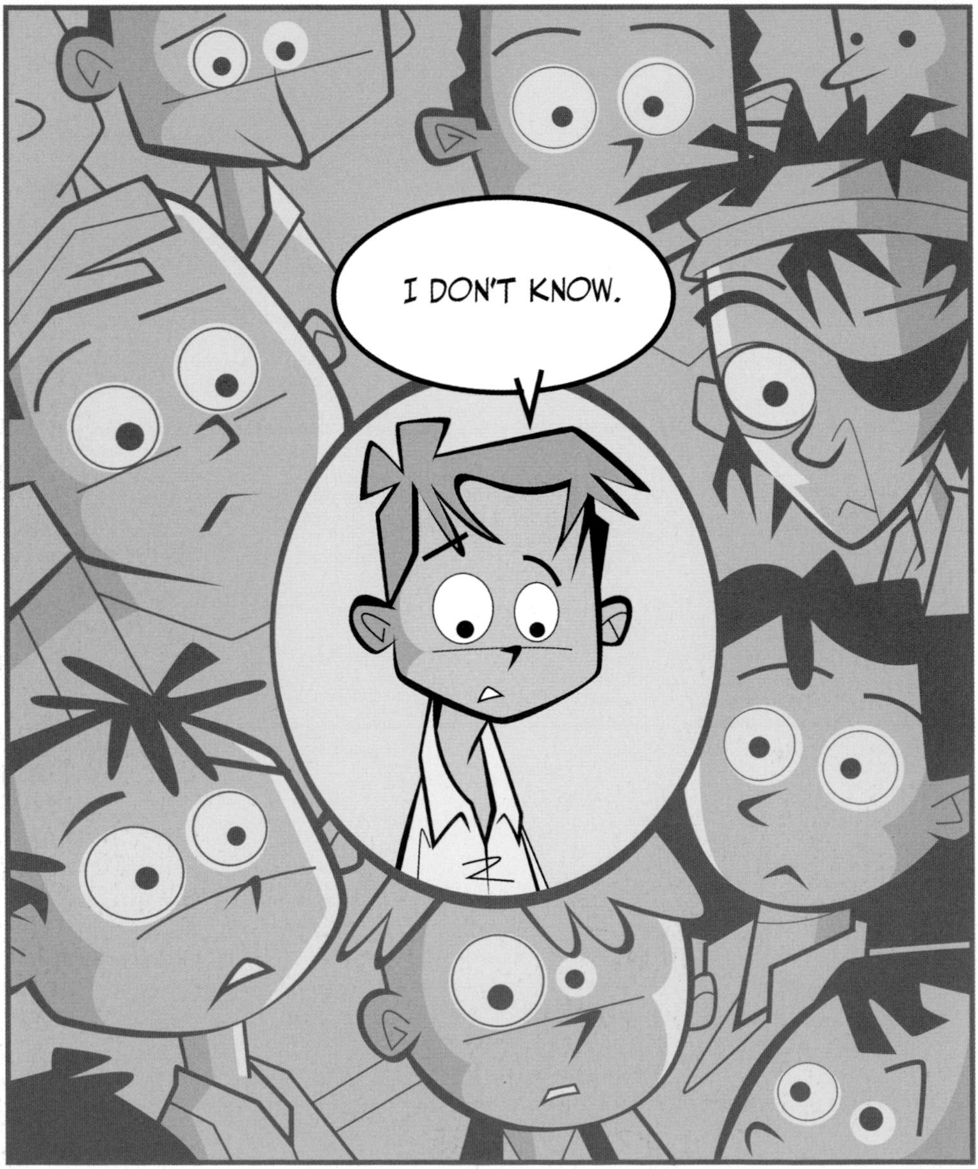
I DON'T KNOW.

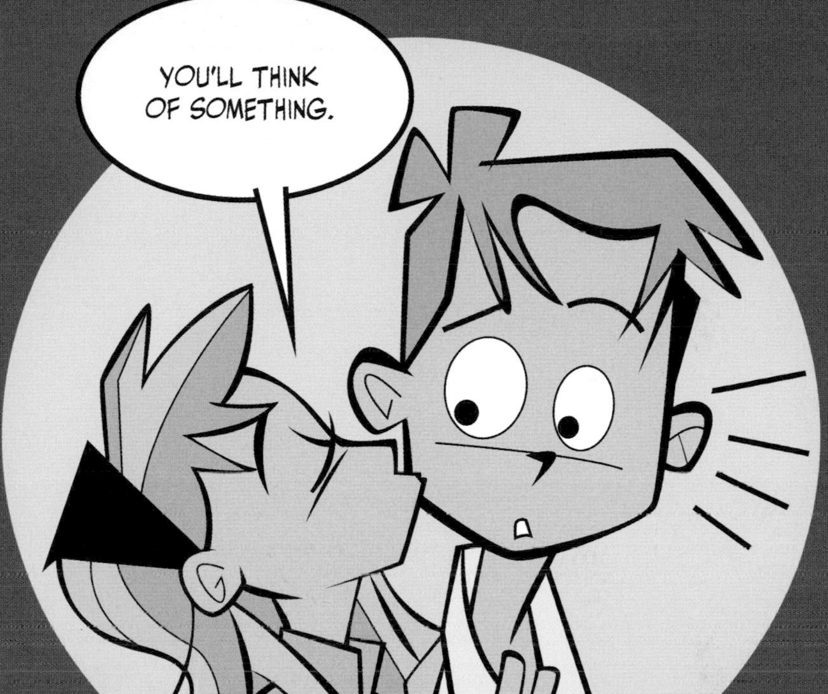
YOU'LL THINK OF SOMETHING.

CHAPTER 2: PETRIFYING PETS

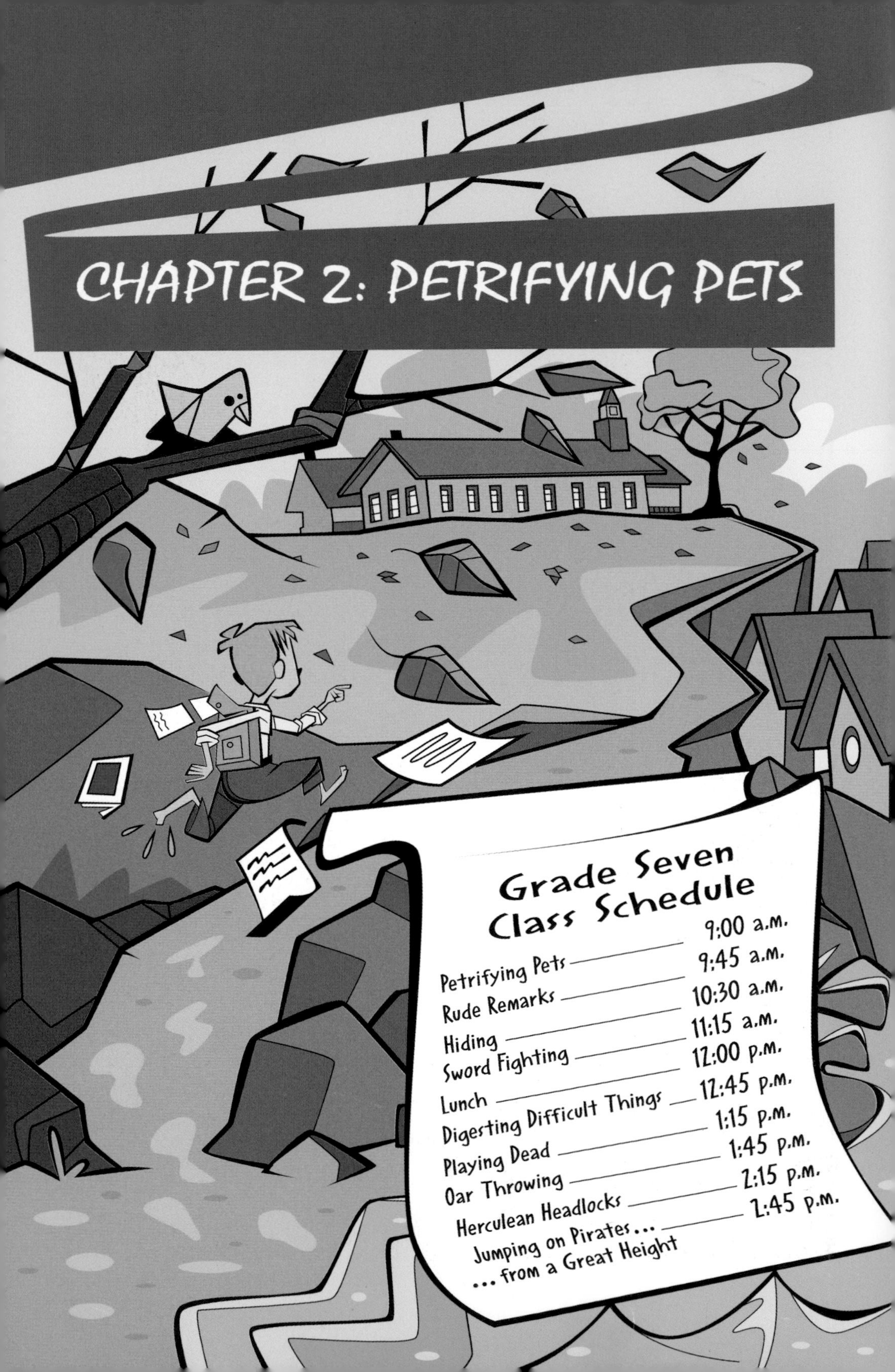
Grade Seven
Class Schedule
Petrifying Pets — 9:00 a.m.
Rude Remarks — 9:45 a.m.
Hiding — 10:30 a.m.
Sword Fighting — 11:15 a.m.
Lunch — 12:00 p.m.
Digesting Difficult Things — 12:45 p.m.
Playing Dead — 1:15 p.m.
Oar Throwing — 1:45 p.m.
Herculean Headlocks — 2:15 p.m.
Jumping on Pirates ...
... from a Great Height — 2:45 p.m.

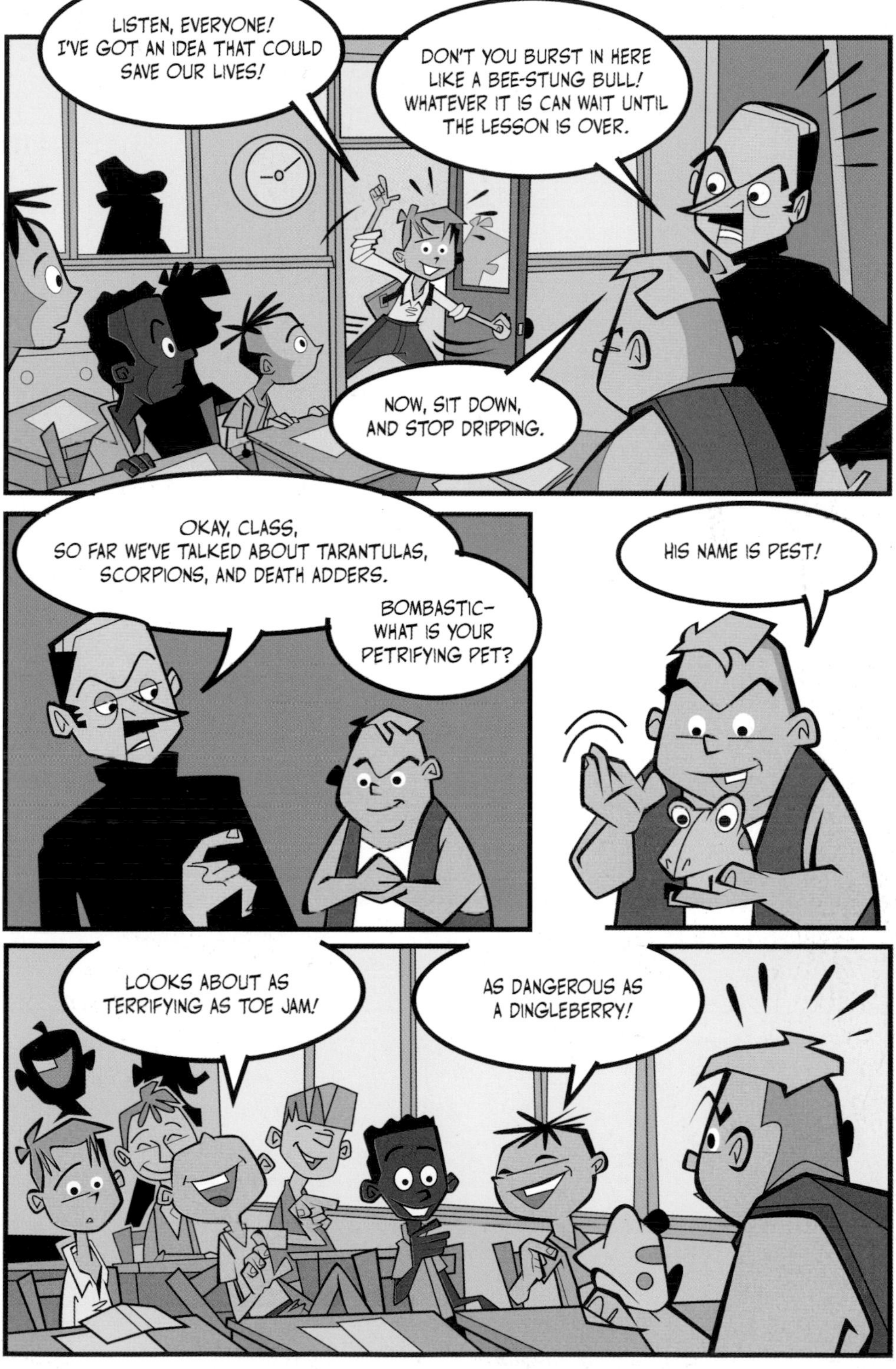
LISTEN, EVERYONE! I'VE GOT AN IDEA THAT COULD SAVE OUR LIVES!
DON'T YOU BURST IN HERE LIKE A BEE-STUNG BULL! WHATEVER IT IS CAN WAIT UNTIL THE LESSON IS OVER.
NOW, SIT DOWN, AND STOP DRIPPING.
OKAY, CLASS, SO FAR WE'VE TALKED ABOUT TARANTULAS, SCORPIONS, AND DEATH ADDERS.
BOMBASTIC- WHAT IS YOUR PETRIFYING PET?
HIS NAME IS PEST!
LOOKS ABOUT AS TERRIFYING AS TOE JAM!
AS DANGEROUS AS A DINGLEBERRY!

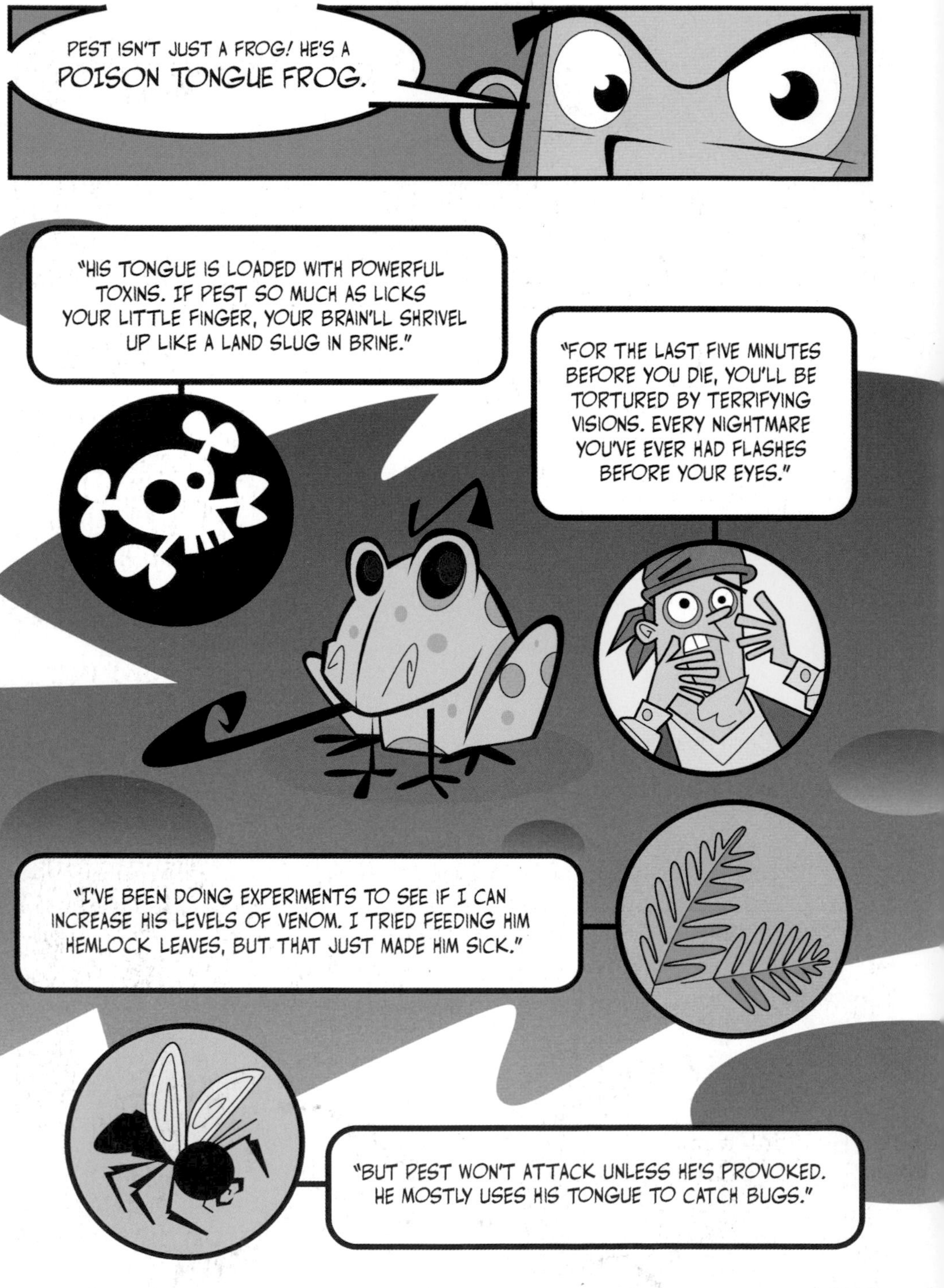
PEST ISN'T JUST A FROG! HE'S A POISON TONGUE FROG.
"HIS TONGUE IS LOADED WITH POWERFUL TOXINS. IF PEST SO MUCH AS LICKS YOUR LITTLE FINGER, YOUR BRAIN'LL SHRIVEL UP LIKE A LAND SLUG IN BRINE."
"FOR THE LAST FIVE MINUTES BEFORE YOU DIE, YOU'LL BE TORTURED BY TERRIFYING VISIONS. EVERY NIGHTMARE YOU'VE EVER HAD FLASHES BEFORE YOUR EYES."
"I'VE BEEN DOING EXPERIMENTS TO SEE IF I CAN INCREASE HIS LEVELS OF VENOM. I TRIED FEEDING HIM HEMLOCK LEAVES, BUT THAT JUST MADE HIM SICK."
"BUT PEST WON'T ATTACK UNLESS HE'S PROVOKED. HE MOSTLY USES HIS TONGUE TO CATCH BUGS."

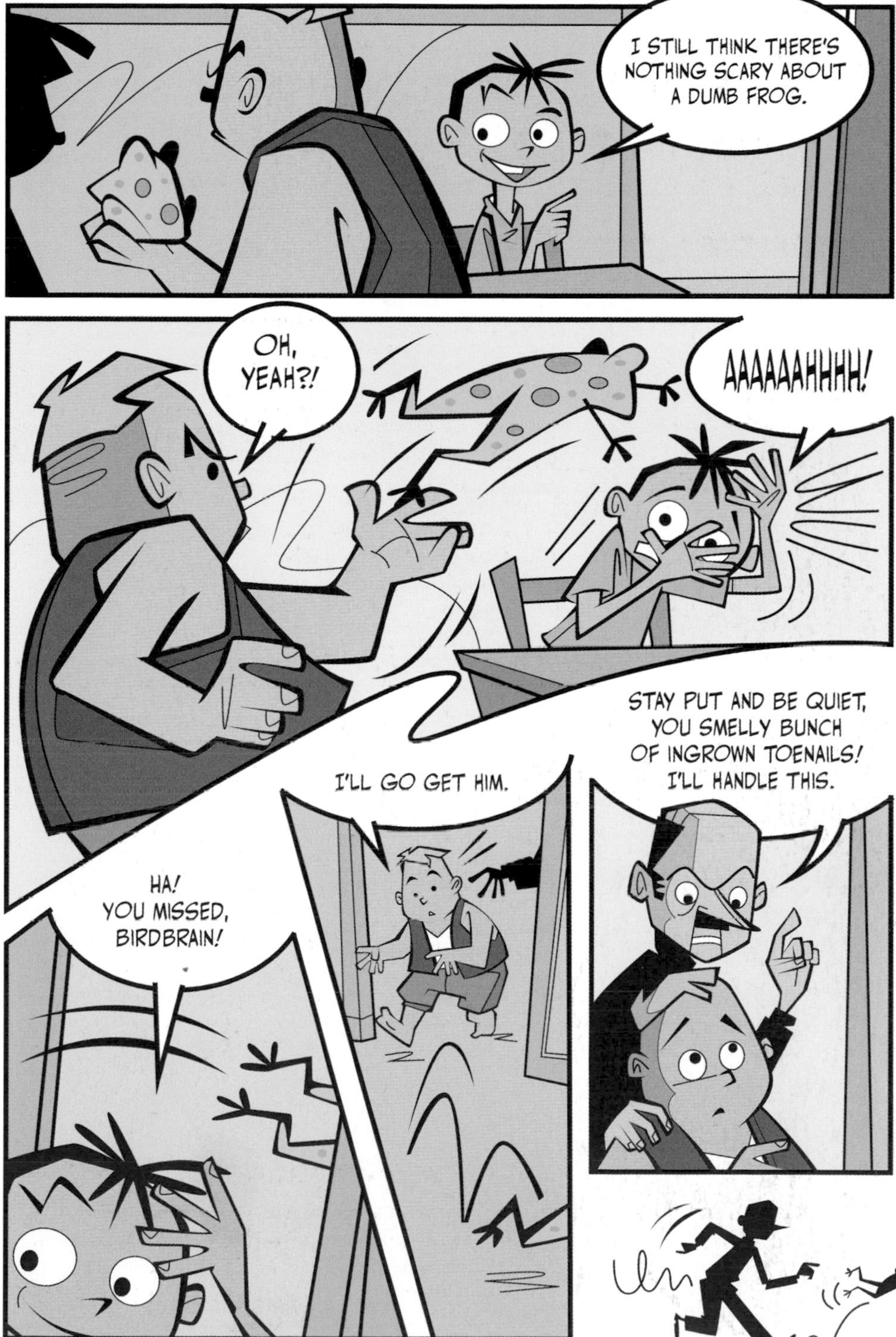
I STILL THINK THERE'S NOTHING SCARY ABOUT A DUMB FROG.
OH, YEAH?!
AAAAAAHHHH!
I'LL GO GET HIM.
STAY PUT AND BE QUIET, YOU SMELLY BUNCH OF INGROWN TOENAILS! I'LL HANDLE THIS.
HA! YOU MISSED, BIRDBRAIN!

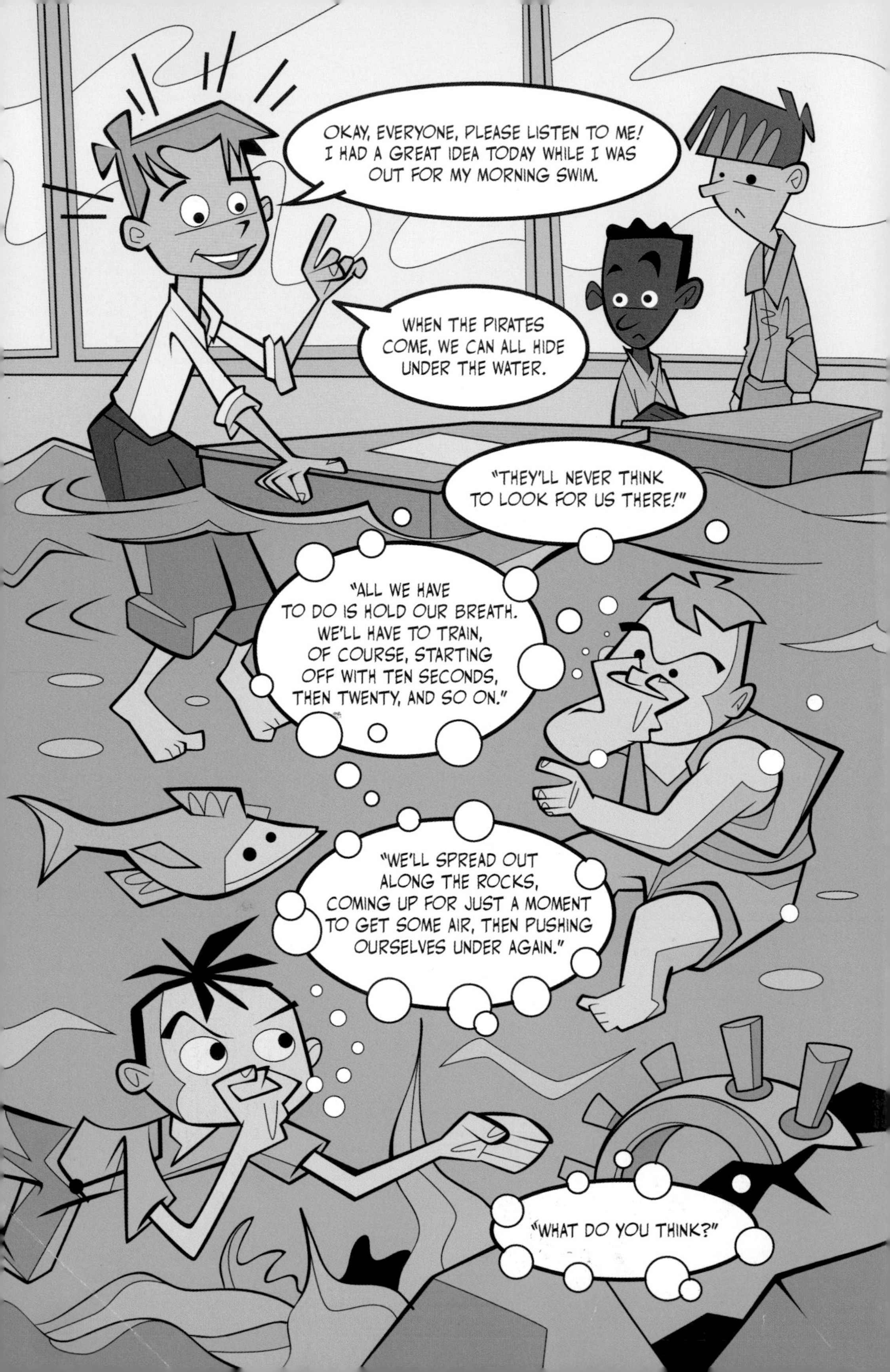
OKAY, EVERYONE, PLEASE LISTEN TO ME! I HAD A GREAT IDEA TODAY WHILE I WAS OUT FOR MY MORNING SWIM.
WHEN THE PIRATES COME, WE CAN ALL HIDE UNDER THE WATER.
"THEY'LL NEVER THINK TO LOOK FOR US THERE!"
"ALL WE HAVE TO DO IS HOLD OUR BREATH. WE'LL HAVE TO TRAIN, OF COURSE, STARTING OFF WITH TEN SECONDS, THEN TWENTY, AND SO ON."
"WE'LL SPREAD OUT ALONG THE ROCKS, COMING UP FOR JUST A MOMENT TO GET SOME AIR, THEN PUSHING OURSELVES UNDER AGAIN."
"WHAT DO YOU THINK?"

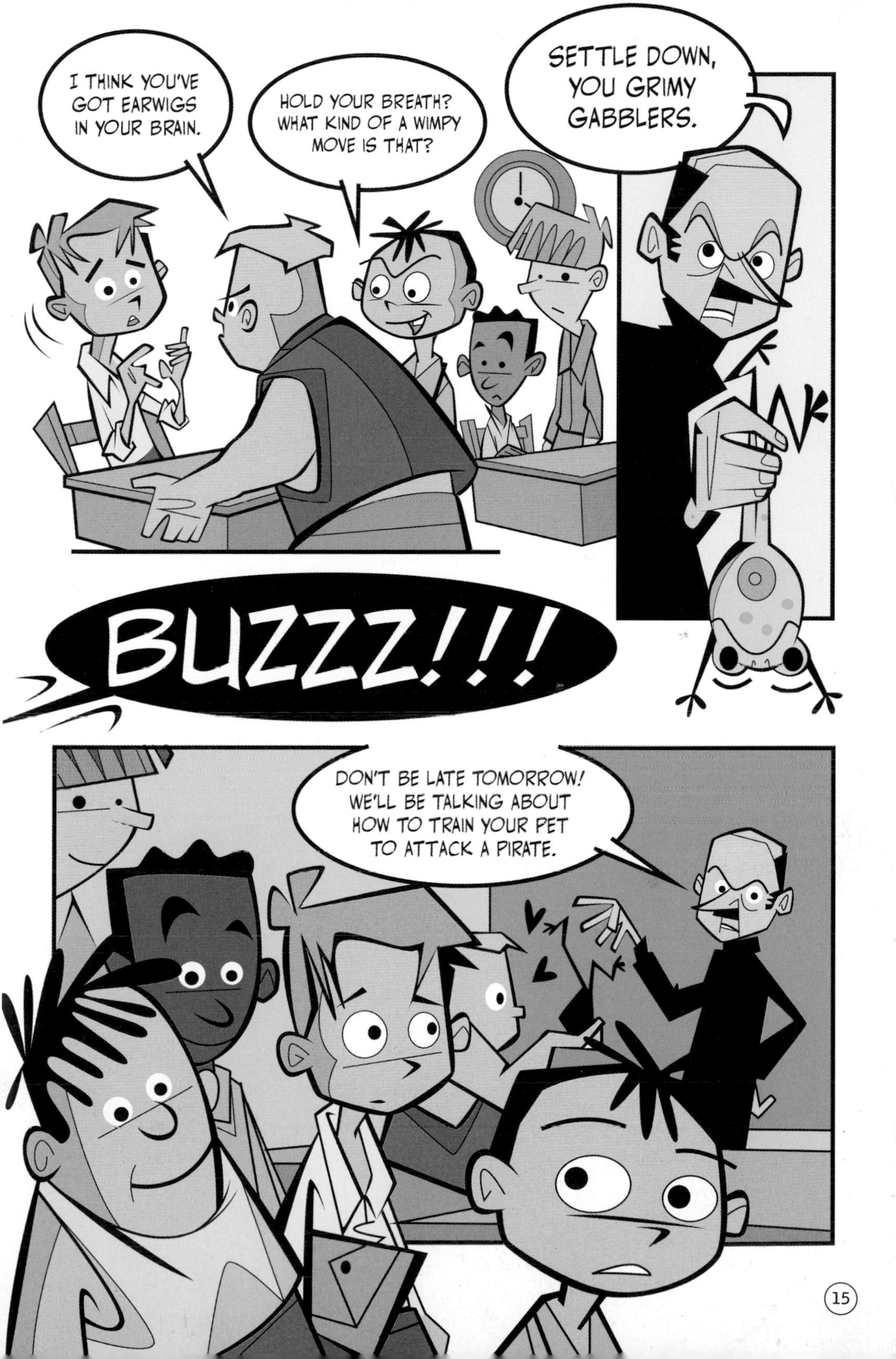
I THINK YOU'VE GOT EARWIGS IN YOUR BRAIN.
HOLD YOUR BREATH? WHAT KIND OF A WIMPY MOVE IS THAT?
SETTLE DOWN, YOU GRIMY GABBLERS.
BUZZZ!!!
DON'T BE LATE TOMORROW! WE'LL BE TALKING ABOUT HOW TO TRAIN YOUR PET TO ATTACK A PIRATE.

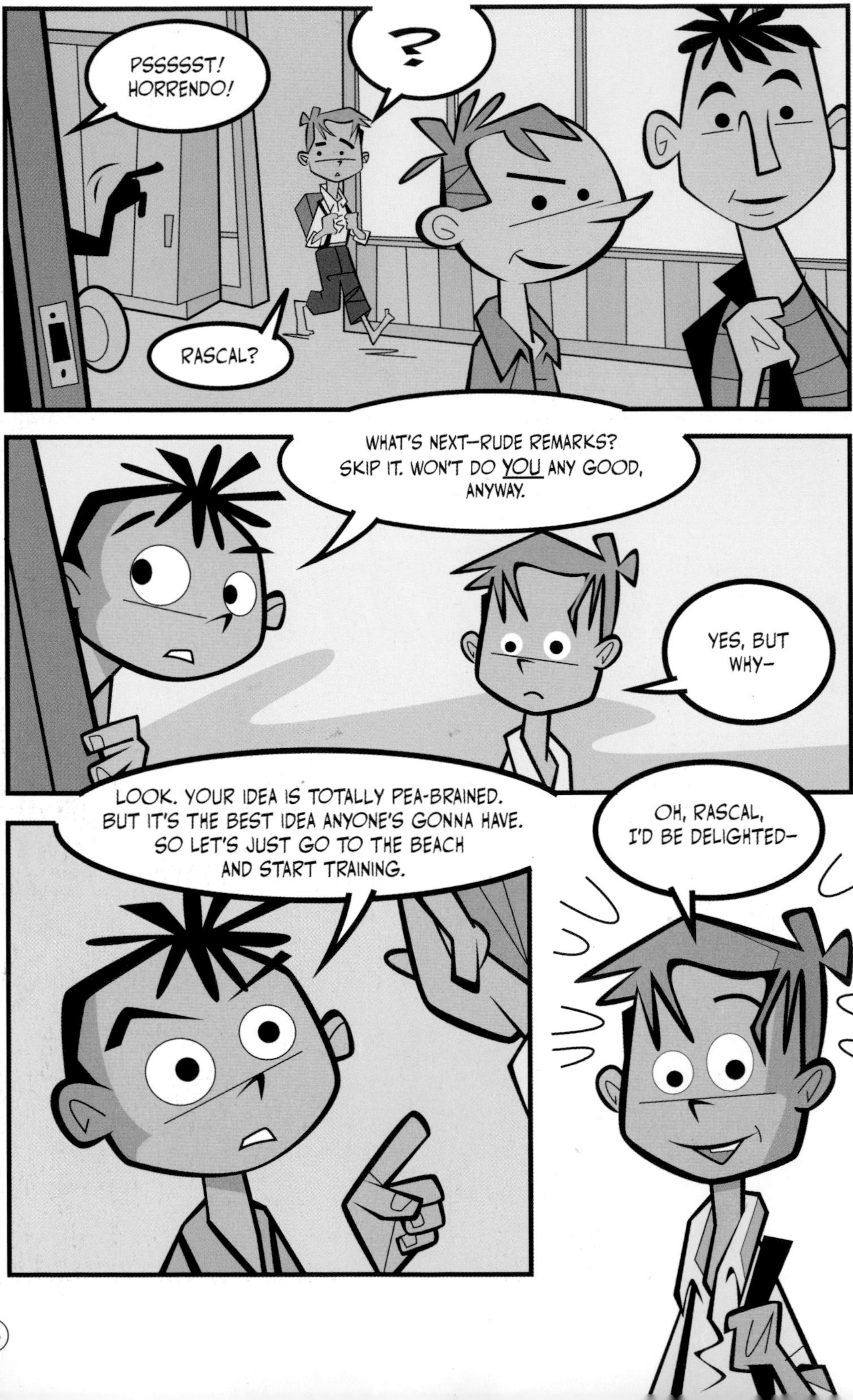
PSSSSST!
HORRENDO!
?
RASCAL?
WHAT'S NEXT—RUDE REMARKS? SKIP IT. WON'T DO YOU ANY GOOD, ANYWAY.
YES, BUT WHY–
LOOK. YOUR IDEA IS TOTALLY PEA-BRAINED. BUT IT'S THE BEST IDEA ANYONE'S GONNA HAVE. SO LET'S JUST GO TO THE BEACH AND START TRAINING.
OH, RASCAL, I'D BE DELIGHTED–

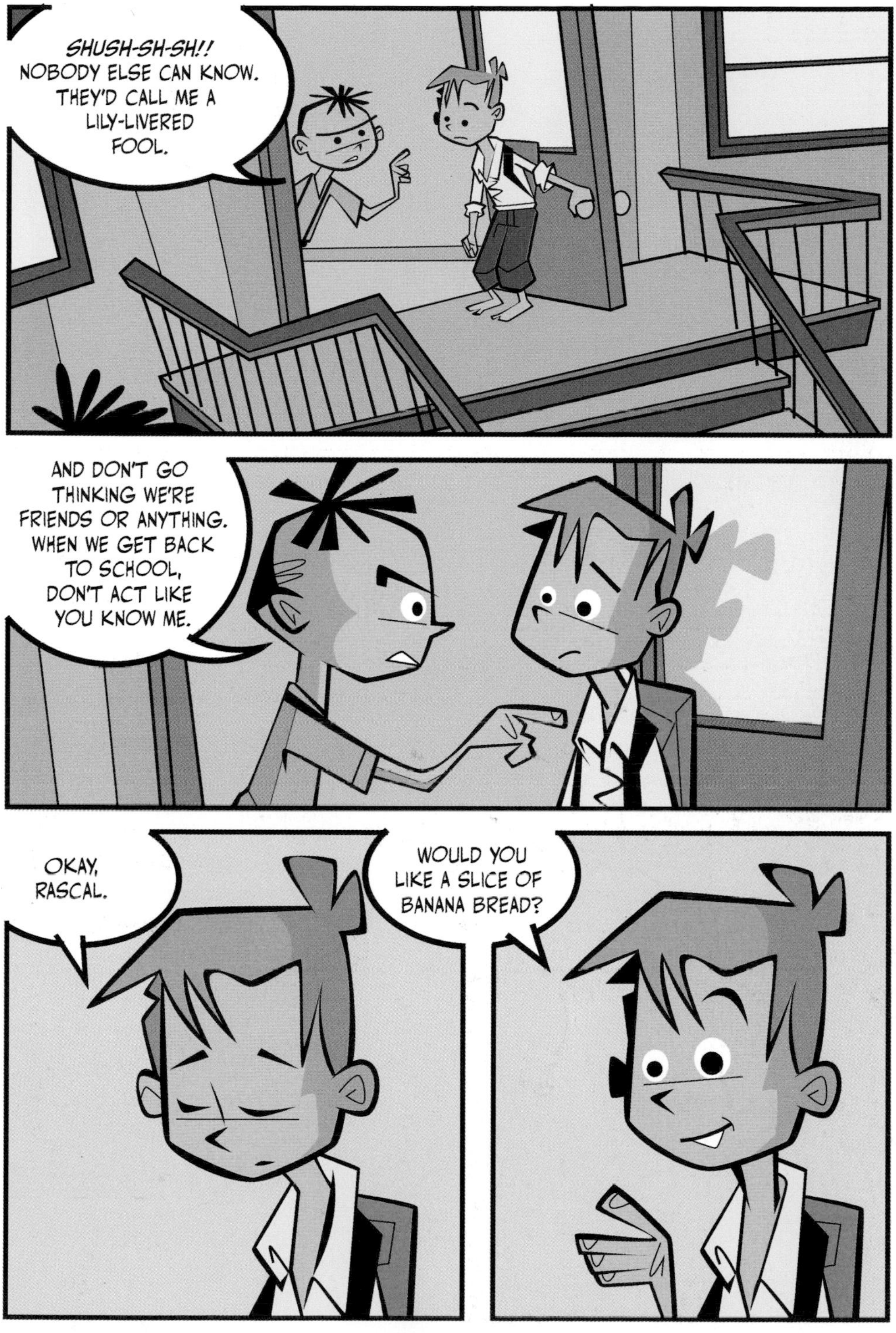
SHUSH-SH-SH!! NOBODY ELSE CAN KNOW. THEY'D CALL ME A LILY-LIVERED FOOL.
AND DON'T GO THINKING WE'RE FRIENDS OR ANYTHING. WHEN WE GET BACK TO SCHOOL, DON'T ACT LIKE YOU KNOW ME.
OKAY, RASCAL.
WOULD YOU LIKE A SLICE OF BANANA BREAD?

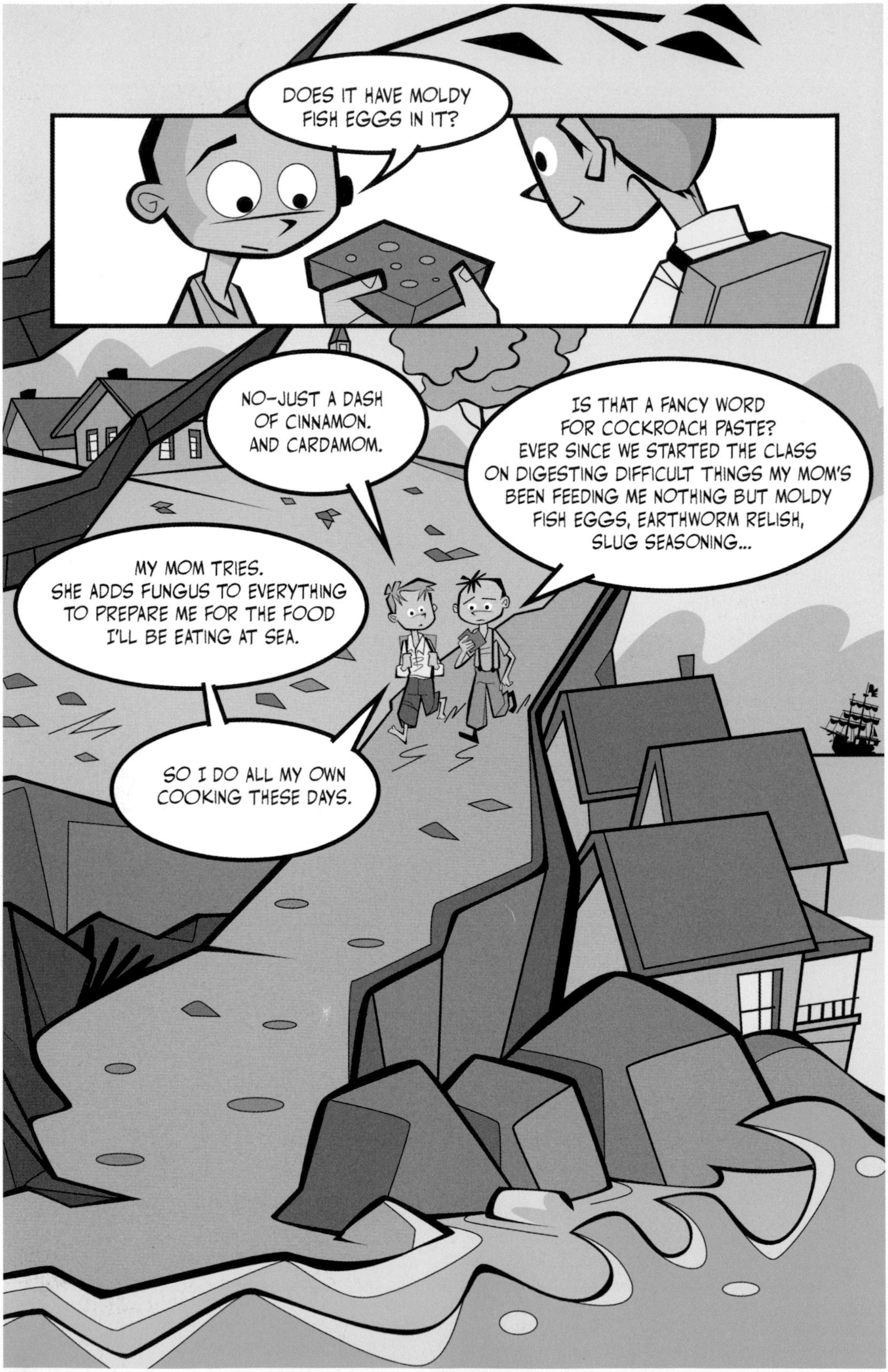
DOES IT HAVE MOLDY FISH EGGS IN IT?
NO–JUST A DASH OF CINNAMON. AND CARDAMOM.
IS THAT A FANCY WORD FOR COCKROACH PASTE? EVER SINCE WE STARTED THE CLASS ON DIGESTING DIFFICULT THINGS MY MOM'S BEEN FEEDING ME NOTHING BUT MOLDY FISH EGGS, EARTHWORM RELISH, SLUG SEASONING...
MY MOM TRIES. SHE ADDS FUNGUS TO EVERYTHING TO PREPARE ME FOR THE FOOD I'LL BE EATING AT SEA.
SO I DO ALL MY OWN COOKING THESE DAYS.

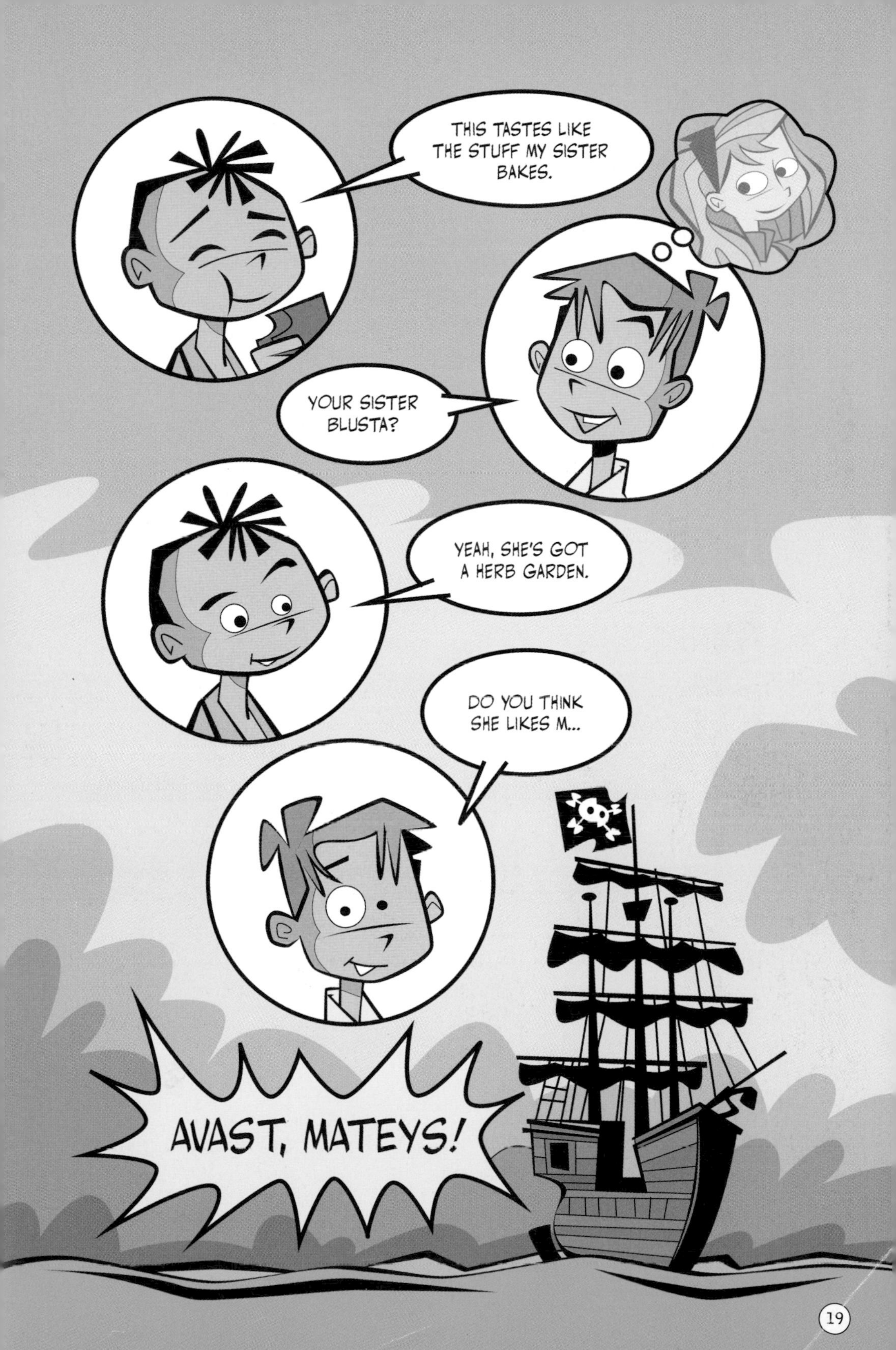
THIS TASTES LIKE THE STUFF MY SISTER BAKES.
YOUR SISTER BLUSTA?
YEAH, SHE'S GOT A HERB GARDEN.
DO YOU THINK SHE LIKES M...
AVAST, MATEYS!

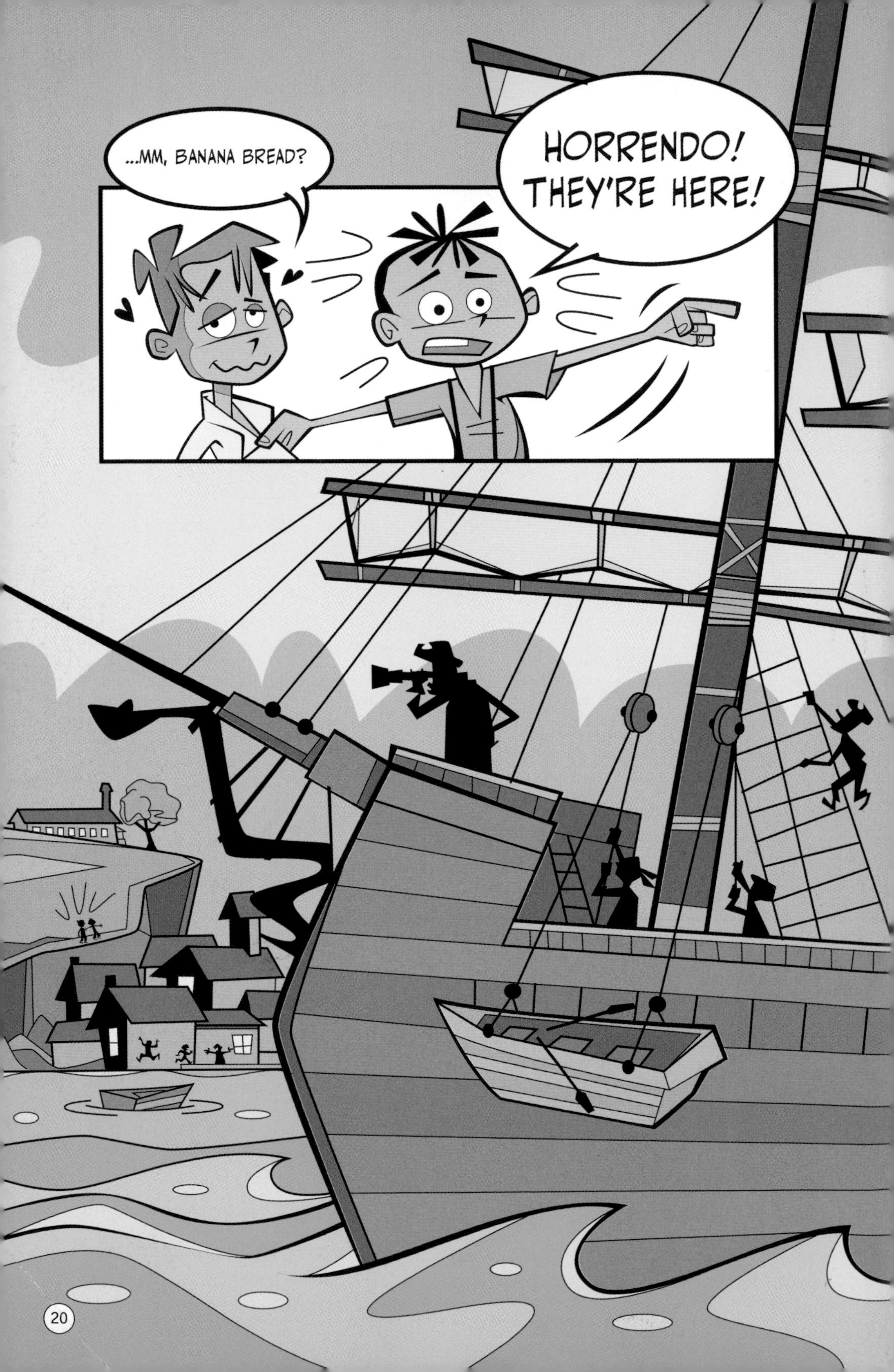
...MM, BANANA BREAD?
HORRENDO! THEY'RE HERE!

CHAPTER 3
DIGESTING DIFFICULT THINGS

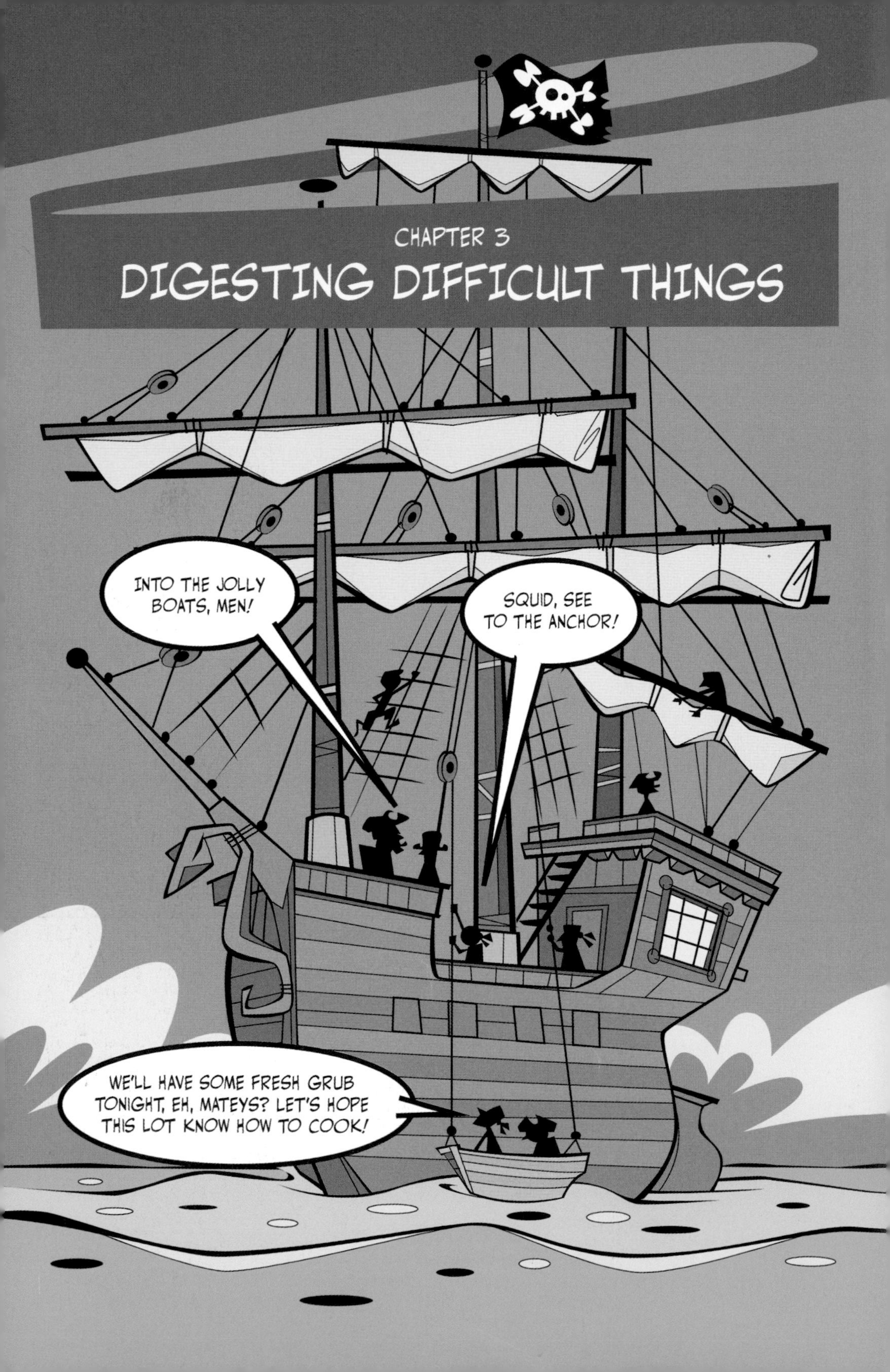
INTO THE JOLLY BOATS, MEN!
SQUID, SEE TO THE ANCHOR!
WE'LL HAVE SOME FRESH GRUB TONIGHT, EH, MATEYS? LET'S HOPE THIS LOT KNOW HOW TO COOK!

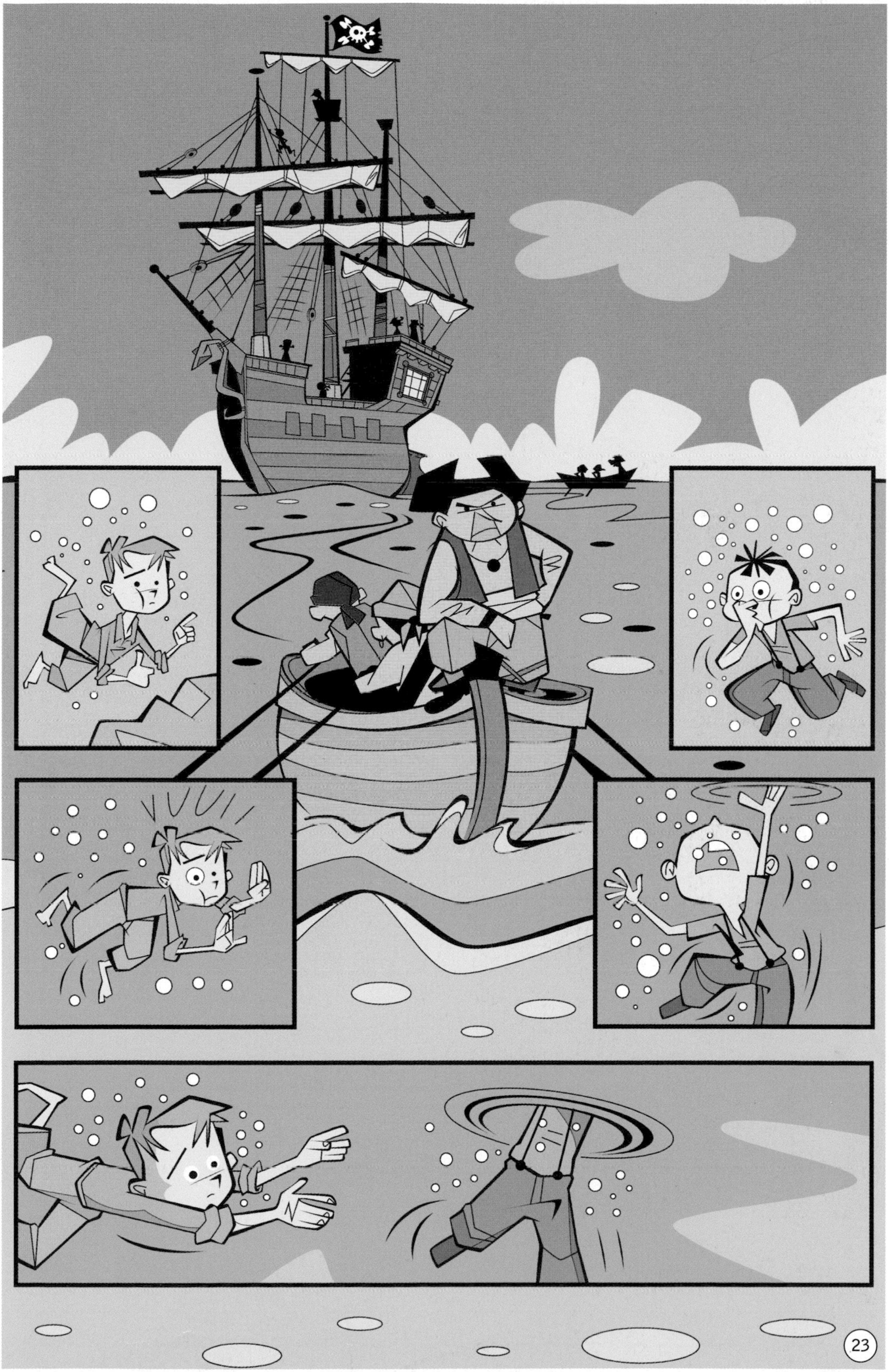

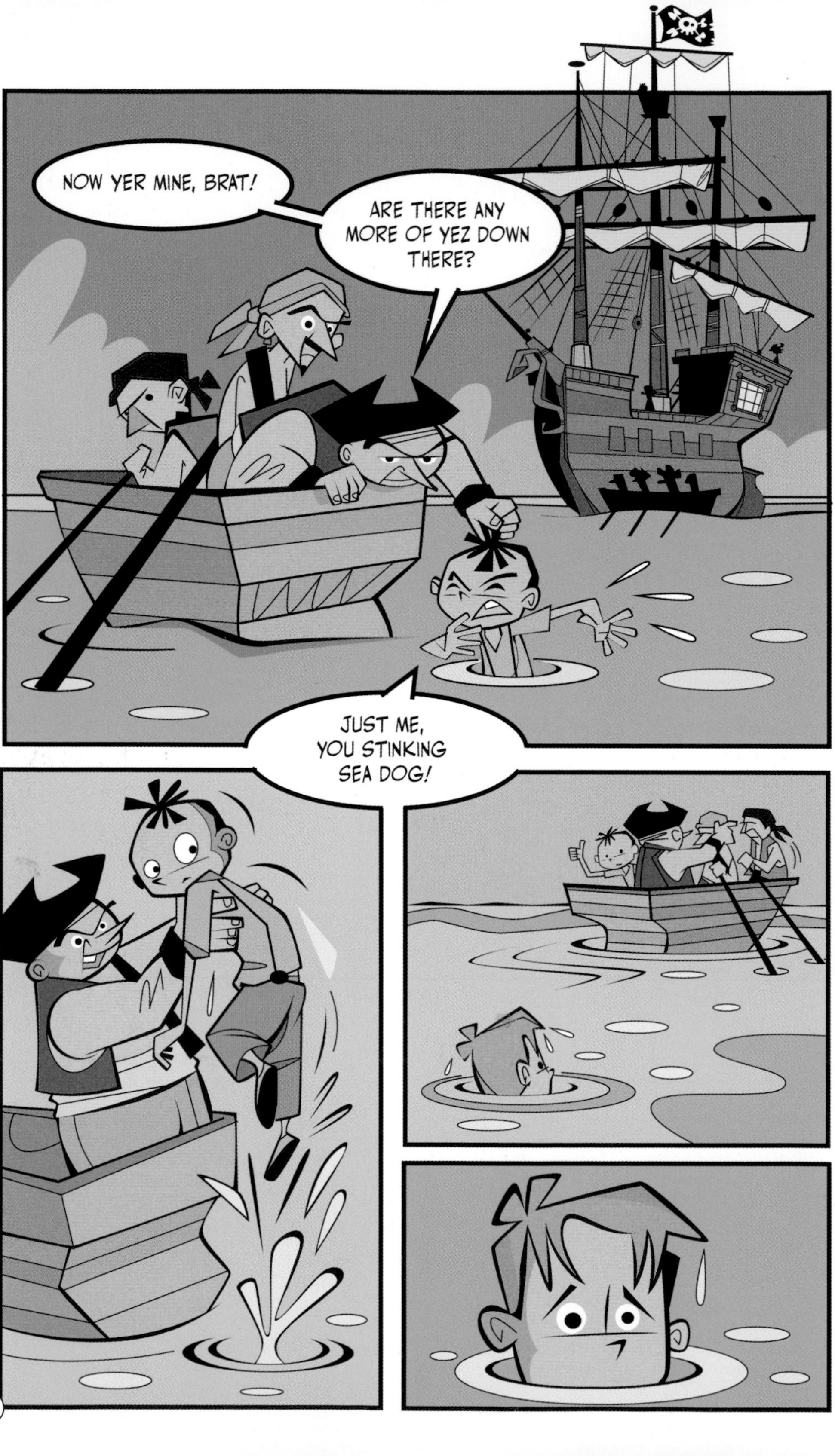
NOW YER MINE, BRAT!
ARE THERE ANY MORE OF YEZ DOWN THERE?
JUST ME, YOU STINKING SEA DOG!

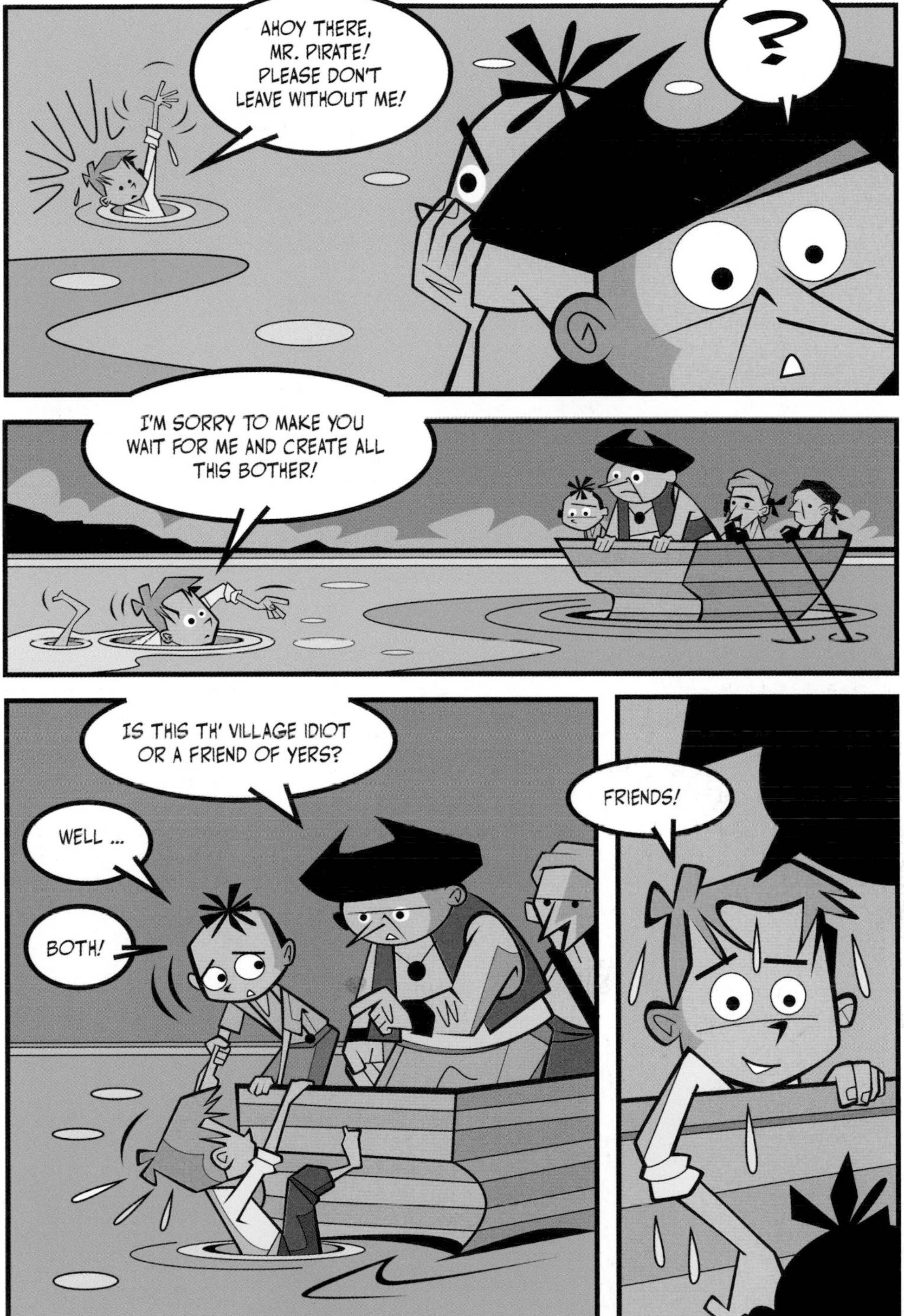
AHOY THERE, MR. PIRATE! PLEASE DON'T LEAVE WITHOUT ME!
?
I'M SORRY TO MAKE YOU WAIT FOR ME AND CREATE ALL THIS BOTHER!
IS THIS TH' VILLAGE IDIOT OR A FRIEND OF YERS?
WELL ...
BOTH!
FRIENDS!

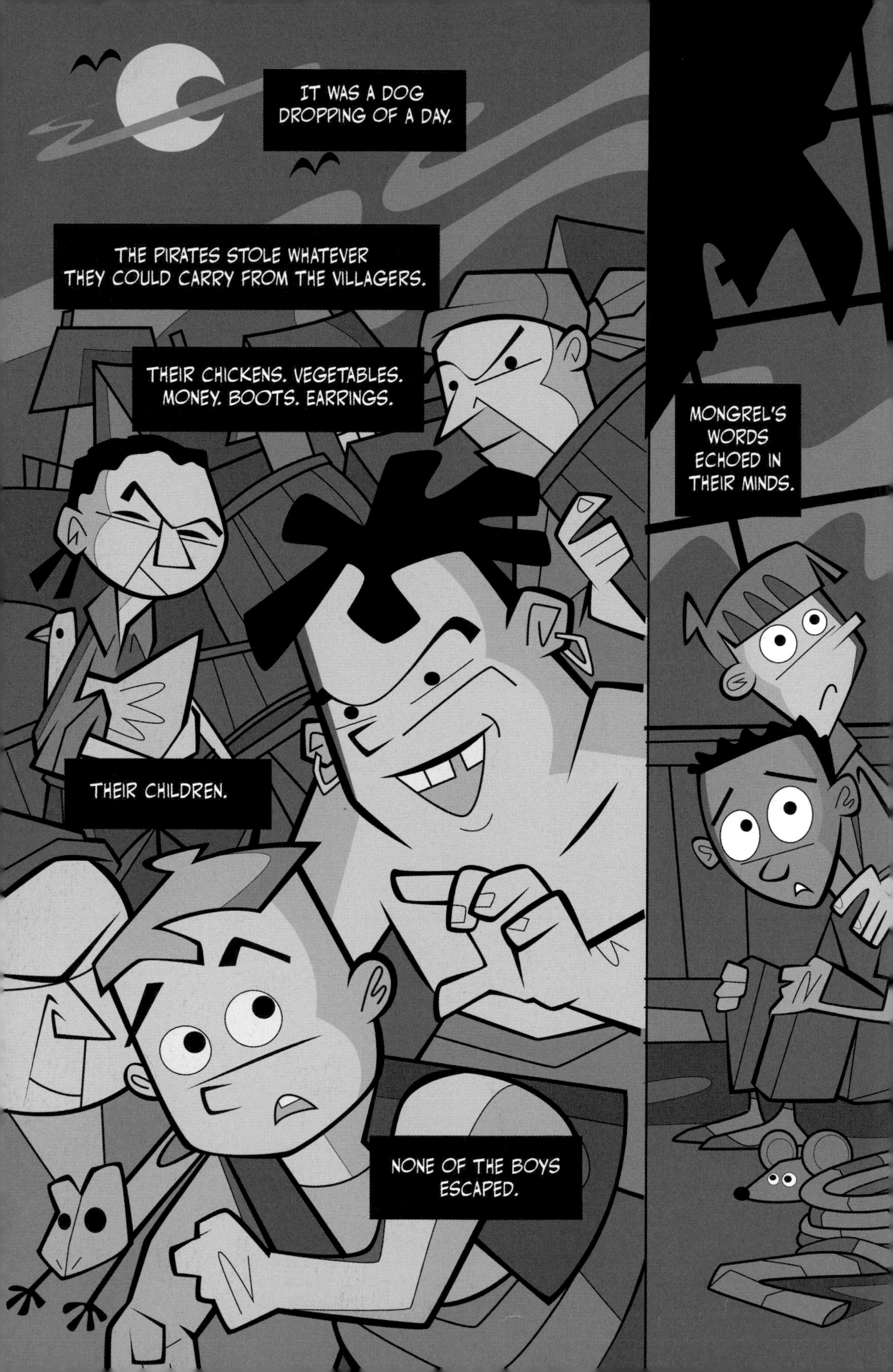
IT WAS A DOG DROPPING OF A DAY.
THE PIRATES STOLE WHATEVER THEY COULD CARRY FROM THE VILLAGERS.
THEIR CHICKENS. VEGETABLES. MONEY. BOOTS. EARRINGS.
THEIR CHILDREN.
NONE OF THE BOYS ESCAPED.
MONGREL'S WORDS ECHOED IN THEIR MINDS.

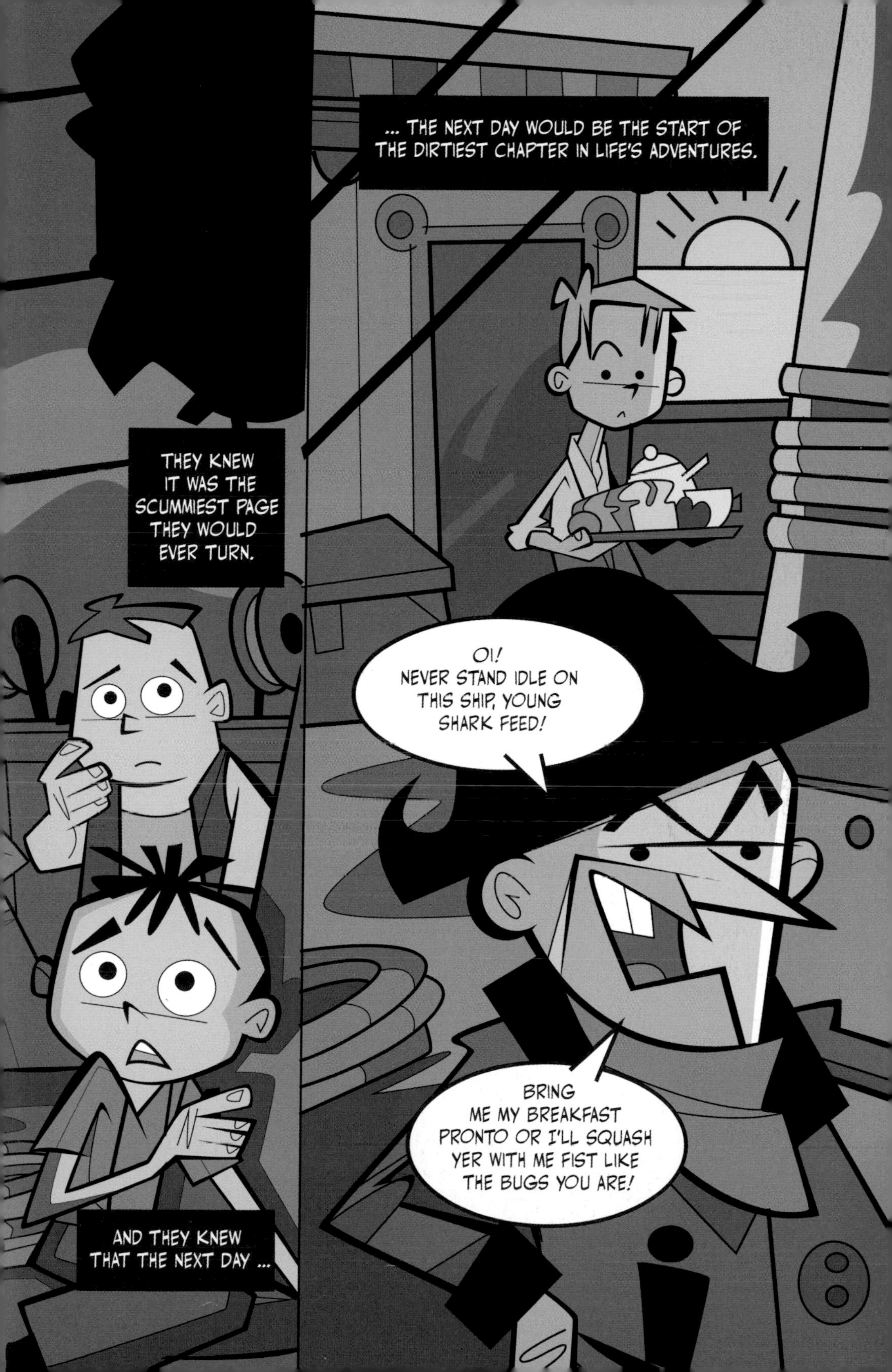
THEY KNEW IT WAS THE SCUMMIEST PAGE THEY WOULD EVER TURN.
AND THEY KNEW THAT THE NEXT DAY ...
... THE NEXT DAY WOULD BE THE START OF THE DIRTIEST CHAPTER IN LIFE'S ADVENTURES.
OI! NEVER STAND IDLE ON THIS SHIP, YOUNG SHARK FEED!
BRING ME MY BREAKFAST PRONTO OR I'LL SQUASH YER WITH ME FIST LIKE THE BUGS YOU ARE!

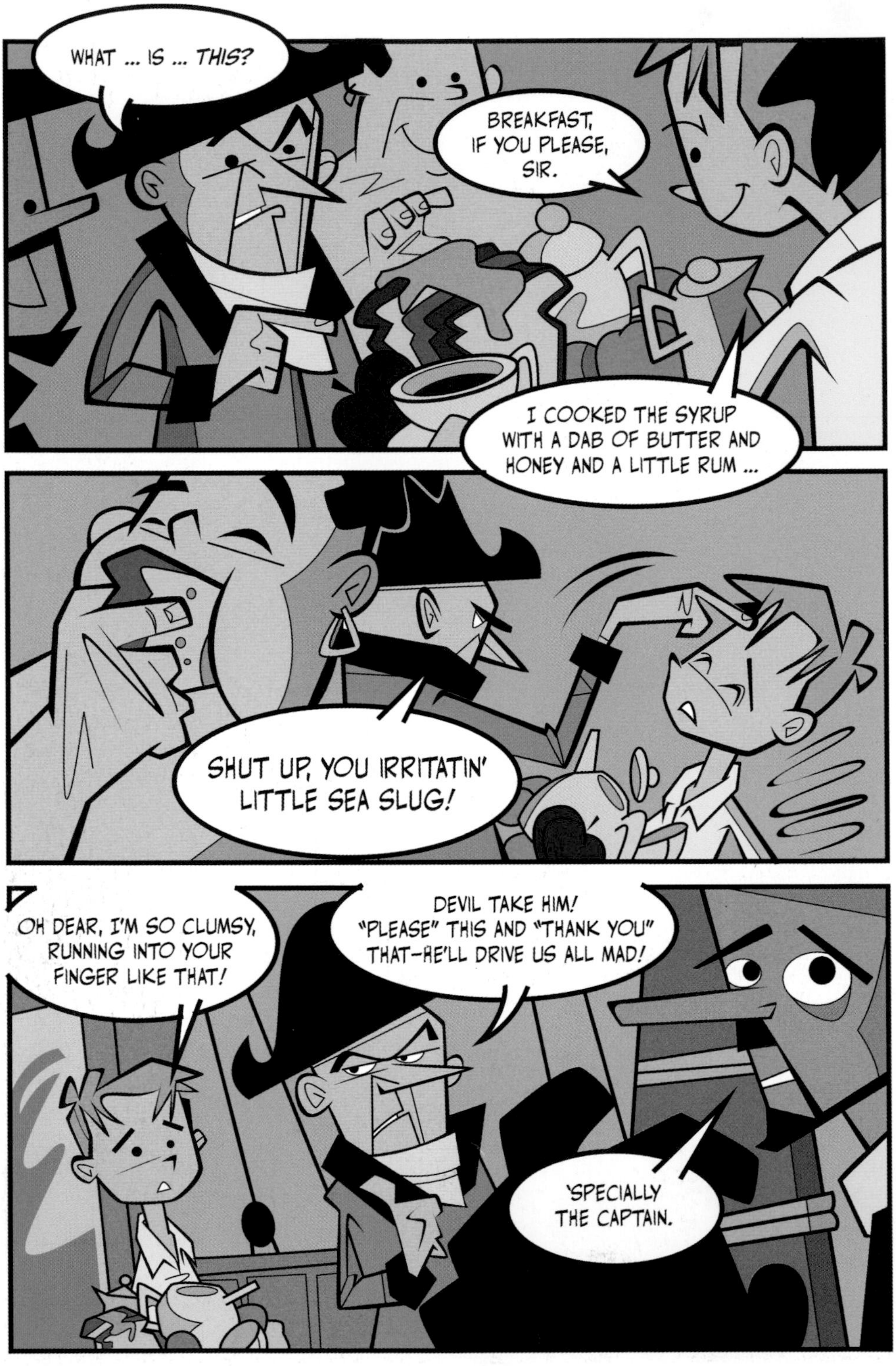
WHAT ... IS ... THIS?
BREAKFAST, IF YOU PLEASE, SIR.
I COOKED THE SYRUP WITH A DAB OF BUTTER AND HONEY AND A LITTLE RUM ...
SHUT UP, YOU IRRITATIN' LITTLE SEA SLUG!
OH DEAR, I'M SO CLUMSY, RUNNING INTO YOUR FINGER LIKE THAT!
DEVIL TAKE HIM! "PLEASE" THIS AND "THANK YOU" THAT—HE'LL DRIVE US ALL MAD!
'SPECIALLY THE CAPTAIN.

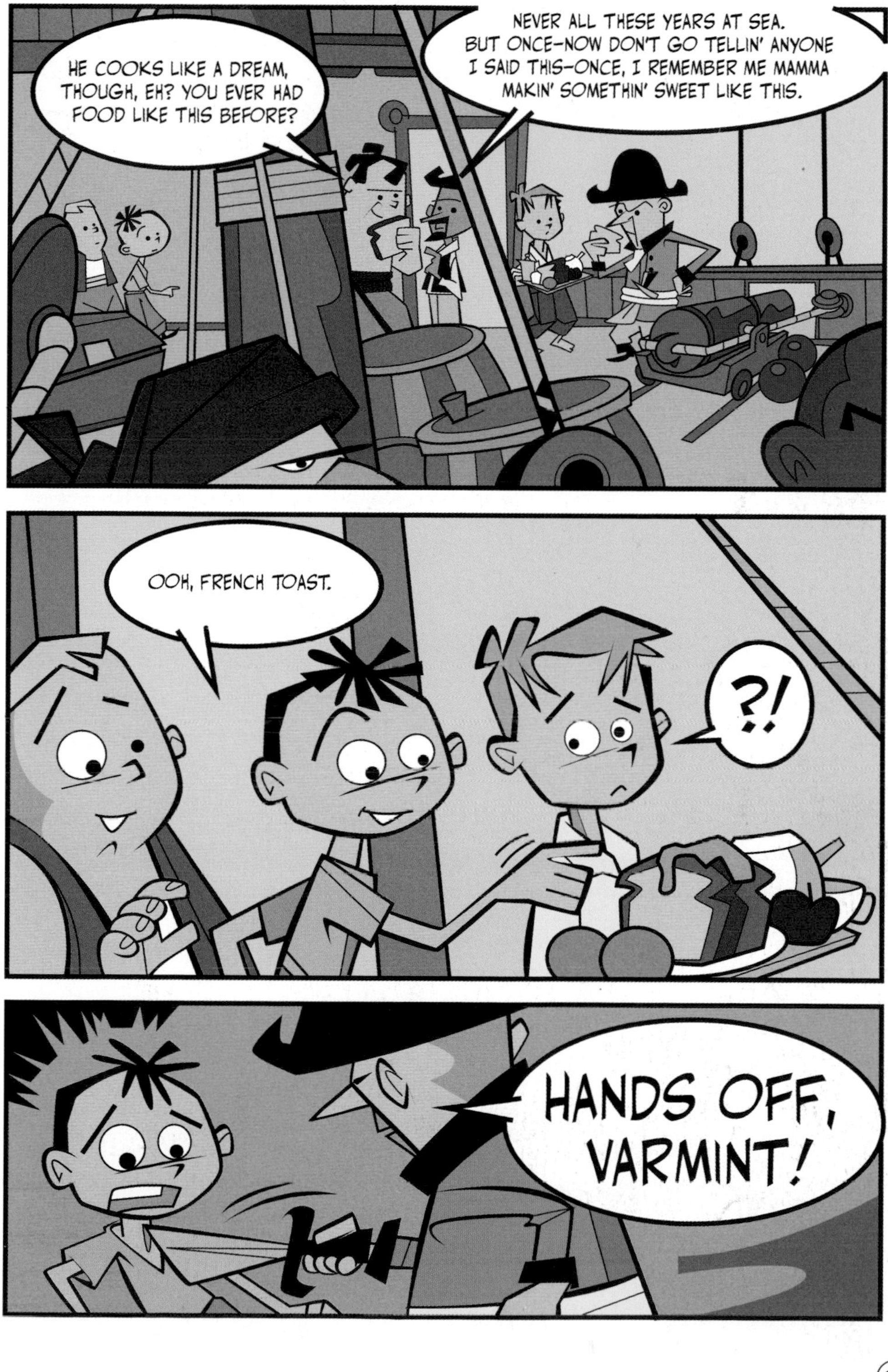

HE COOKS LIKE A DREAM, THOUGH, EH? YOU EVER HAD FOOD LIKE THIS BEFORE?
NEVER ALL THESE YEARS AT SEA. BUT ONCE–NOW DON'T GO TELLIN' ANYONE I SAID THIS–ONCE, I REMEMBER ME MAMMA MAKIN' SOMETHIN' SWEET LIKE THIS.
OOH, FRENCH TOAST.
?!
HANDS OFF, VARMINT!

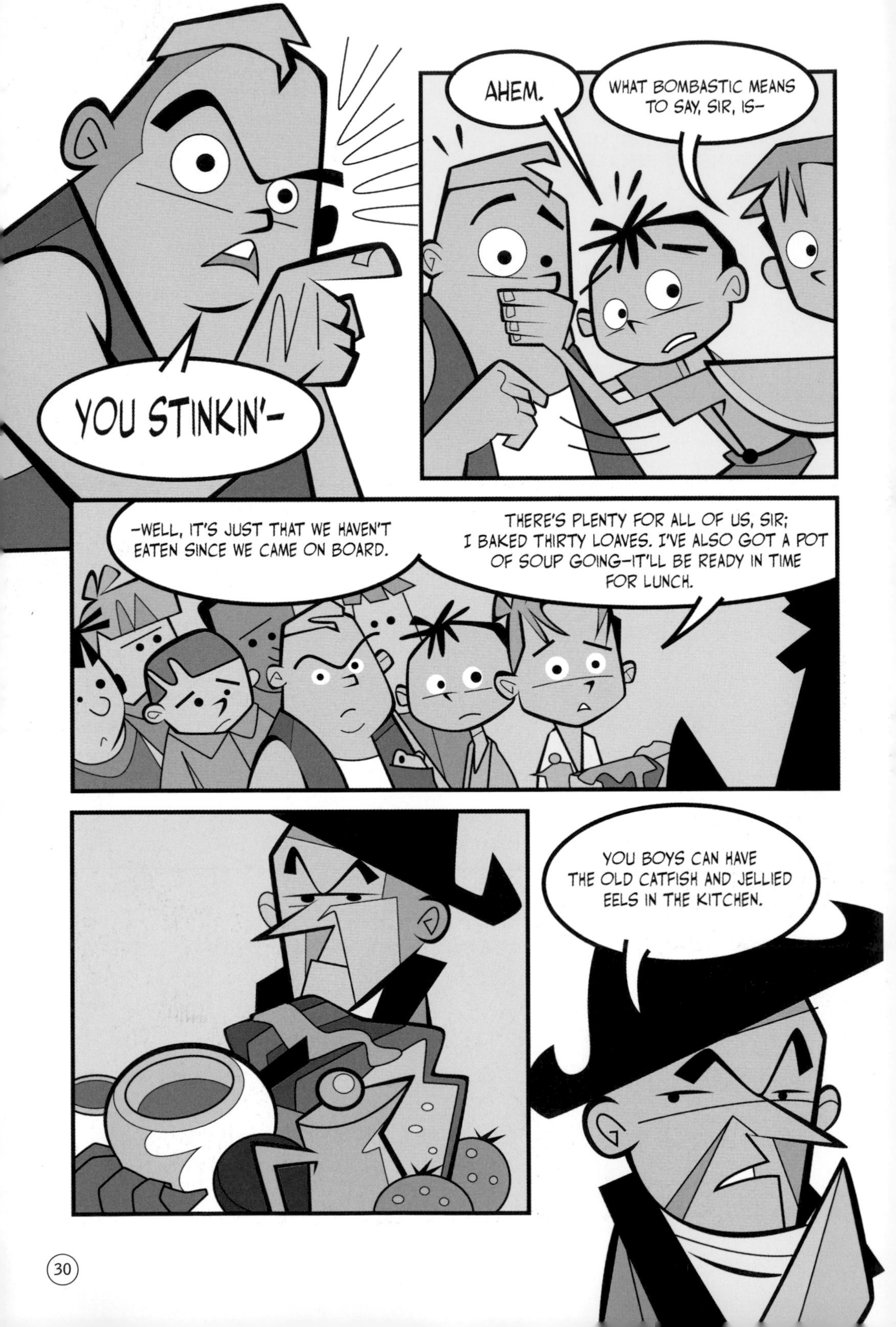
YOU STINKIN'-
AHEM.
WHAT BOMBASTIC MEANS TO SAY, SIR, IS-
-WELL, IT'S JUST THAT WE HAVEN'T EATEN SINCE WE CAME ON BOARD.
THERE'S PLENTY FOR ALL OF US, SIR; I BAKED THIRTY LOAVES. I'VE ALSO GOT A POT OF SOUP GOING-IT'LL BE READY IN TIME FOR LUNCH.
YOU BOYS CAN HAVE THE OLD CATFISH AND JELLIED EELS IN THE KITCHEN.

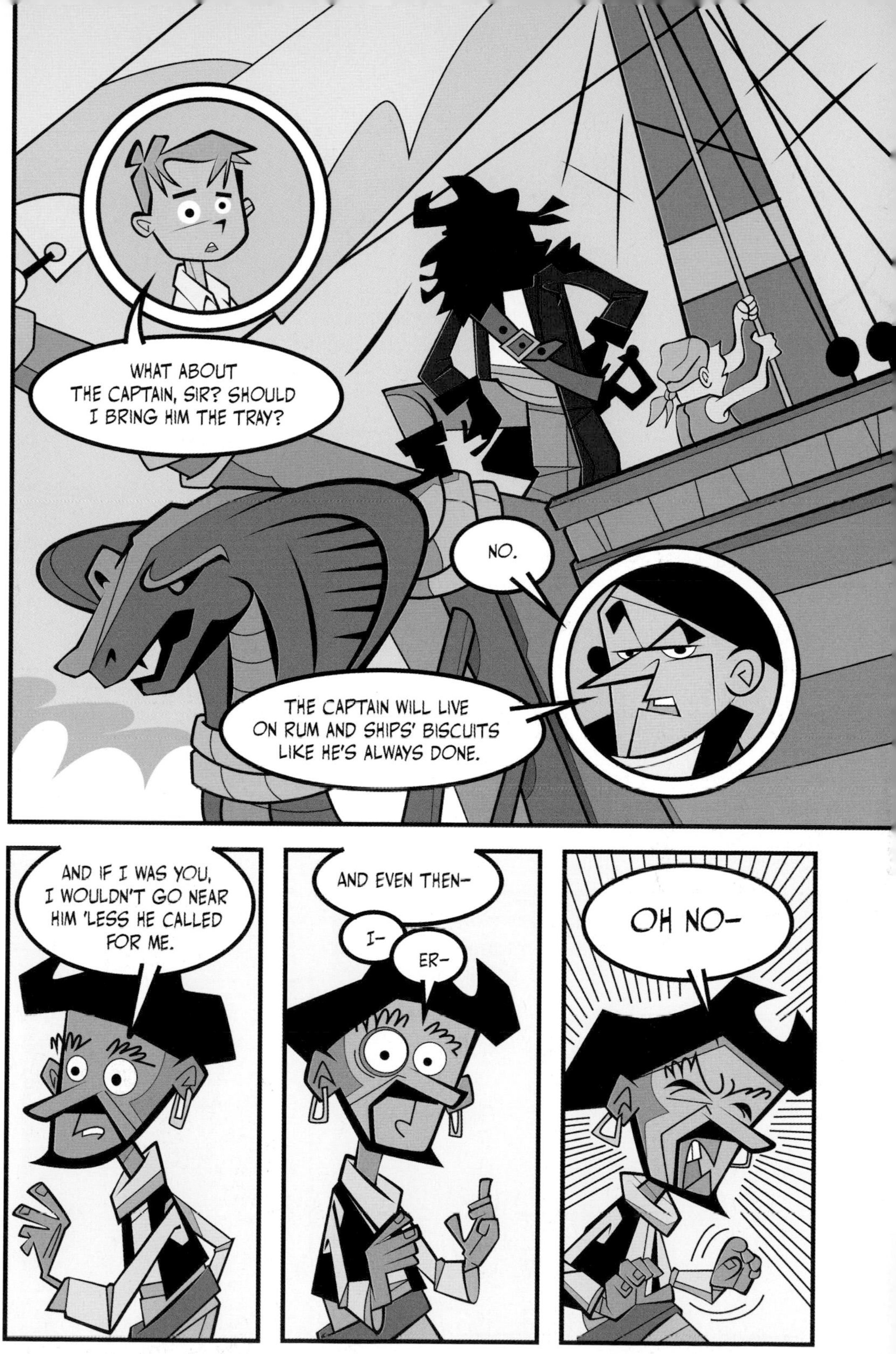
WHAT ABOUT THE CAPTAIN, SIR? SHOULD I BRING HIM THE TRAY?
NO.
THE CAPTAIN WILL LIVE ON RUM AND SHIPS' BISCUITS LIKE HE'S ALWAYS DONE.
AND IF I WAS YOU, I WOULDN'T GO NEAR HIM 'LESS HE CALLED FOR ME.
AND EVEN THEN-
I-
ER-
OH NO-

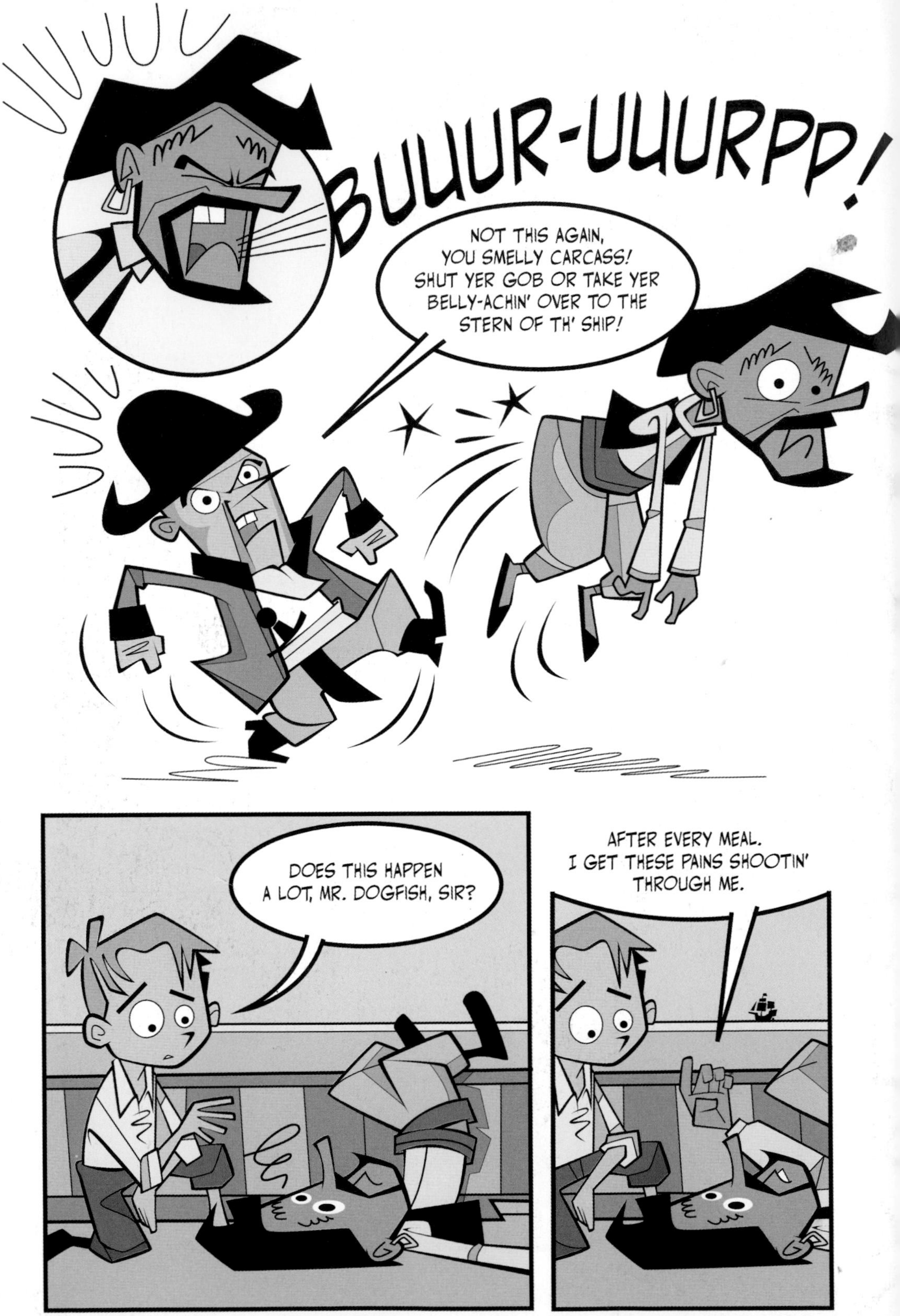
BUUUR-UUURPP!
NOT THIS AGAIN, YOU SMELLY CARCASS! SHUT YER GOB OR TAKE YER BELLY-ACHIN' OVER TO THE STERN OF TH' SHIP!
DOES THIS HAPPEN A LOT, MR. DOGFISH, SIR?
AFTER EVERY MEAL. I GET THESE PAINS SHOOTIN' THROUGH ME.

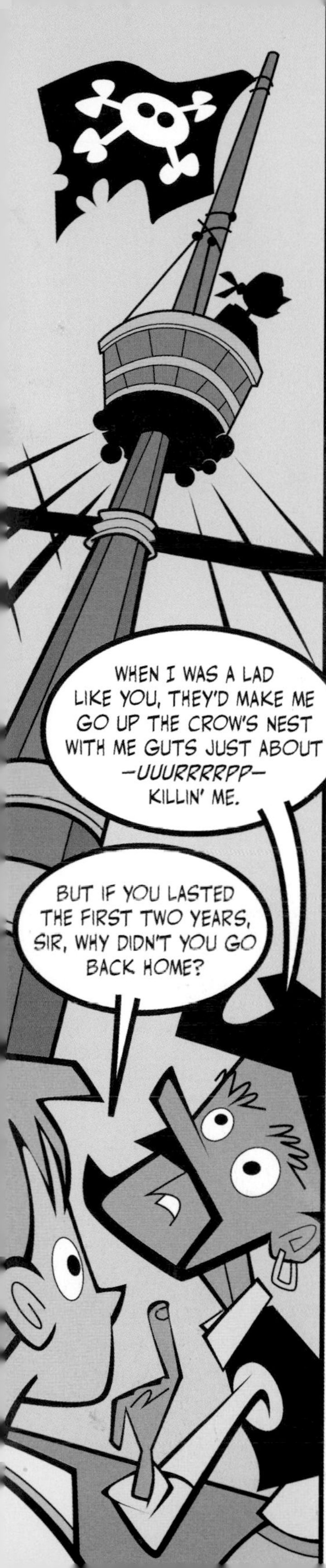
WHEN I WAS A LAD LIKE YOU, THEY'D MAKE ME GO UP THE CROW'S NEST WITH ME GUTS JUST ABOUT —UUURRRRPP— KILLIN' ME.
BUT IF YOU LASTED THE FIRST TWO YEARS, SIR, WHY DIDN'T YOU GO BACK HOME?

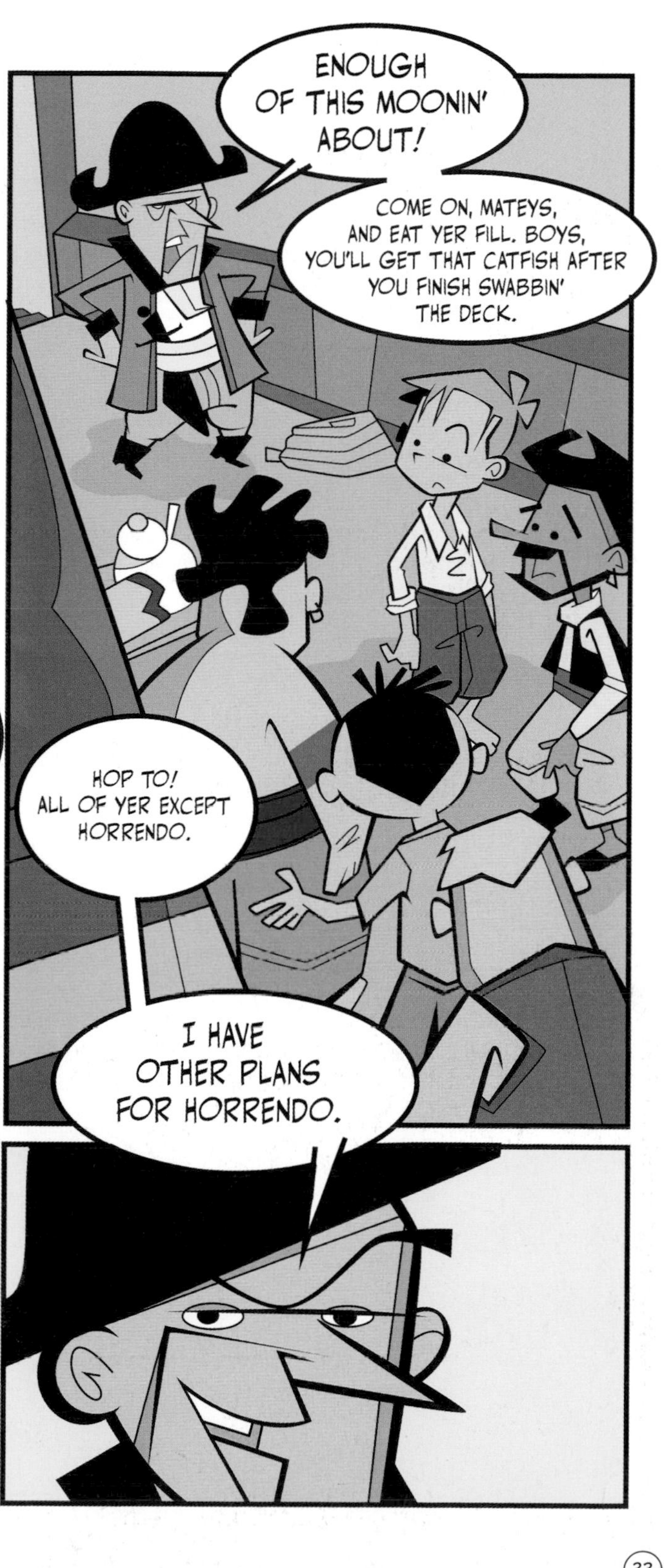
ENOUGH OF THIS MOONIN' ABOUT!
COME ON, MATEYS, AND EAT YER FILL. BOYS, YOU'LL GET THAT CATFISH AFTER YOU FINISH SWABBIN' THE DECK.
HOP TO! ALL OF YER EXCEPT HORRENDO.
I HAVE OTHER PLANS FOR HORRENDO.

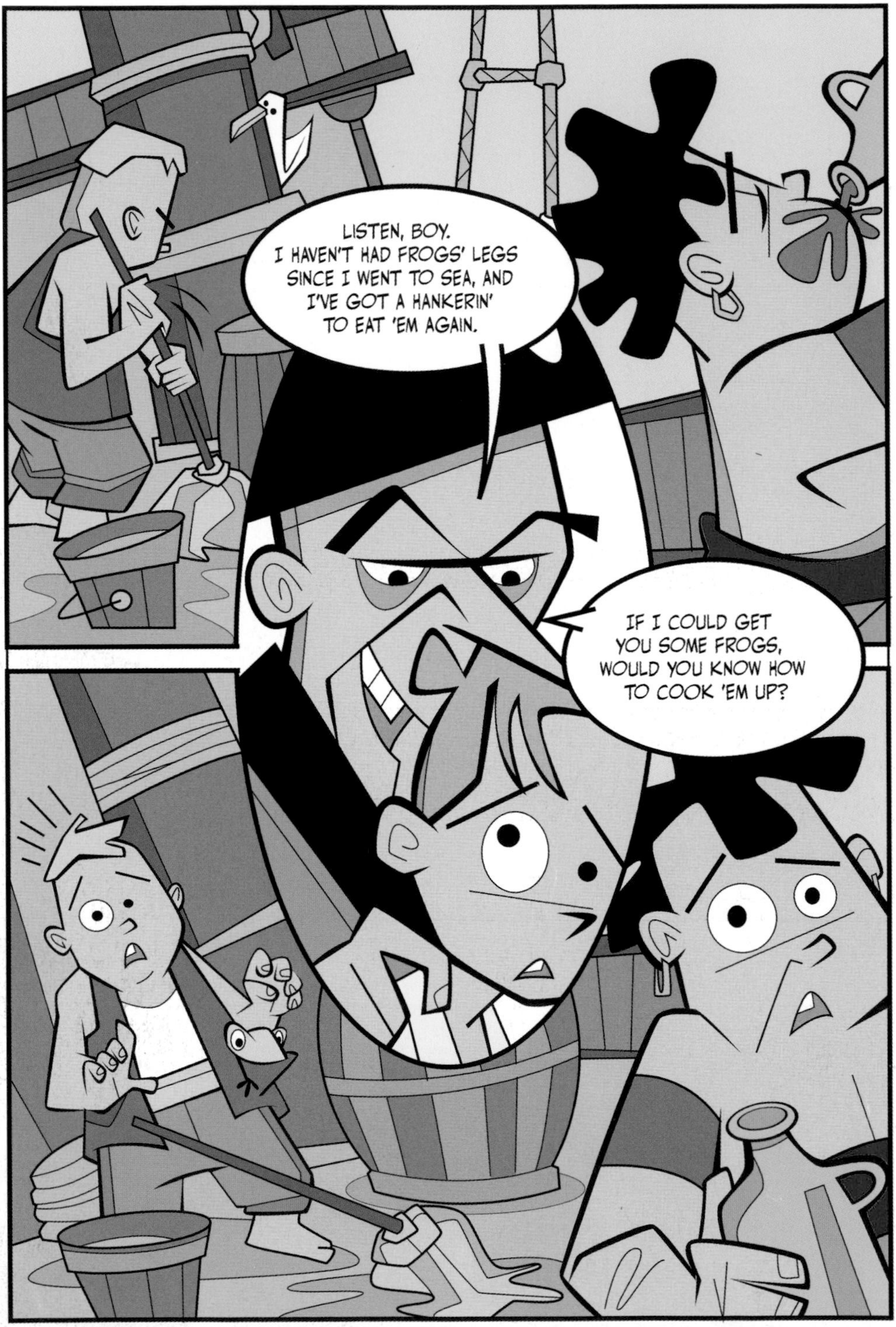
LISTEN, BOY. I HAVEN'T HAD FROGS' LEGS SINCE I WENT TO SEA, AND I'VE GOT A HANKERIN' TO EAT 'EM AGAIN.
IF I COULD GET YOU SOME FROGS, WOULD YOU KNOW HOW TO COOK 'EM UP?

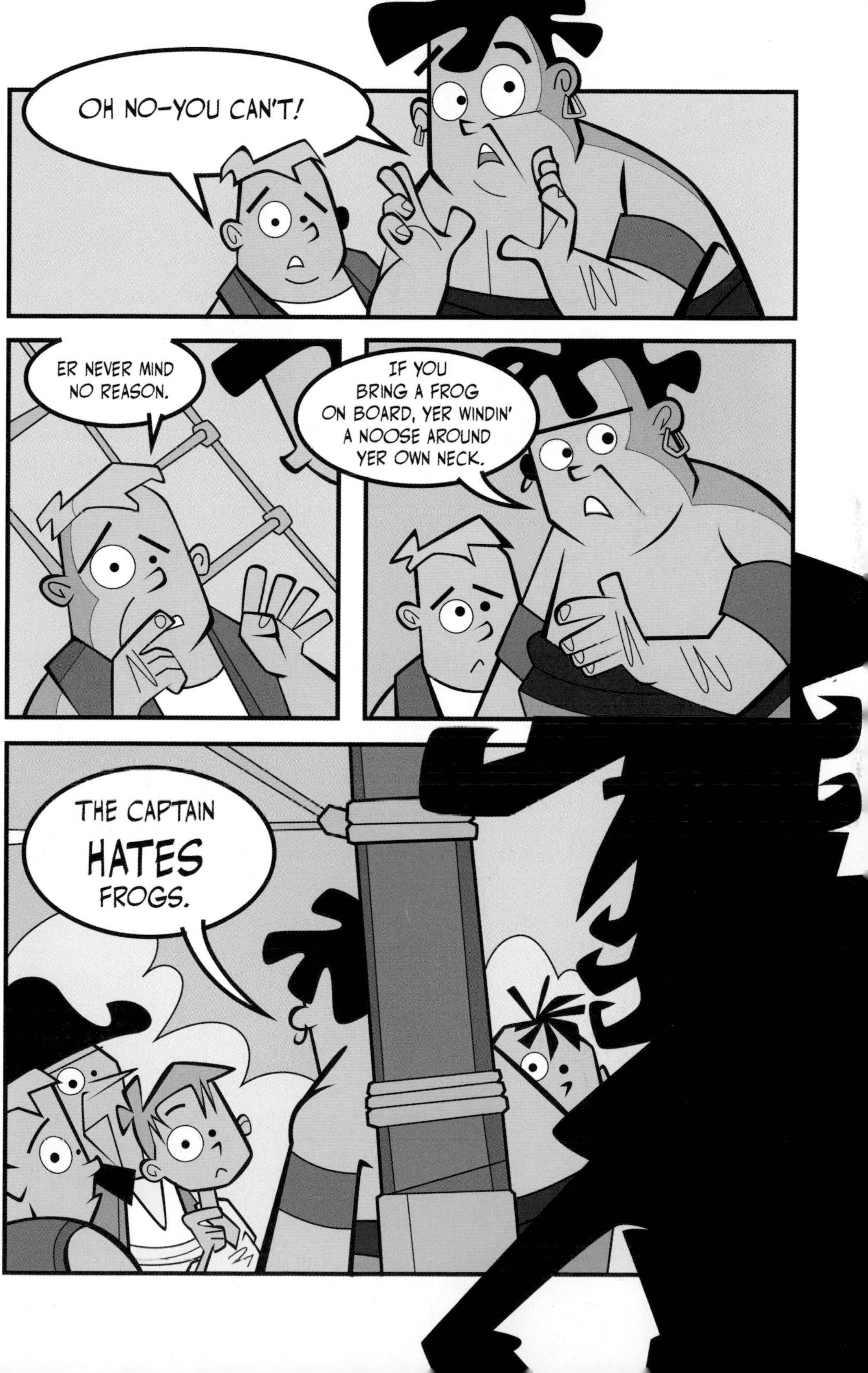
OH NO—YOU CAN'T!
ER NEVER MIND NO REASON.
IF YOU BRING A FROG ON BOARD, YER WINDIN' A NOOSE AROUND YER OWN NECK.
THE CAPTAIN HATES FROGS.

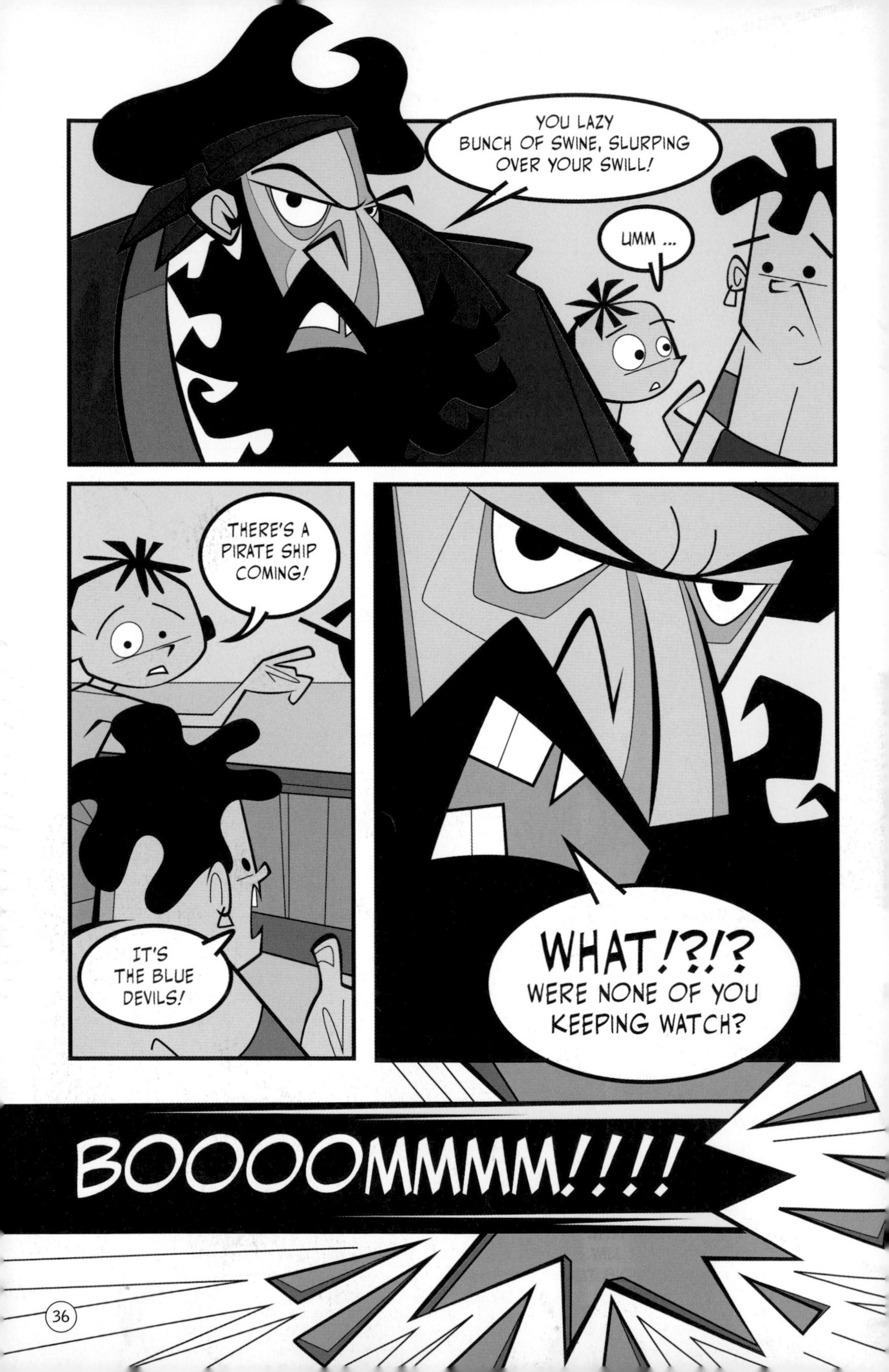
YOU LAZY BUNCH OF SWINE, SLURPING OVER YOUR SWILL!
UMM ...
THERE'S A PIRATE SHIP COMING!
IT'S THE BLUE DEVILS!
WHAT!?!? WERE NONE OF YOU KEEPING WATCH?
BOOOOMMMM!!!!

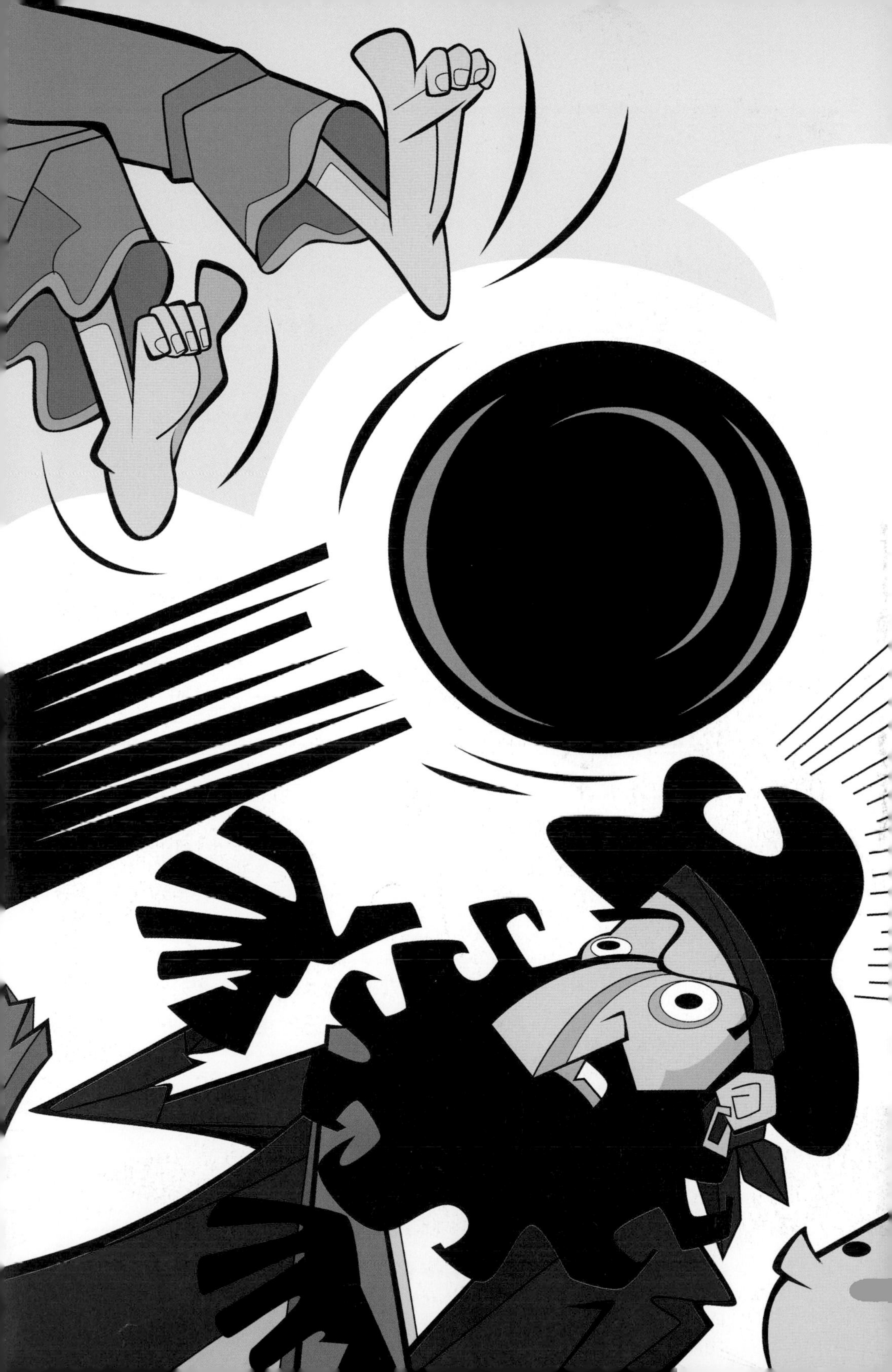

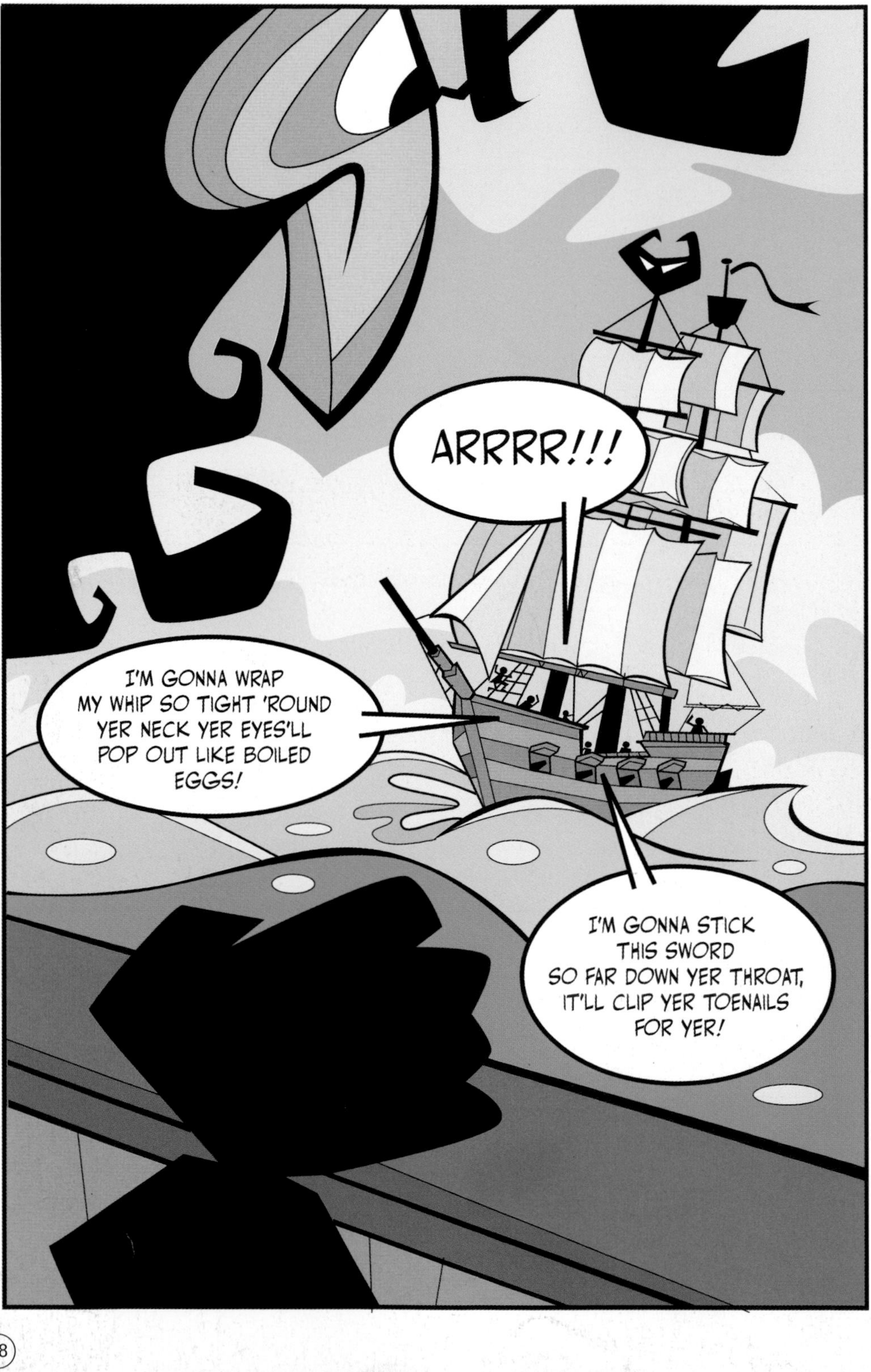
ARRRR!!!
I'M GONNA WRAP MY WHIP SO TIGHT 'ROUND YER NECK YER EYES'LL POP OUT LIKE BOILED EGGS!
I'M GONNA STICK THIS SWORD SO FAR DOWN YER THROAT, IT'LL CLIP YER TOENAILS FOR YER!

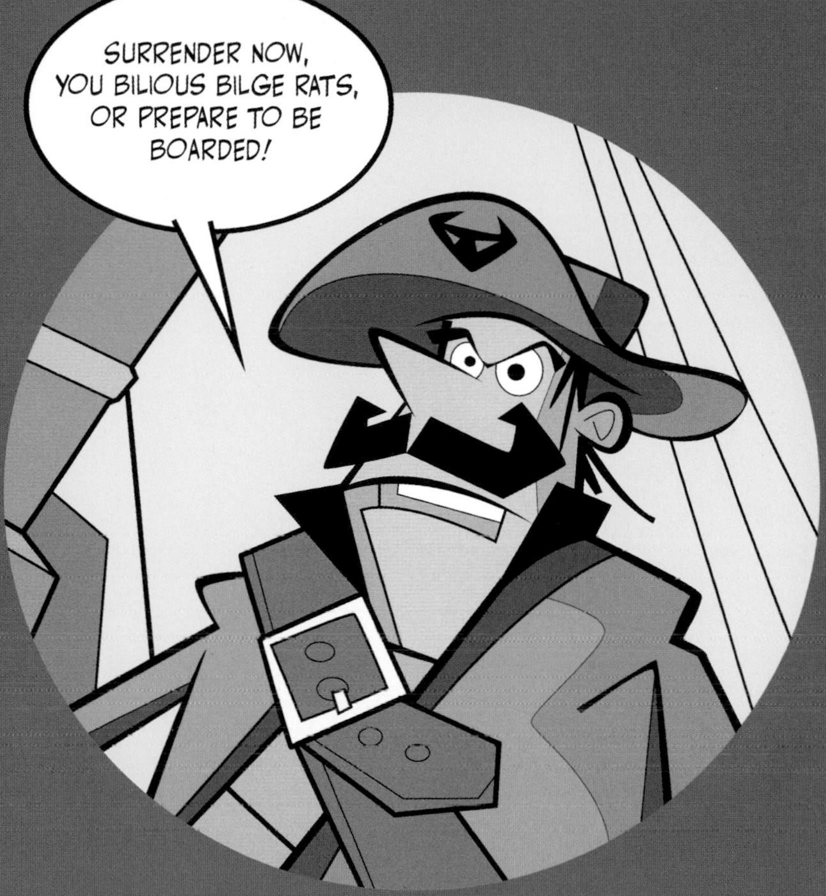
SURRENDER NOW, YOU BILIOUS BILGE RATS, OR PREPARE TO BE BOARDED!

CHAPTER 4
SWORD FIGHTING

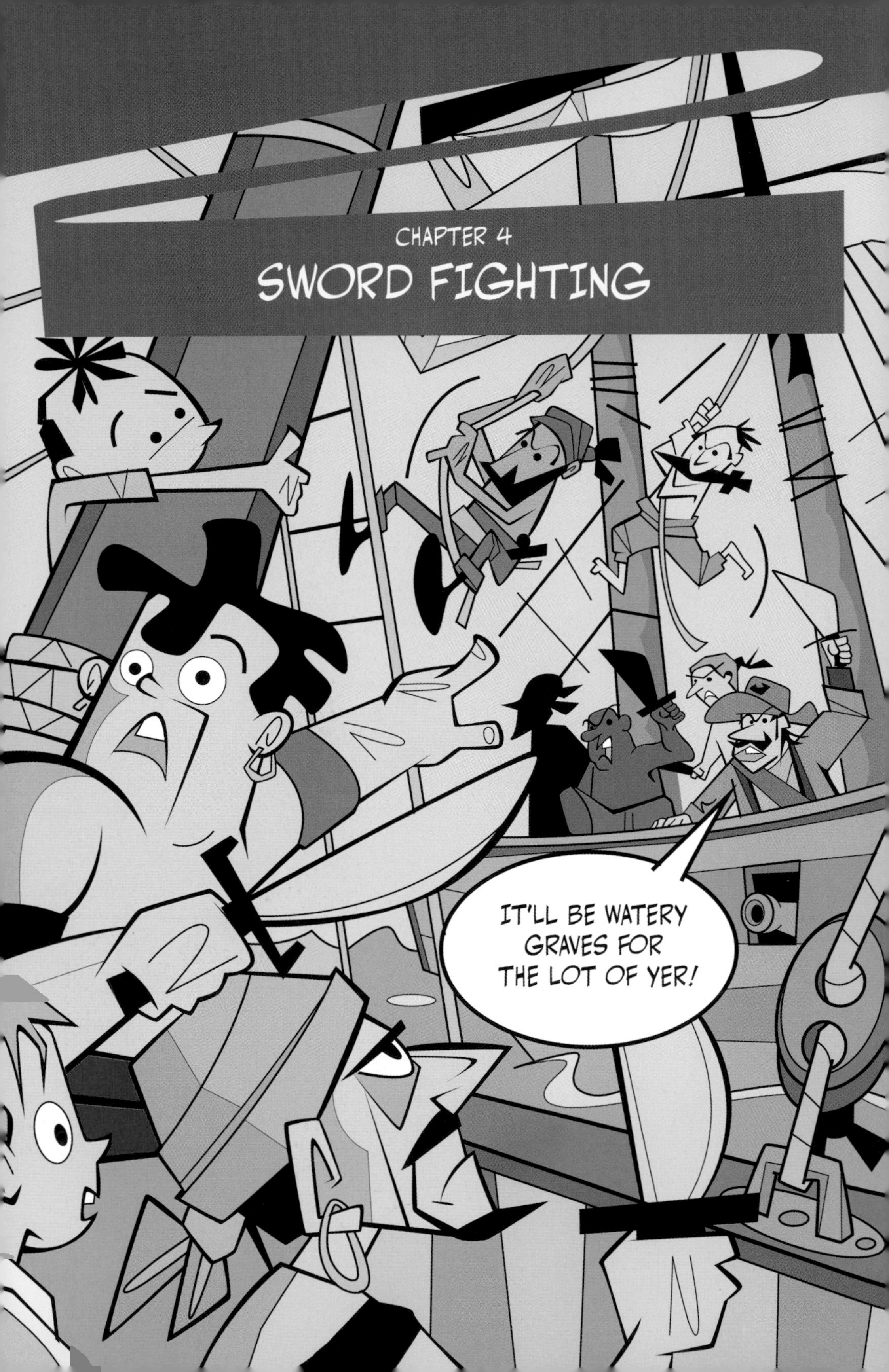
IT'LL BE WATERY GRAVES FOR THE LOT OF YER!

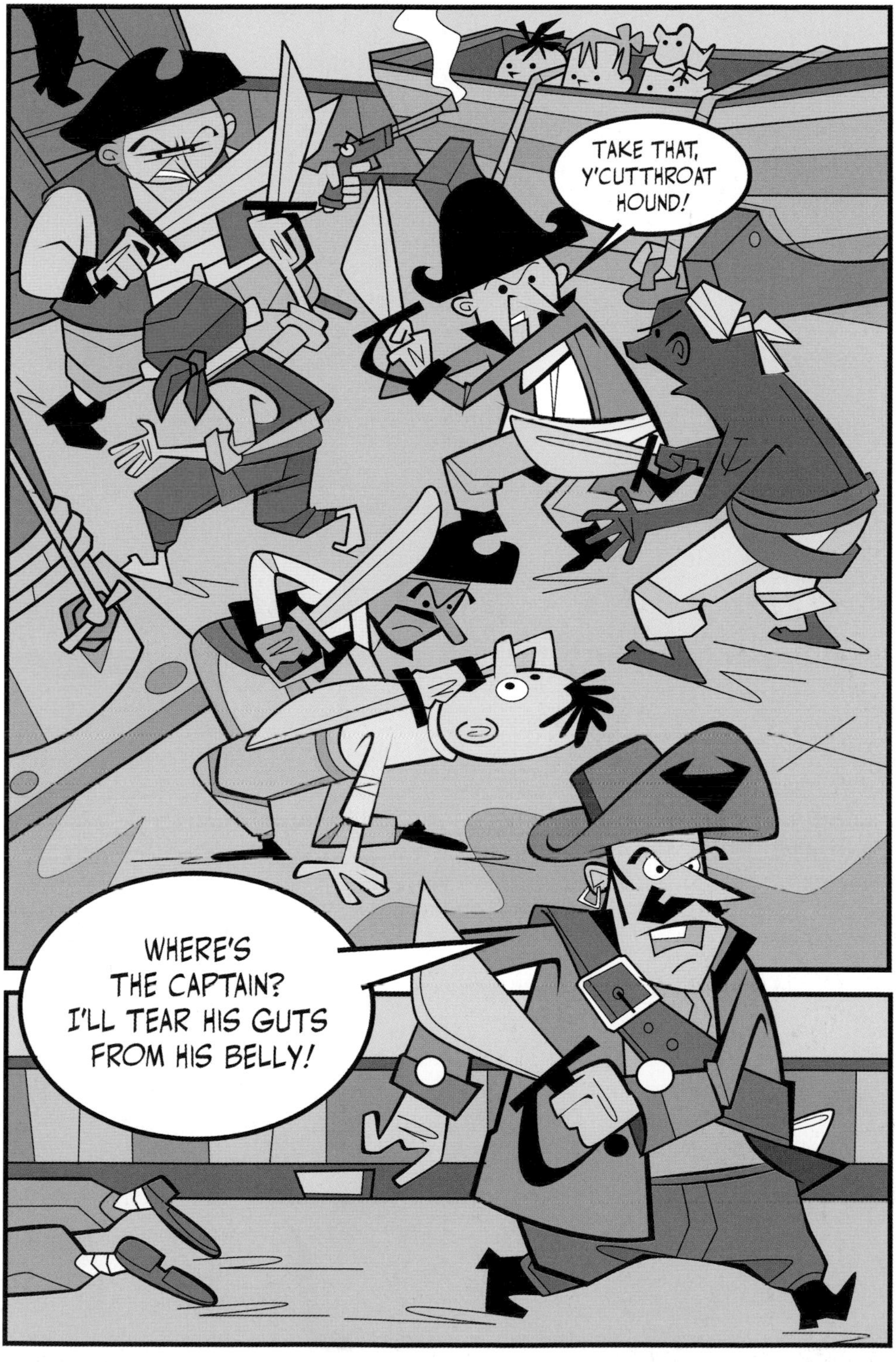
TAKE THAT, Y'CUTTHROAT HOUND!
WHERE'S THE CAPTAIN? I'LL TEAR HIS GUTS FROM HIS BELLY!

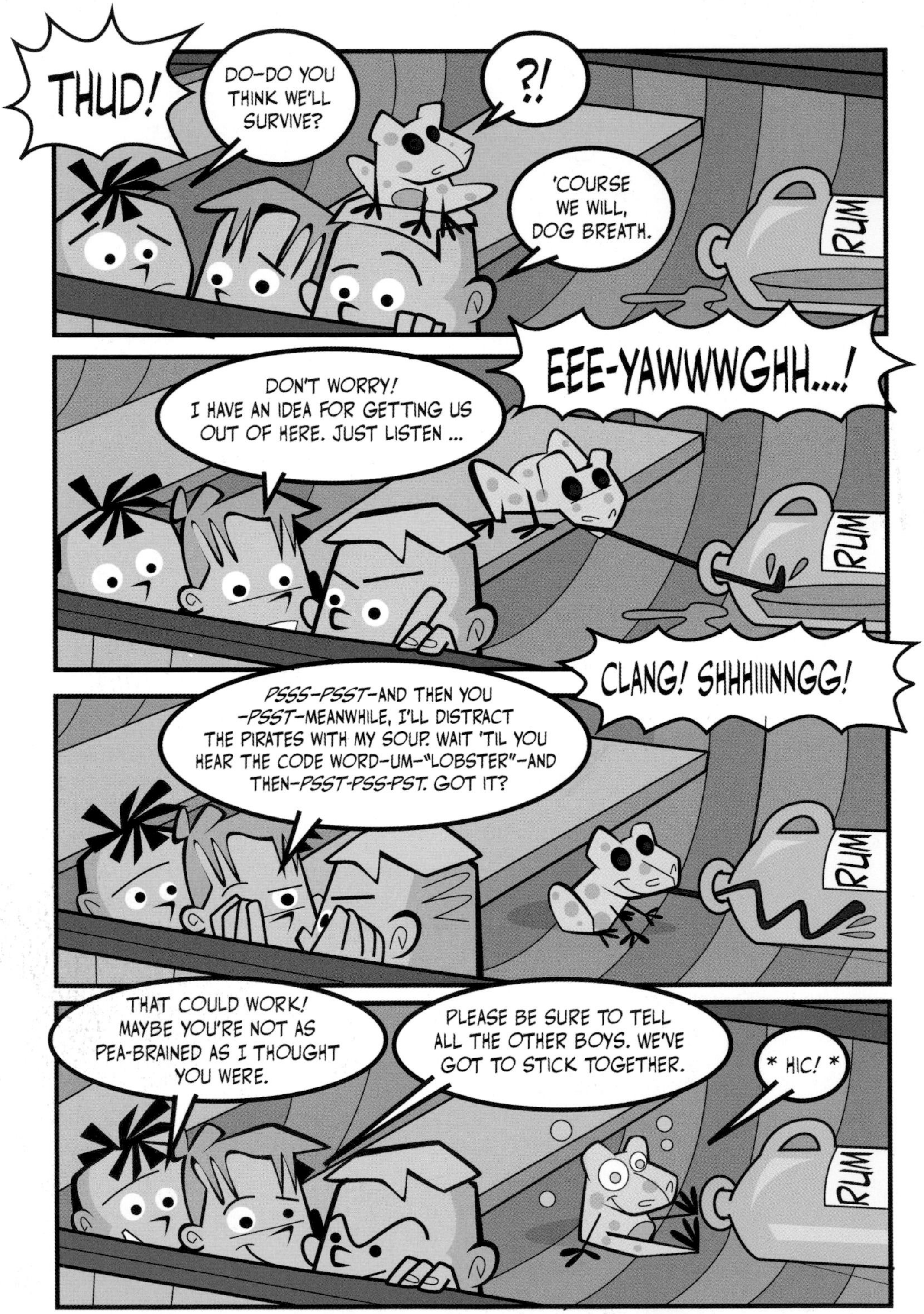
THUD!
DO-DO YOU THINK WE'LL SURVIVE?
?!
'COURSE WE WILL, DOG BREATH.
RUM
EEE-YAWWWGHH...!
DON'T WORRY! I HAVE AN IDEA FOR GETTING US OUT OF HERE. JUST LISTEN ...
RUM
CLANG! SHHHIIINNGG!
PSSS-PSST-AND THEN YOU -PSST-MEANWHILE, I'LL DISTRACT THE PIRATES WITH MY SOUP. WAIT 'TIL YOU HEAR THE CODE WORD-UM-"LOBSTER"-AND THEN-PSST-PSS-PST. GOT IT?
RUM
THAT COULD WORK! MAYBE YOU'RE NOT AS PEA-BRAINED AS I THOUGHT YOU WERE.
PLEASE BE SURE TO TELL ALL THE OTHER BOYS. WE'VE GOT TO STICK TOGETHER.
* HIC! *
RUM

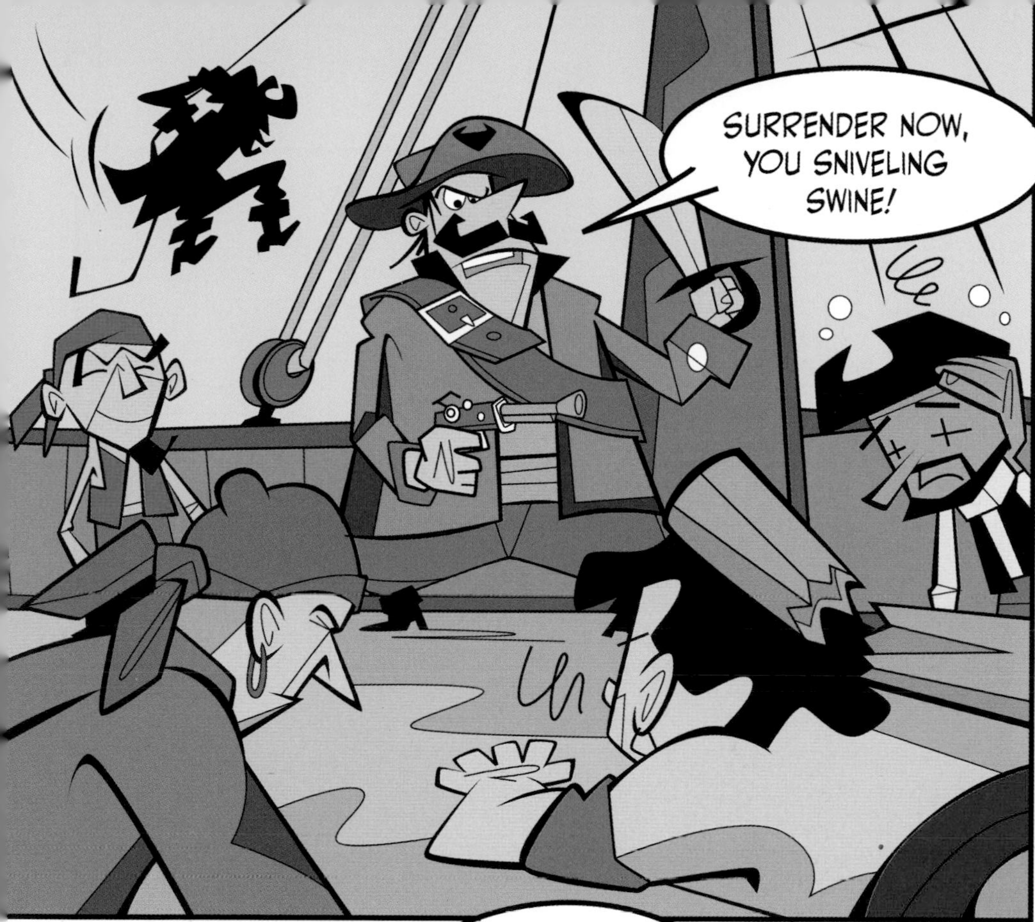
SURRENDER NOW, YOU SNIVELING SWINE!

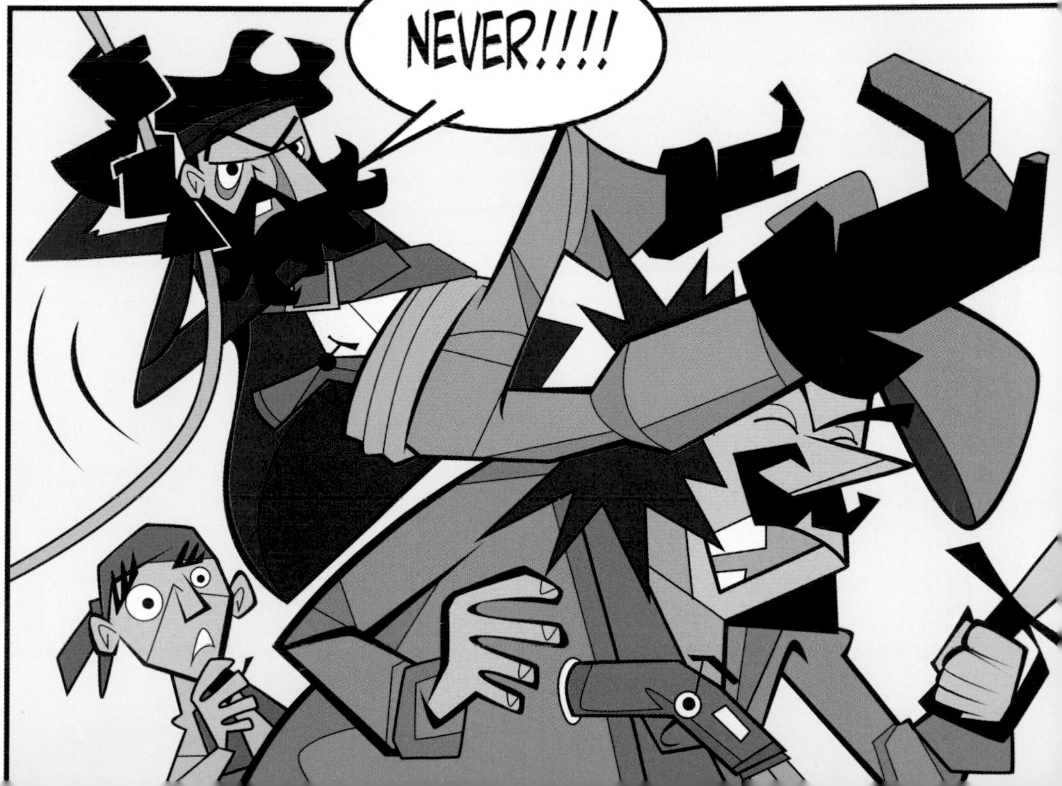
NEVER!!!!

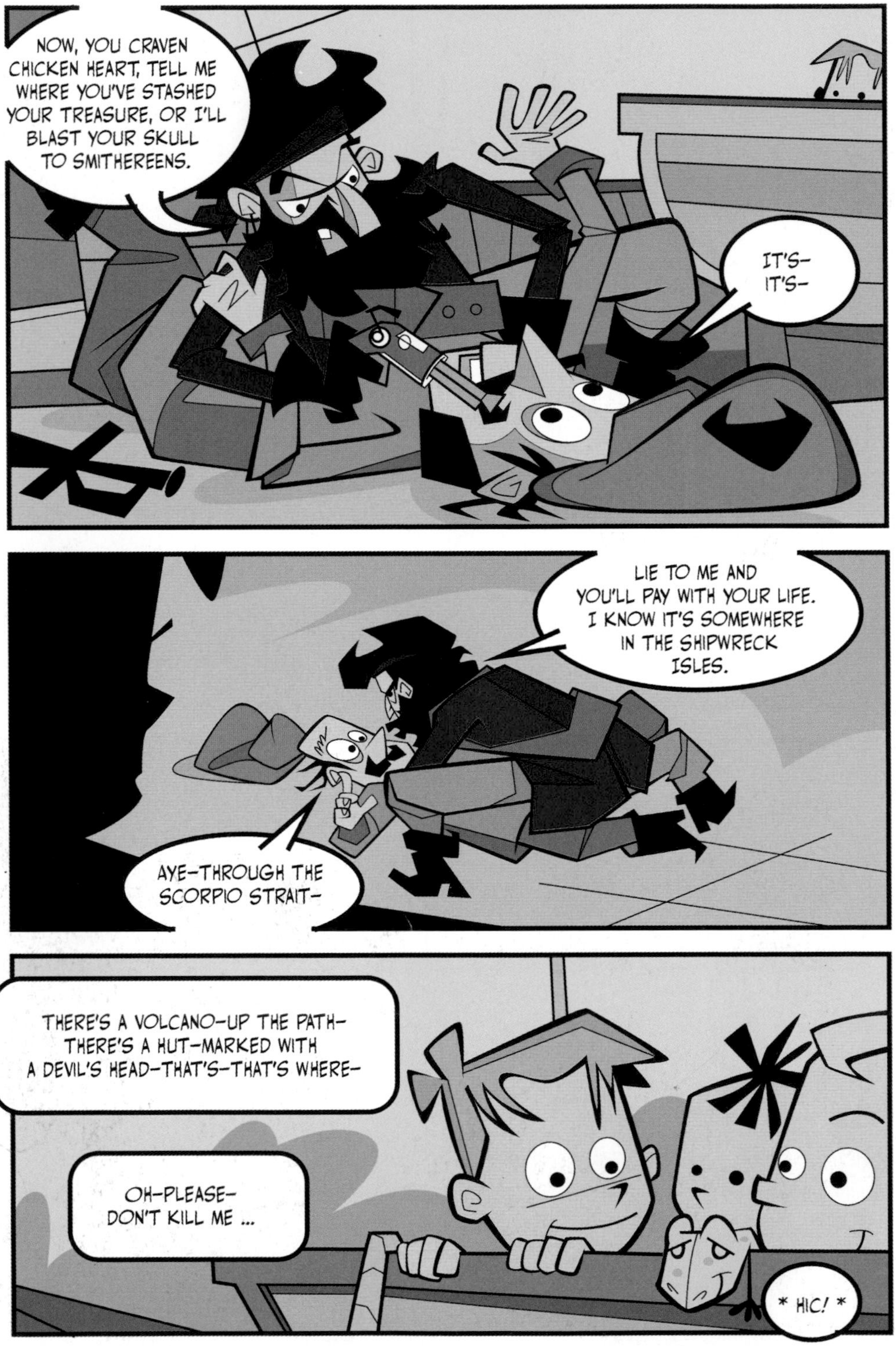
NOW, YOU CRAVEN CHICKEN HEART, TELL ME WHERE YOU'VE STASHED YOUR TREASURE, OR I'LL BLAST YOUR SKULL TO SMITHEREENS.
IT'S- IT'S-
LIE TO ME AND YOU'LL PAY WITH YOUR LIFE. I KNOW IT'S SOMEWHERE IN THE SHIPWRECK ISLES.
AYE-THROUGH THE SCORPIO STRAIT-
THERE'S A VOLCANO-UP THE PATH-THERE'S A HUT-MARKED WITH A DEVIL'S HEAD-THAT'S-THAT'S WHERE-
OH-PLEASE-DON'T KILL ME ...
* HIC! *

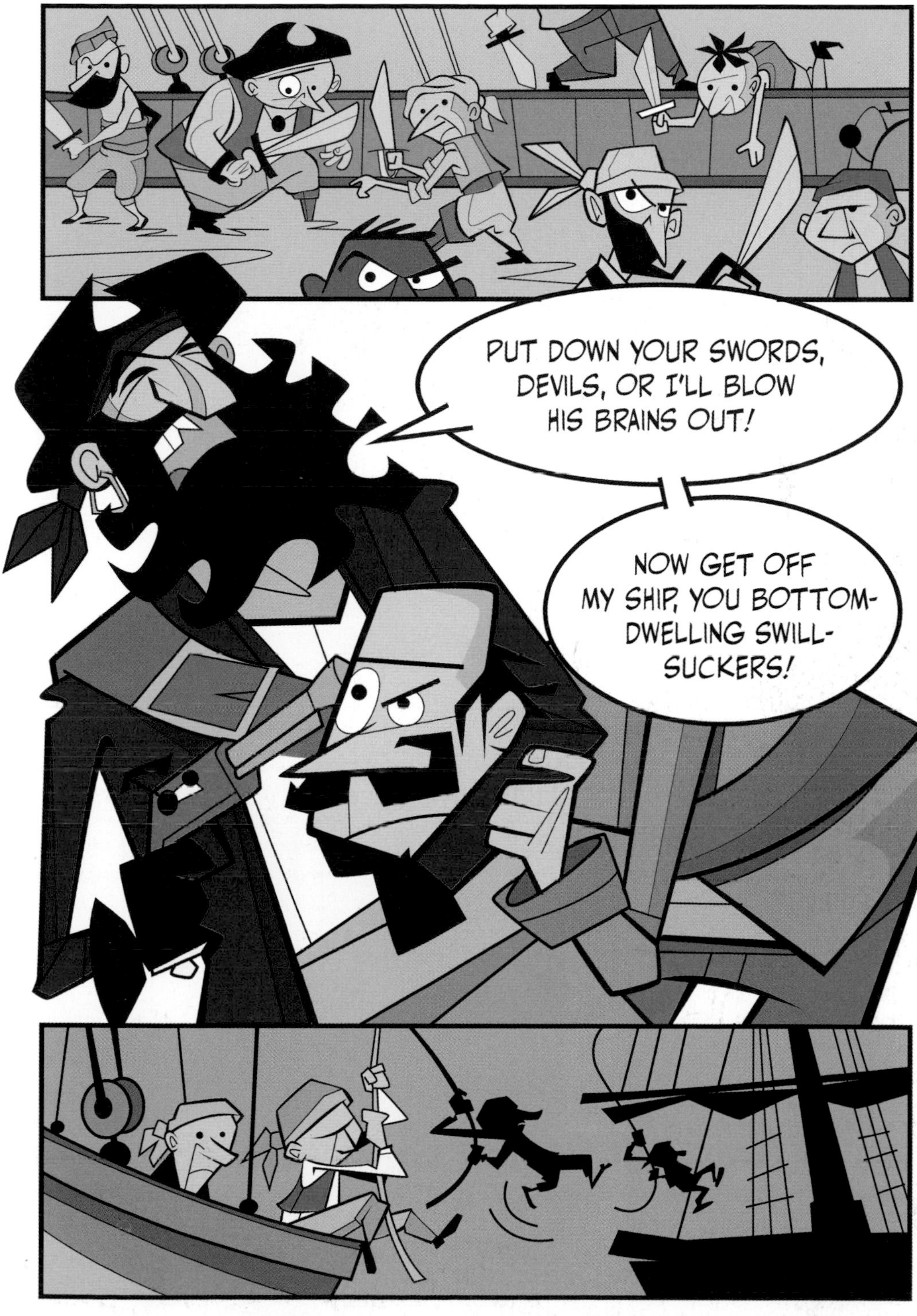
PUT DOWN YOUR SWORDS, DEVILS, OR I'LL BLOW HIS BRAINS OUT!
NOW GET OFF MY SHIP, YOU BOTTOM-DWELLING SWILL-SUCKERS!

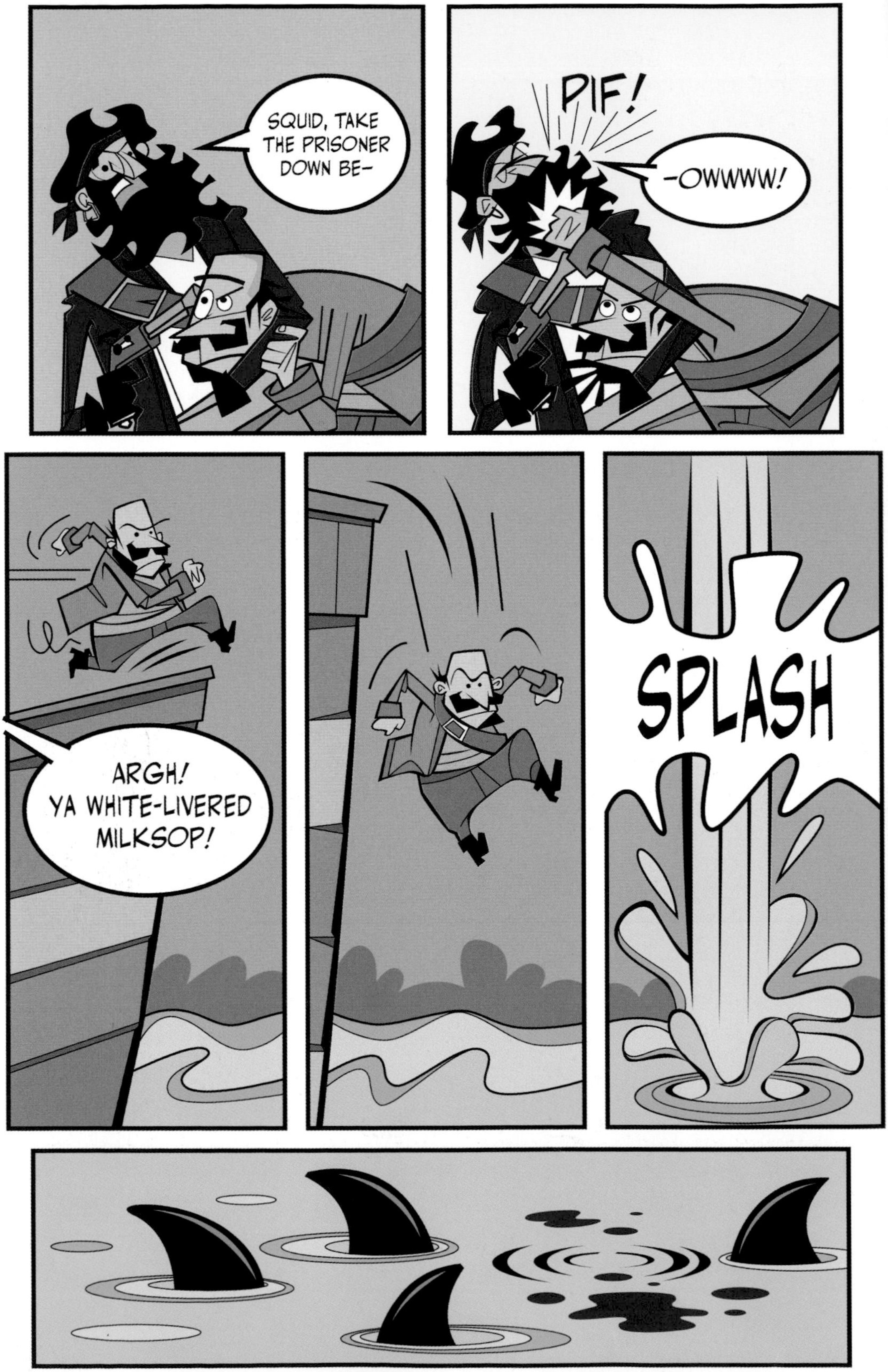
SQUID, TAKE THE PRISONER DOWN BE-
PIF!
-OWWWW!
ARGH! YA WHITE-LIVERED MILKSOP!
SPLASH

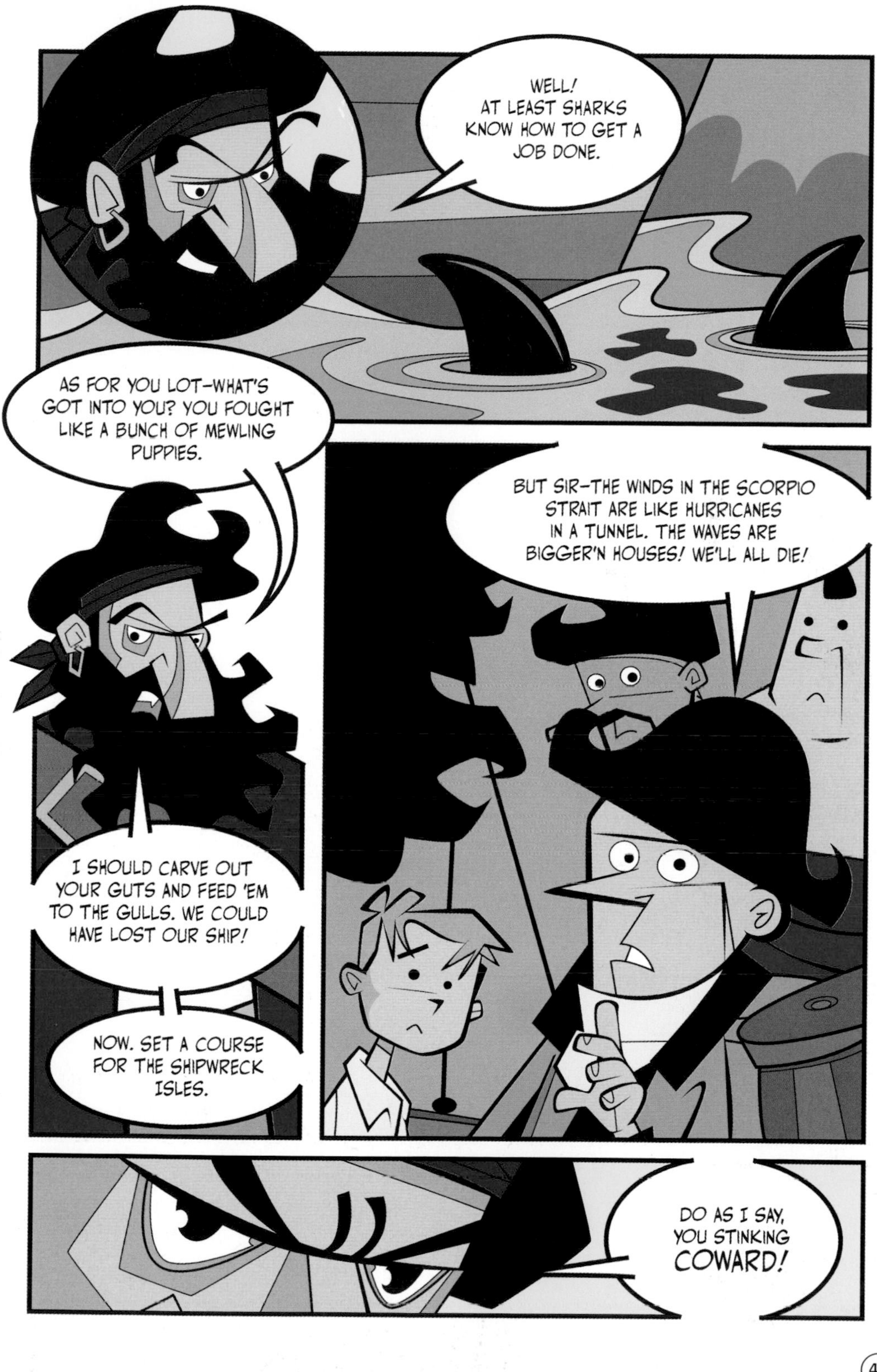
WELL! AT LEAST SHARKS KNOW HOW TO GET A JOB DONE.
AS FOR YOU LOT–WHAT'S GOT INTO YOU? YOU FOUGHT LIKE A BUNCH OF MEWLING PUPPIES.
I SHOULD CARVE OUT YOUR GUTS AND FEED 'EM TO THE GULLS. WE COULD HAVE LOST OUR SHIP!
NOW. SET A COURSE FOR THE SHIPWRECK ISLES.
BUT SIR–THE WINDS IN THE SCORPIO STRAIT ARE LIKE HURRICANES IN A TUNNEL. THE WAVES ARE BIGGER'N HOUSES! WE'LL ALL DIE!
DO AS I SAY, YOU STINKING COWARD!

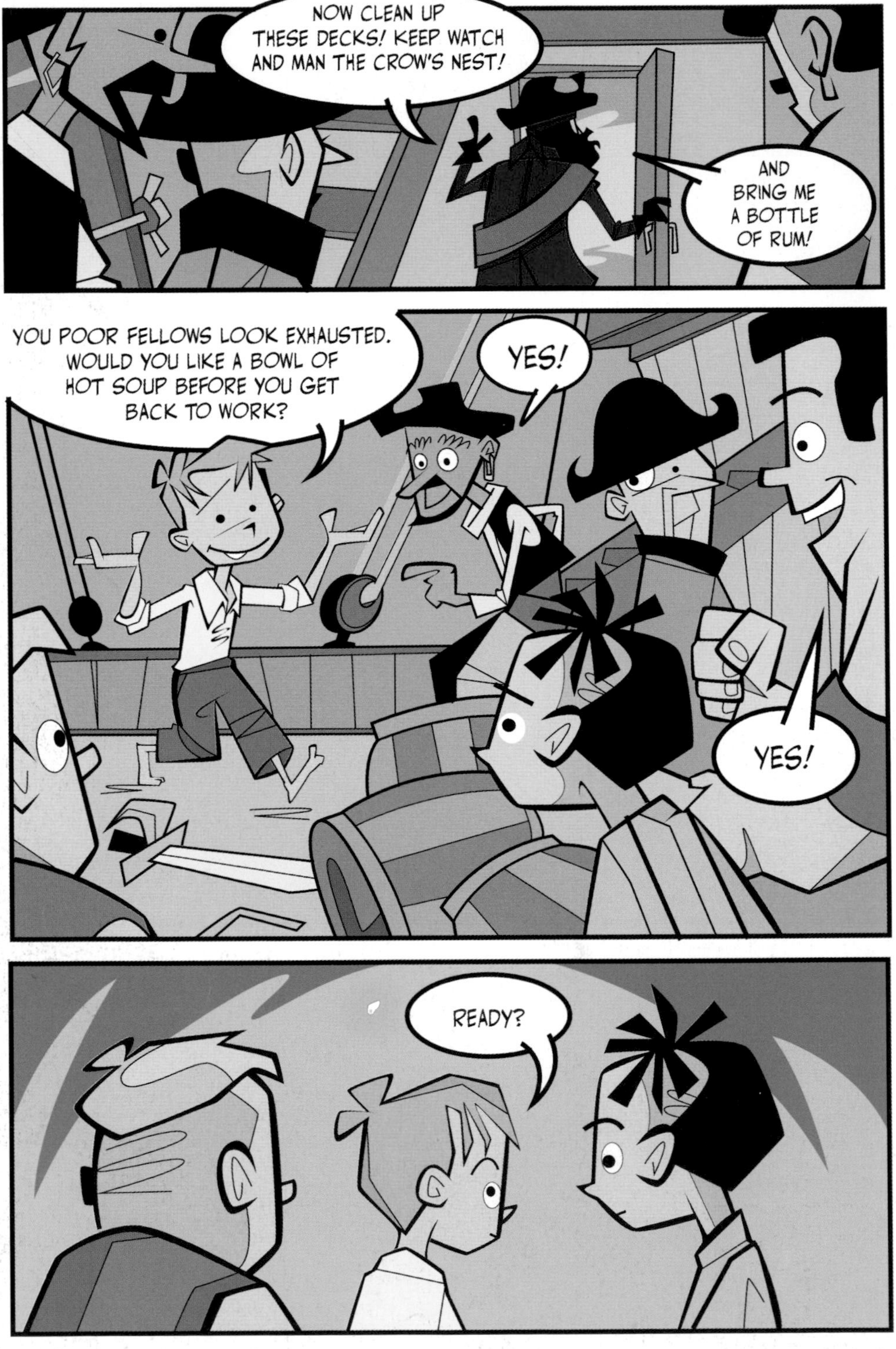
NOW CLEAN UP THESE DECKS! KEEP WATCH AND MAN THE CROW'S NEST!
AND BRING ME A BOTTLE OF RUM!
YOU POOR FELLOWS LOOK EXHAUSTED. WOULD YOU LIKE A BOWL OF HOT SOUP BEFORE YOU GET BACK TO WORK?
YES!
YES!
READY?

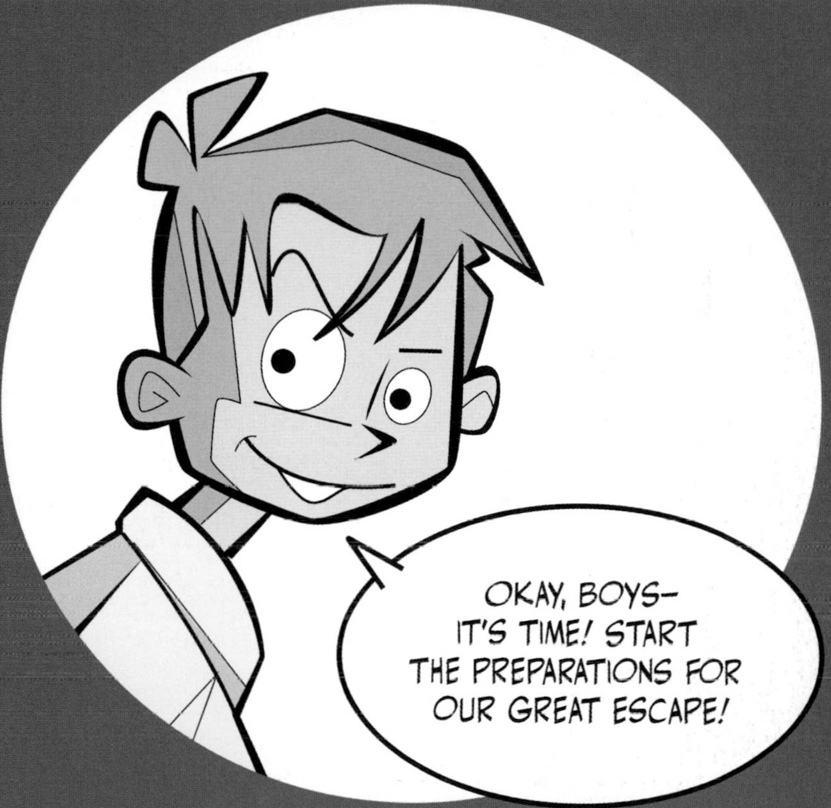
OKAY, BOYS–
IT'S TIME! START
THE PREPARATIONS FOR
OUR GREAT ESCAPE!

CHAPTER 5
HERCULEAN HEADLOCKS

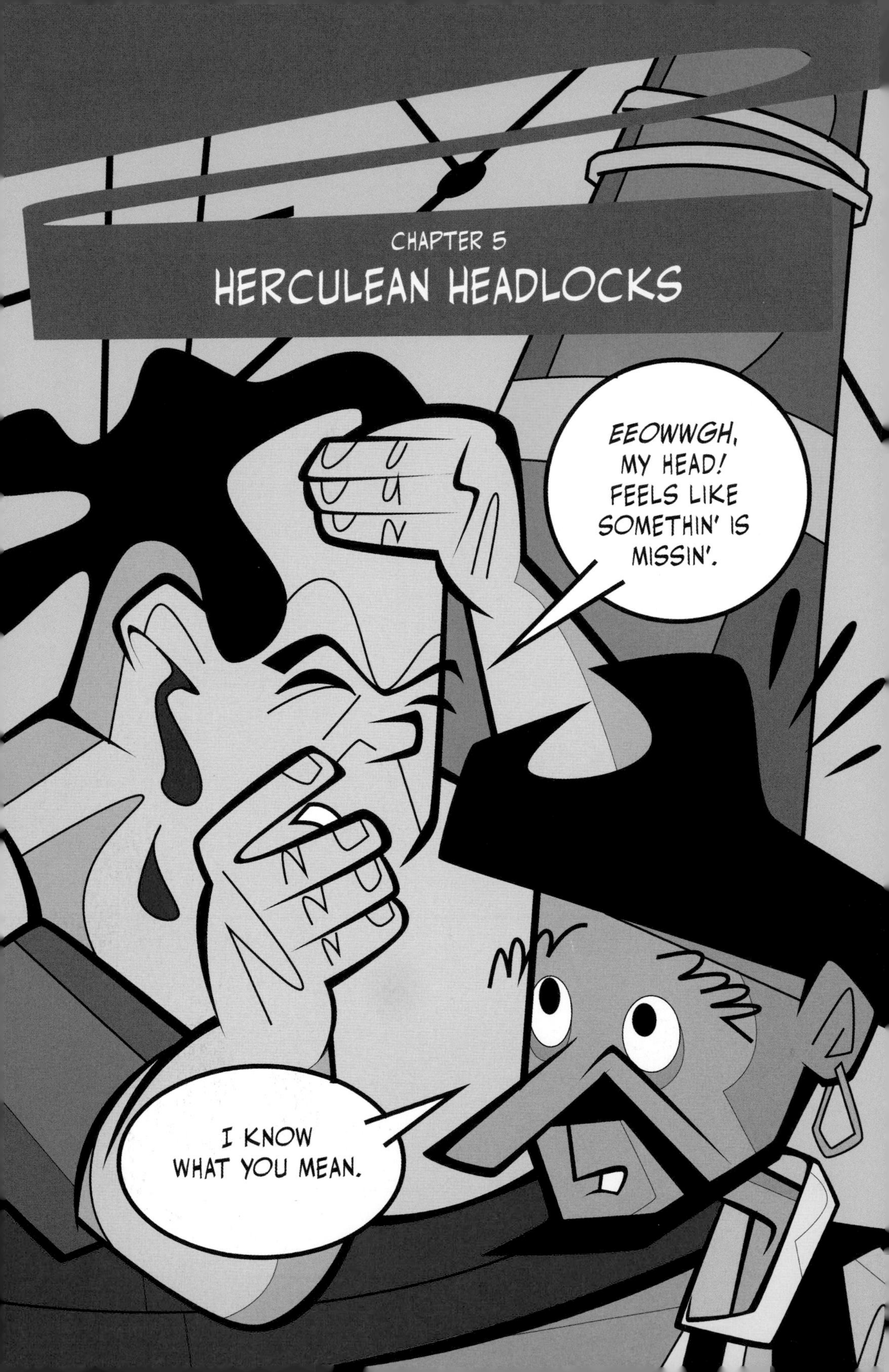
EEOWWGH, MY HEAD! FEELS LIKE SOMETHIN' IS MISSIN'.
I KNOW WHAT YOU MEAN.

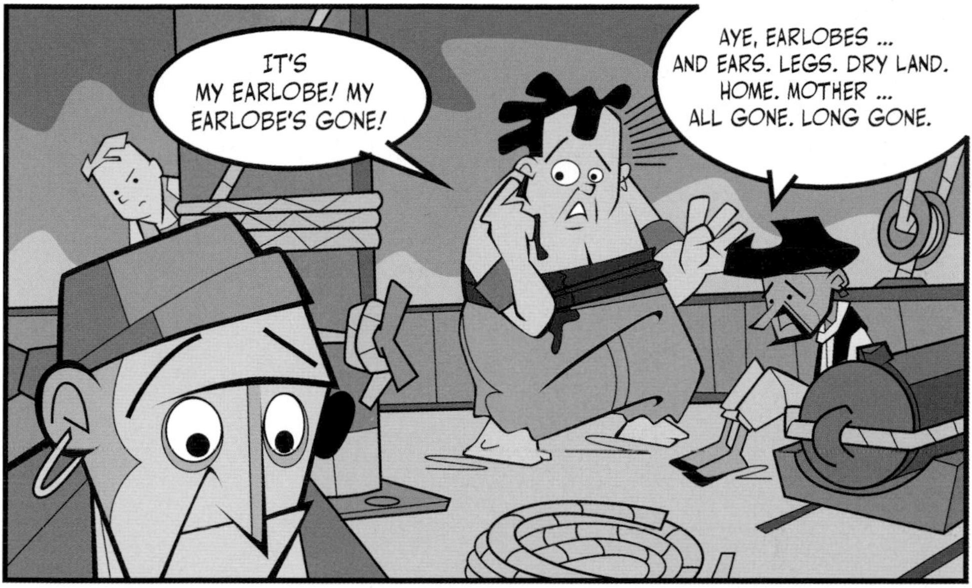
IT'S MY EARLOBE! MY EARLOBE'S GONE!
AYE, EARLOBES ... AND EARS. LEGS. DRY LAND. HOME. MOTHER ... ALL GONE. LONG GONE.

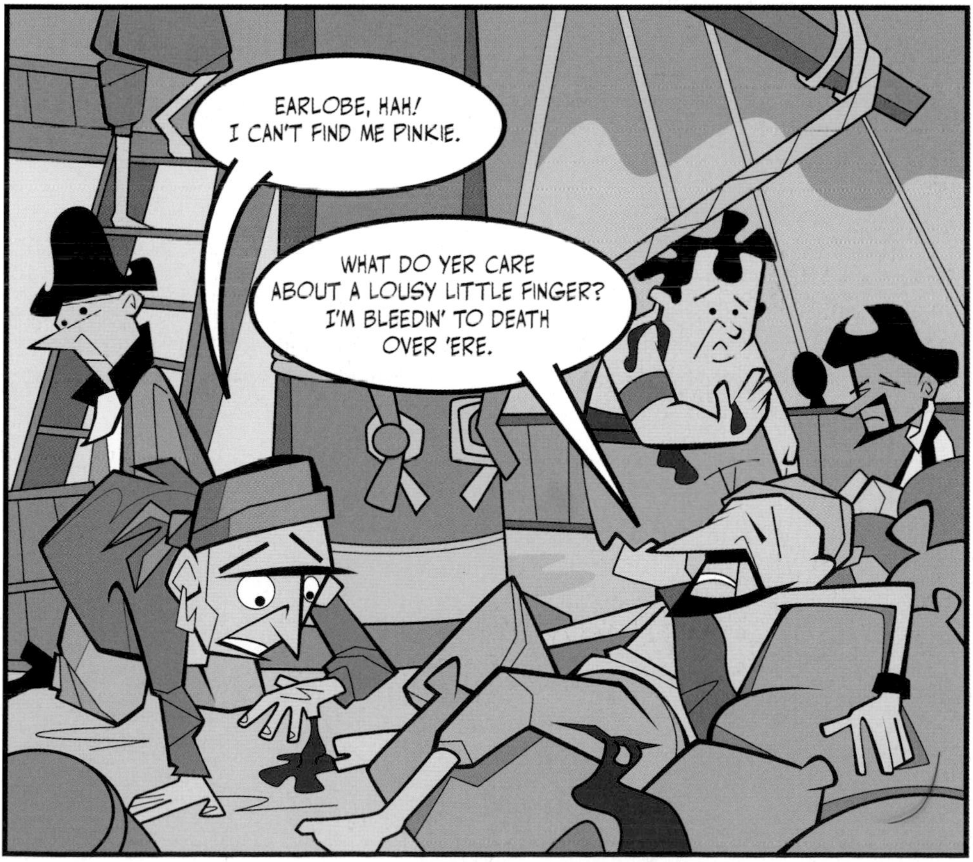
EARLOBE, HAH! I CAN'T FIND ME PINKIE.
WHAT DO YER CARE ABOUT A LOUSY LITTLE FINGER? I'M BLEEDIN' TO DEATH OVER 'ERE.

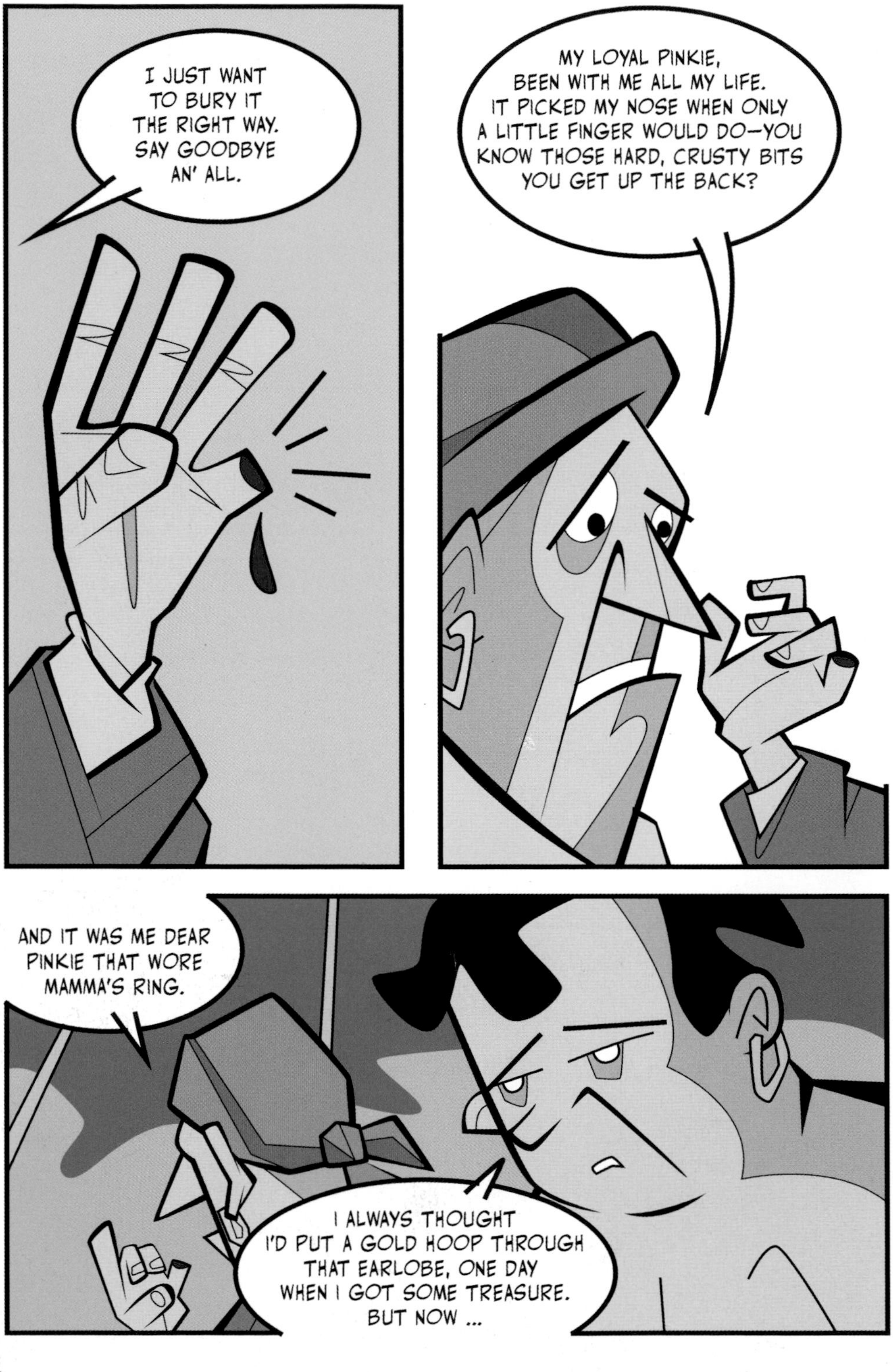
I JUST WANT TO BURY IT THE RIGHT WAY. SAY GOODBYE AN' ALL.
MY LOYAL PINKIE, BEEN WITH ME ALL MY LIFE. IT PICKED MY NOSE WHEN ONLY A LITTLE FINGER WOULD DO—YOU KNOW THOSE HARD, CRUSTY BITS YOU GET UP THE BACK?
AND IT WAS ME DEAR PINKIE THAT WORE MAMMA'S RING.
I ALWAYS THOUGHT I'D PUT A GOLD HOOP THROUGH THAT EARLOBE, ONE DAY WHEN I GOT SOME TREASURE. BUT NOW ...

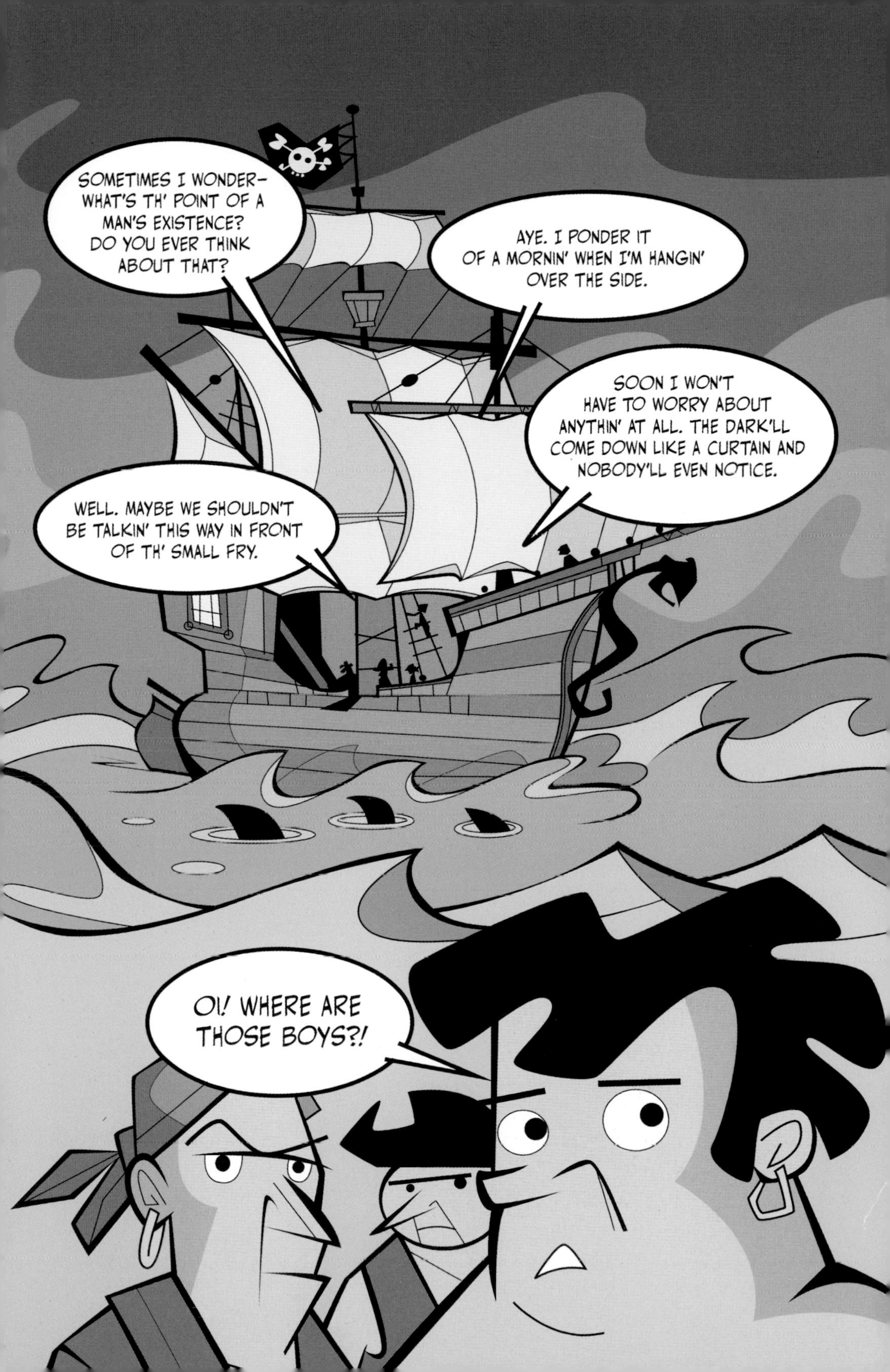
SOMETIMES I WONDER–WHAT'S TH' POINT OF A MAN'S EXISTENCE? DO YOU EVER THINK ABOUT THAT?
AYE. I PONDER IT OF A MORNIN' WHEN I'M HANGIN' OVER THE SIDE.
SOON I WON'T HAVE TO WORRY ABOUT ANYTHIN' AT ALL. THE DARK'LL COME DOWN LIKE A CURTAIN AND NOBODY'LL EVEN NOTICE.
WELL. MAYBE WE SHOULDN'T BE TALKIN' THIS WAY IN FRONT OF TH' SMALL FRY.
OI! WHERE ARE THOSE BOYS?!

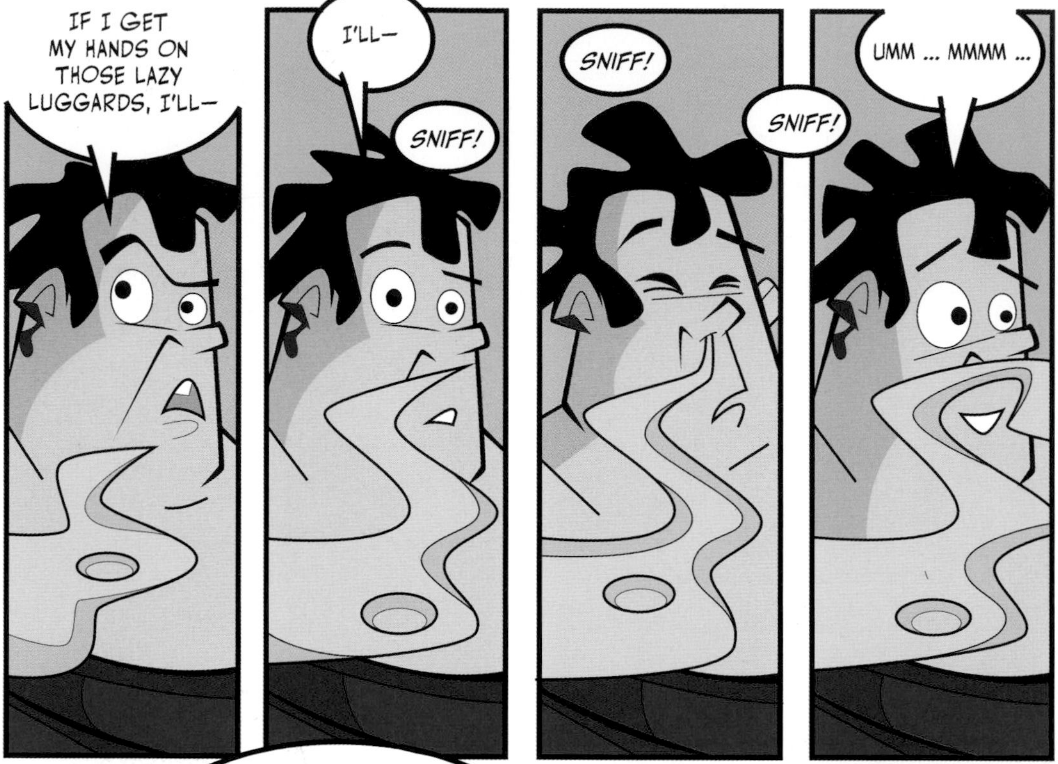
IF I GET MY HANDS ON THOSE LAZY LUGGARDS, I'LL—
I'LL—
SNIFF!
SNIFF!
SNIFF!
UMM ... MMMM ...

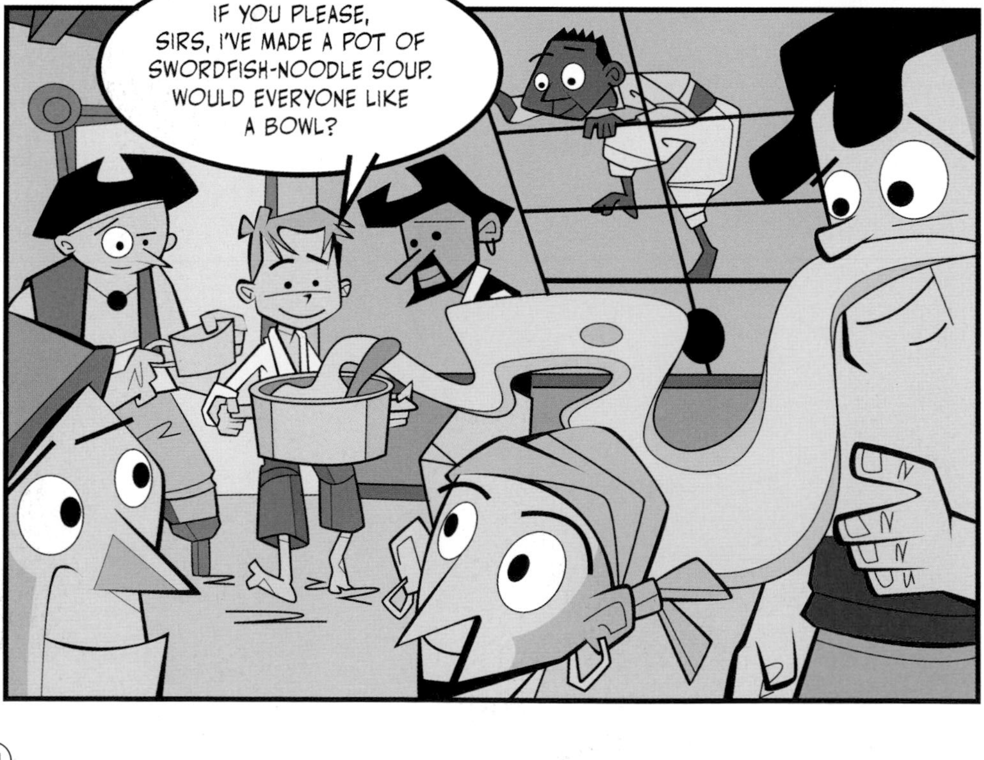
IF YOU PLEASE, SIRS, I'VE MADE A POT OF SWORDFISH-NOODLE SOUP. WOULD EVERYONE LIKE A BOWL?

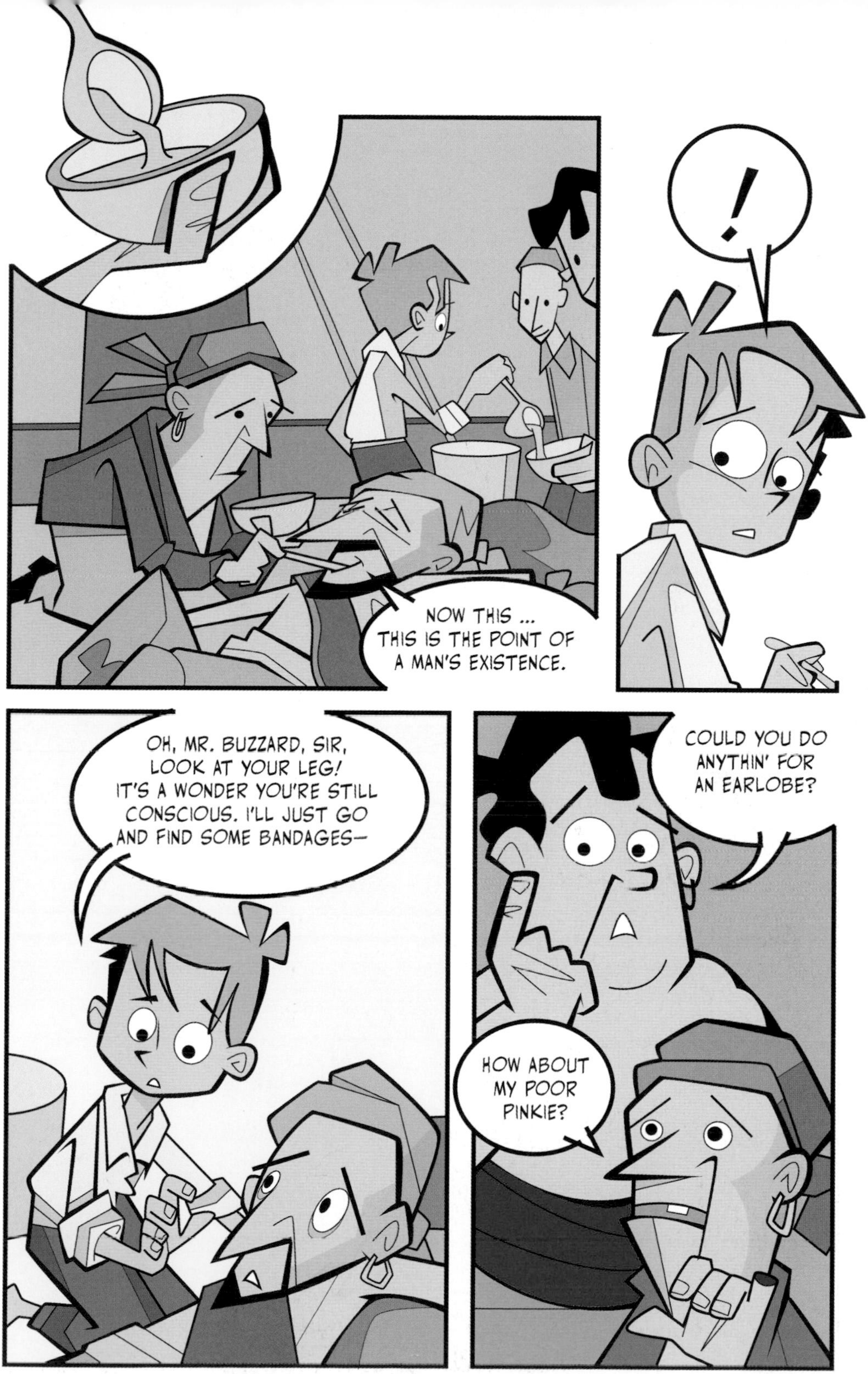
NOW THIS ...
THIS IS THE POINT OF
A MAN'S EXISTENCE.
!
OH, MR. BUZZARD, SIR,
LOOK AT YOUR LEG!
IT'S A WONDER YOU'RE STILL
CONSCIOUS. I'LL JUST GO
AND FIND SOME BANDAGES—
COULD YOU DO
ANYTHIN' FOR
AN EARLOBE?
HOW ABOUT
MY POOR
PINKIE?

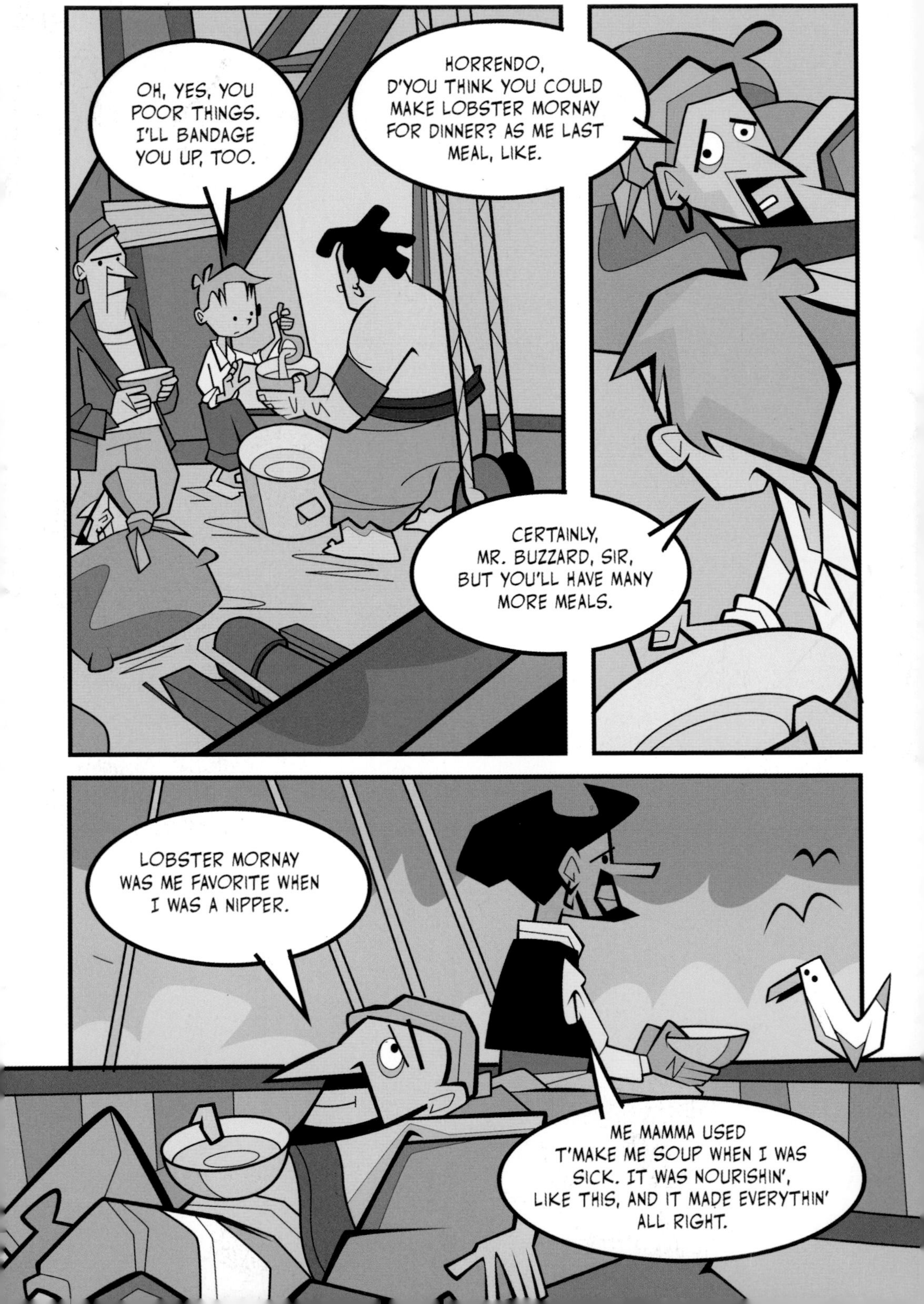
OH, YES, YOU POOR THINGS. I'LL BANDAGE YOU UP, TOO.
HORRENDO, D'YOU THINK YOU COULD MAKE LOBSTER MORNAY FOR DINNER? AS ME LAST MEAL, LIKE.
CERTAINLY, MR. BUZZARD, SIR, BUT YOU'LL HAVE MANY MORE MEALS.
LOBSTER MORNAY WAS ME FAVORITE WHEN I WAS A NIPPER.
ME MAMMA USED T'MAKE ME SOUP WHEN I WAS SICK. IT WAS NOURISHIN', LIKE THIS, AND IT MADE EVERYTHIN' ALL RIGHT.

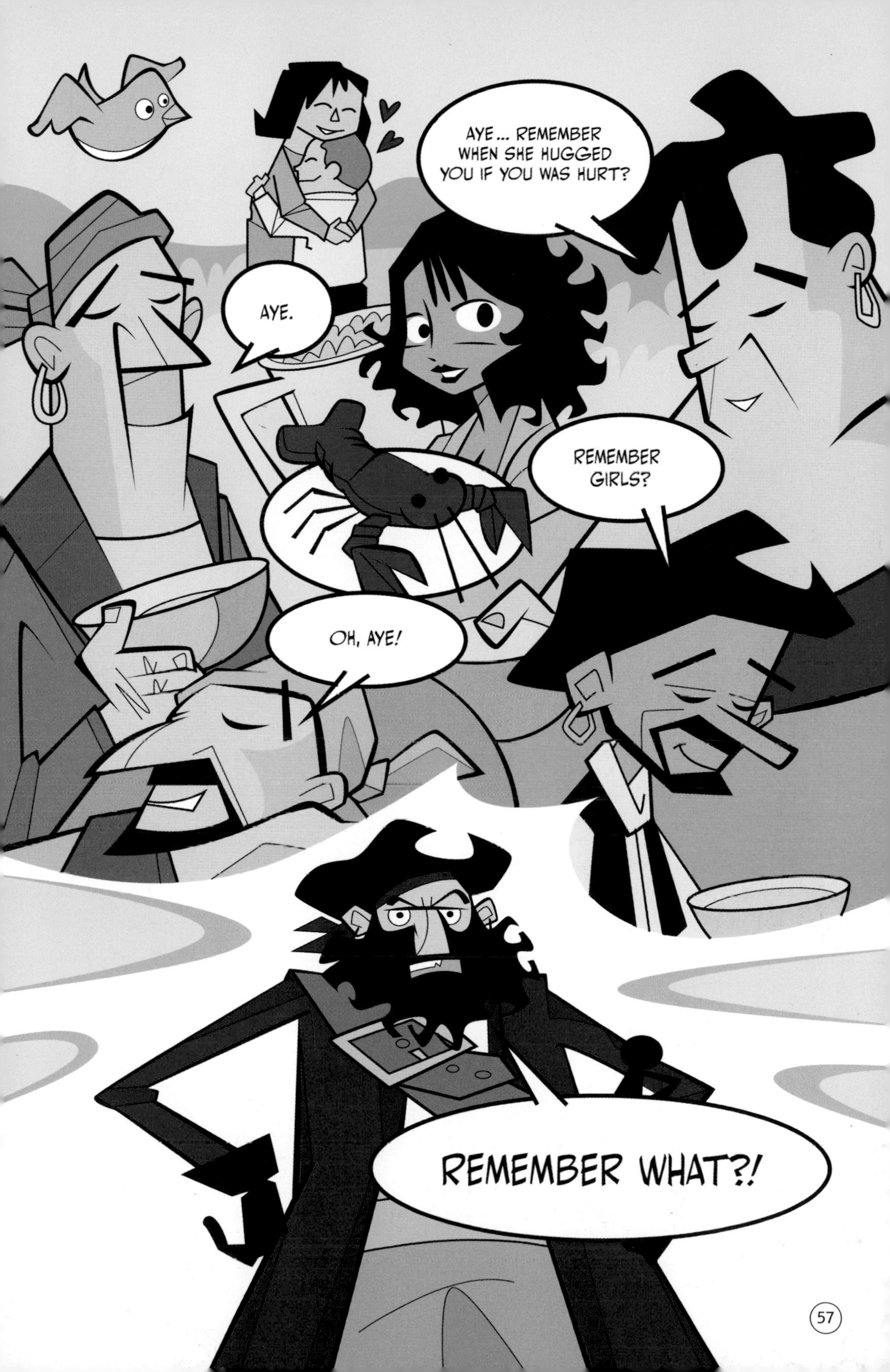
AYE... REMEMBER WHEN SHE HUGGED YOU IF YOU WAS HURT?
AYE.
REMEMBER GIRLS?
OH, AYE!
REMEMBER WHAT?!

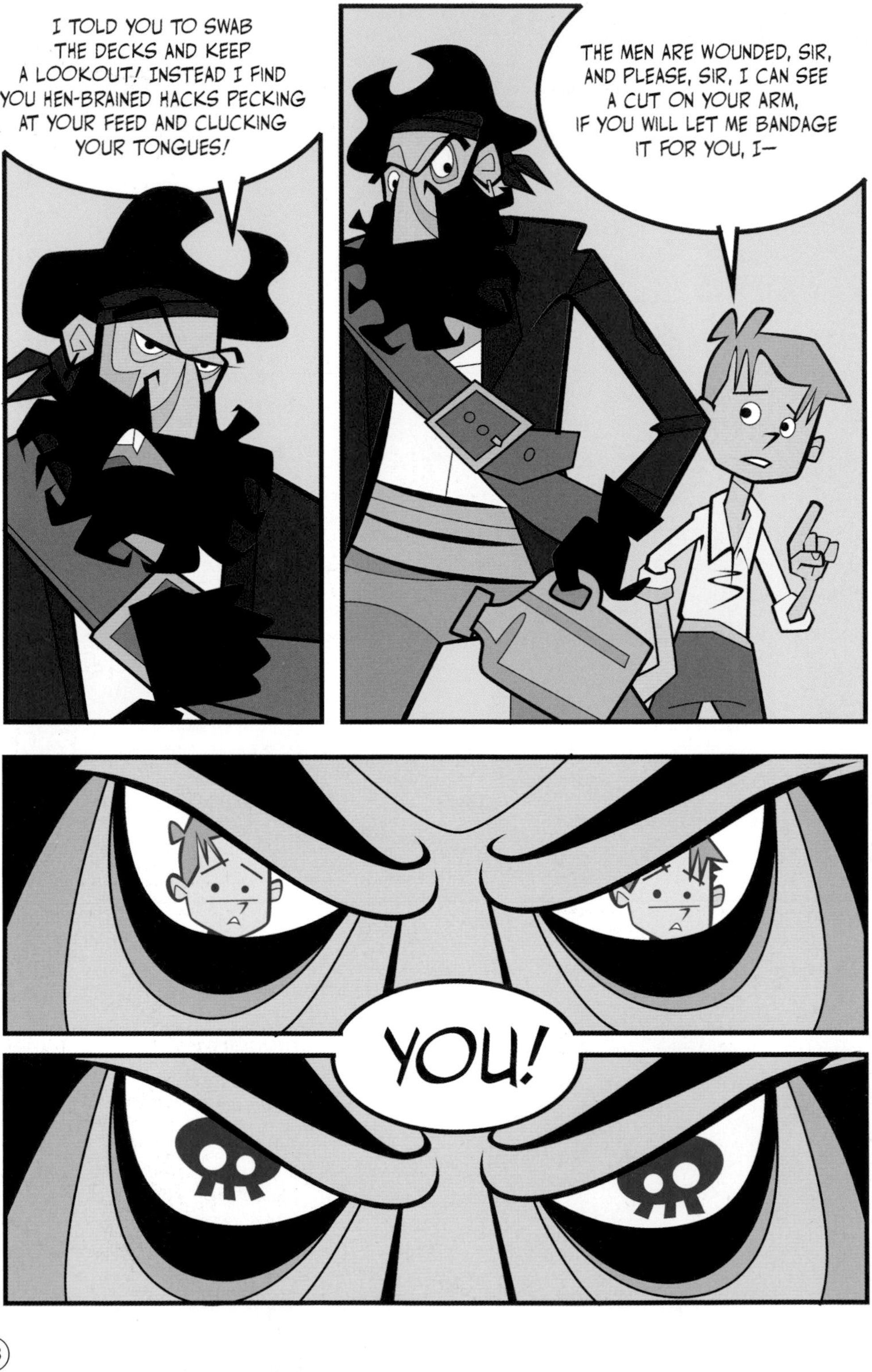
I TOLD YOU TO SWAB THE DECKS AND KEEP A LOOKOUT! INSTEAD I FIND YOU HEN-BRAINED HACKS PECKING AT YOUR FEED AND CLUCKING YOUR TONGUES!
THE MEN ARE WOUNDED, SIR, AND PLEASE, SIR, I CAN SEE A CUT ON YOUR ARM, IF YOU WILL LET ME BANDAGE IT FOR YOU, I—
YOU!

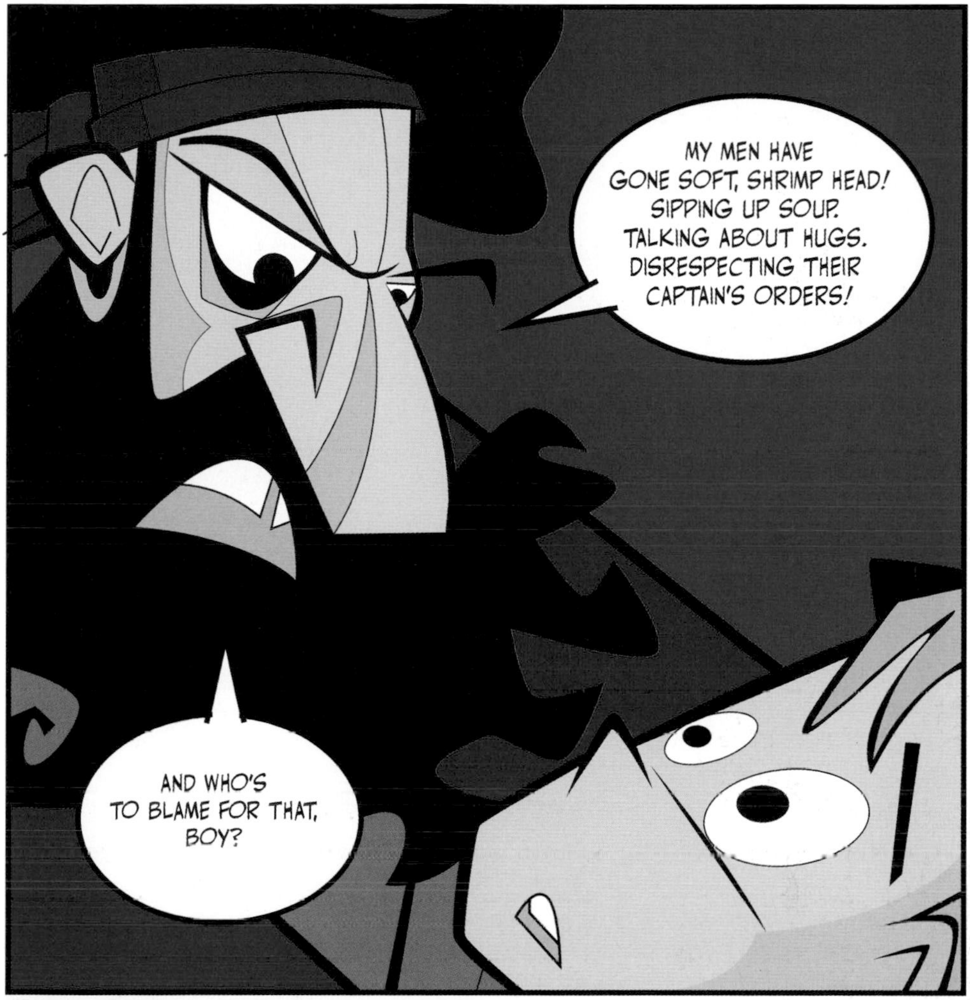
MY MEN HAVE GONE SOFT, SHRIMP HEAD! SIPPING UP SOUP. TALKING ABOUT HUGS. DISRESPECTING THEIR CAPTAIN'S ORDERS!
AND WHO'S TO BLAME FOR THAT, BOY?

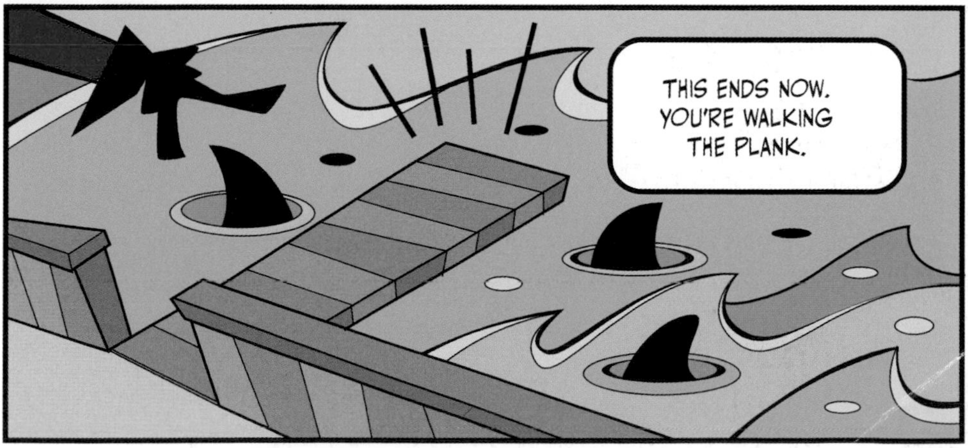
THIS ENDS NOW. YOU'RE WALKING THE PLANK.

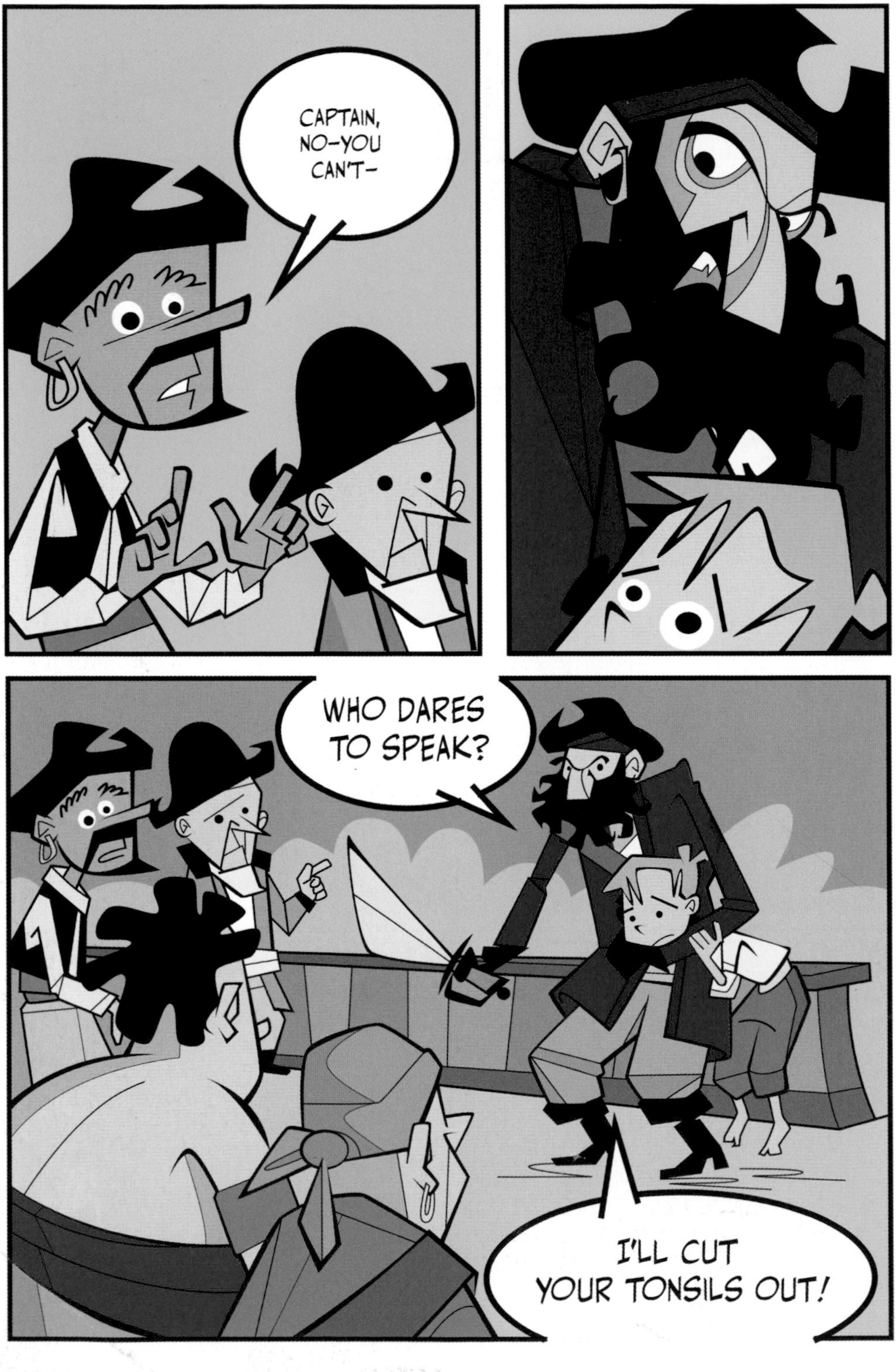
CAPTAIN, NO–YOU CAN'T–
WHO DARES TO SPEAK?
I'LL CUT YOUR TONSILS OUT!

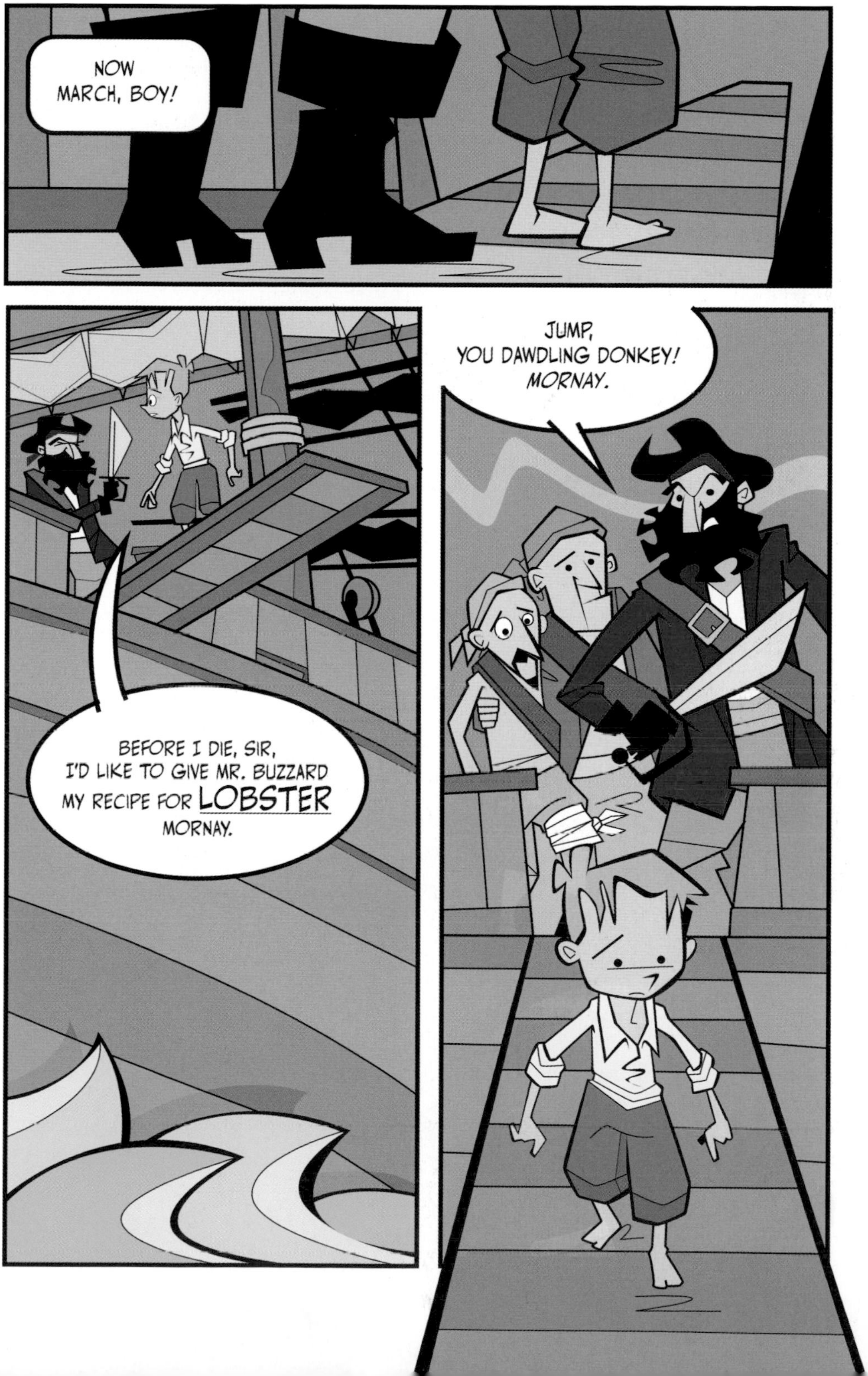
NOW MARCH, BOY!
BEFORE I DIE, SIR, I'D LIKE TO GIVE MR. BUZZARD MY RECIPE FOR LOBSTER MORNAY.
JUMP, YOU DAWDLING DONKEY! MORNAY.

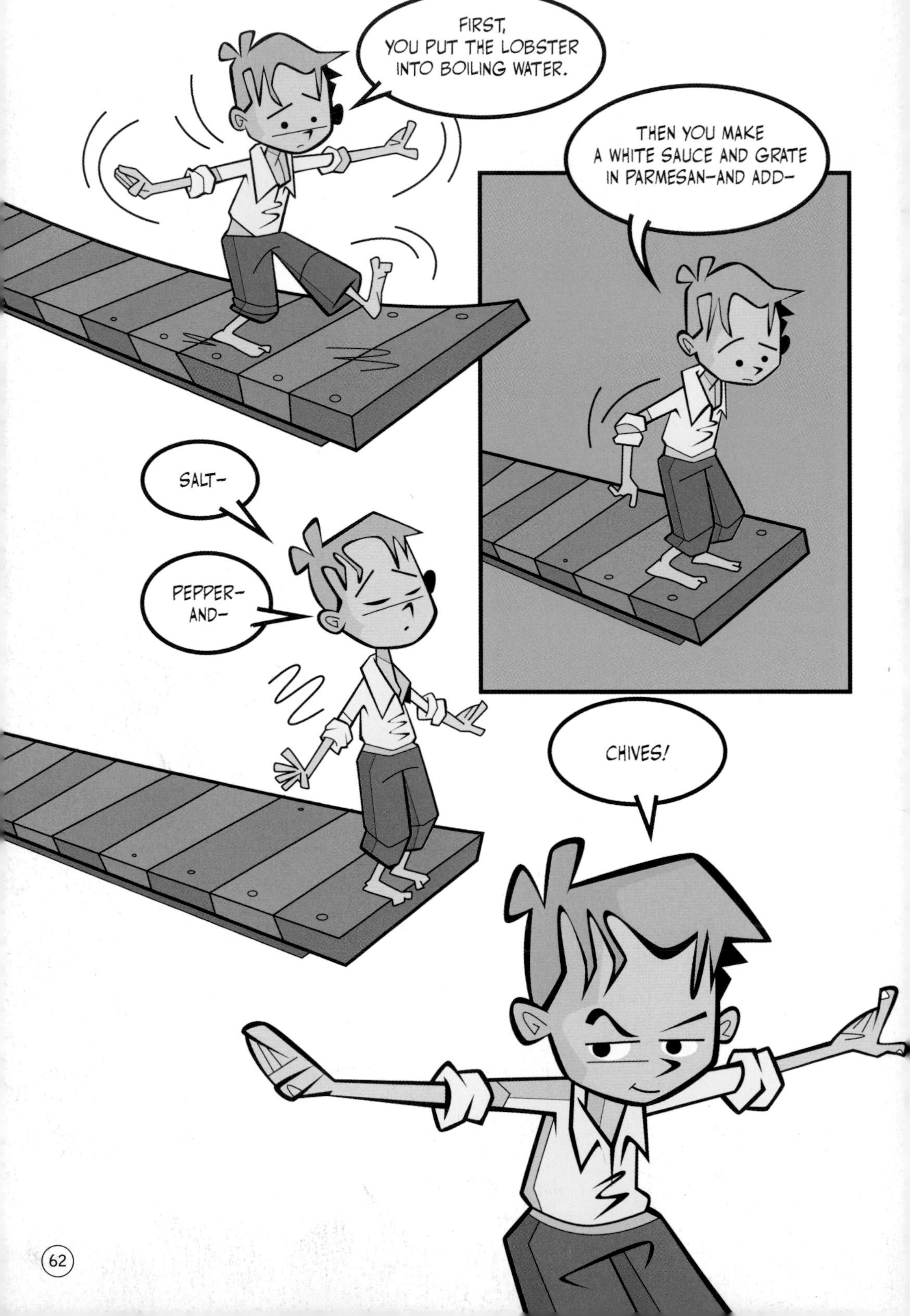
FIRST, YOU PUT THE LOBSTER INTO BOILING WATER.
THEN YOU MAKE A WHITE SAUCE AND GRATE IN PARMESAN—AND ADD—
SALT—
PEPPER—AND—
CHIVES!

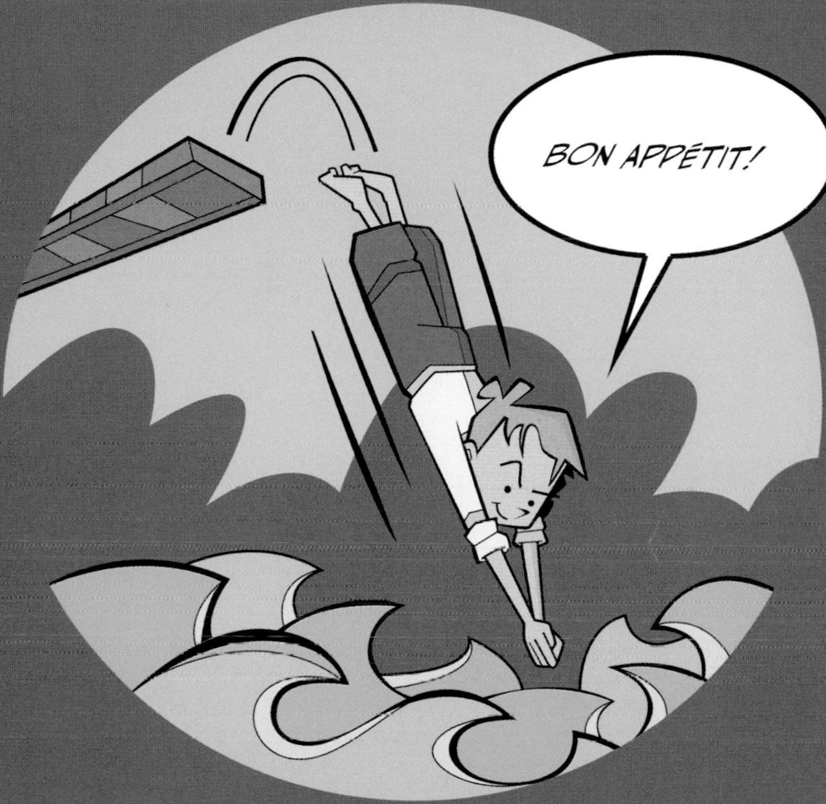
BON APPÉTIT!

CHAPTER 6
PLAYING DEAD

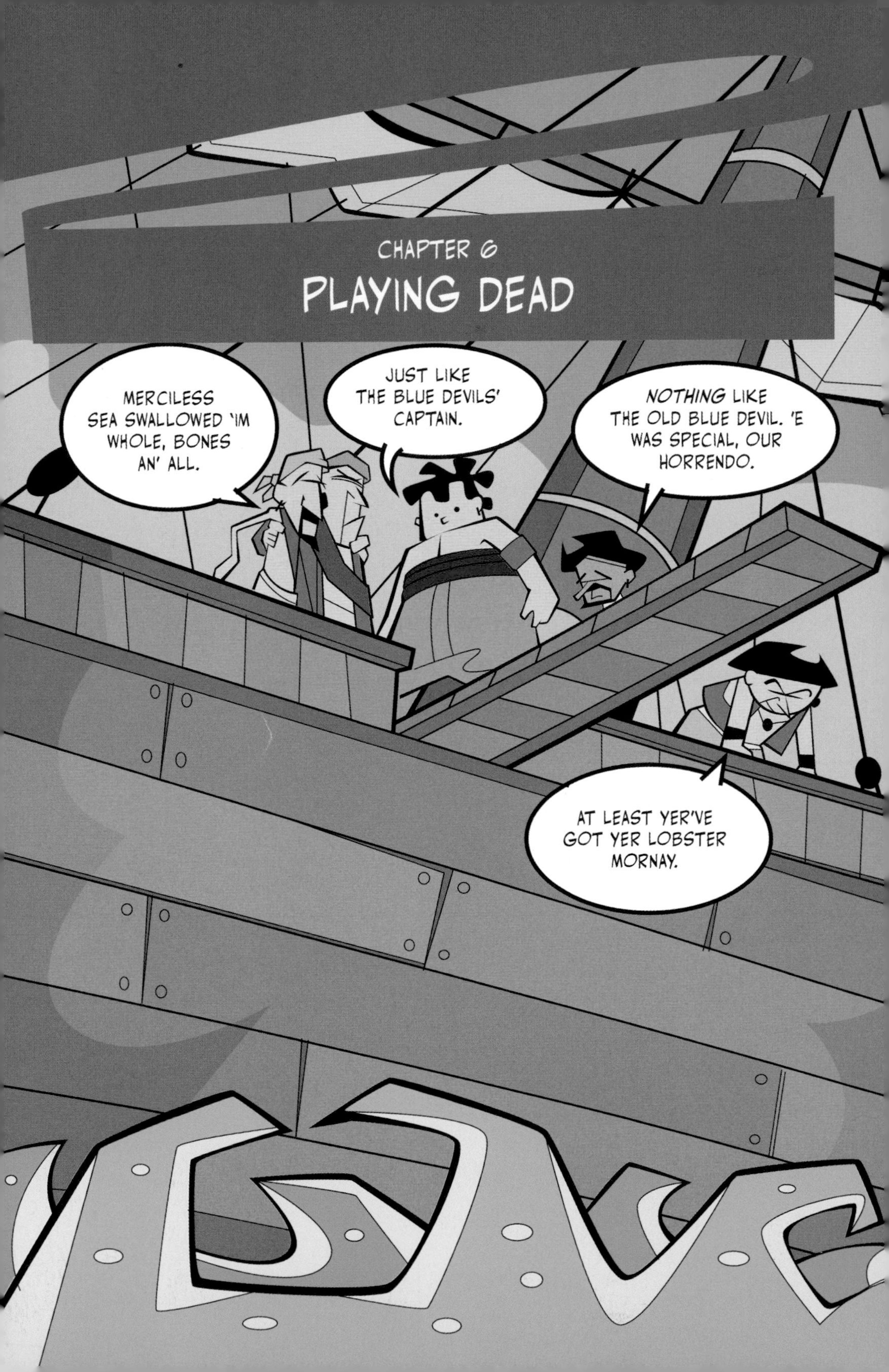
MERCILESS SEA SWALLOWED 'IM WHOLE, BONES AN' ALL.
JUST LIKE THE BLUE DEVILS' CAPTAIN.
NOTHING LIKE THE OLD BLUE DEVIL. 'E WAS SPECIAL, OUR HORRENDO.
AT LEAST YER'VE GOT YER LOBSTER MORNAY.

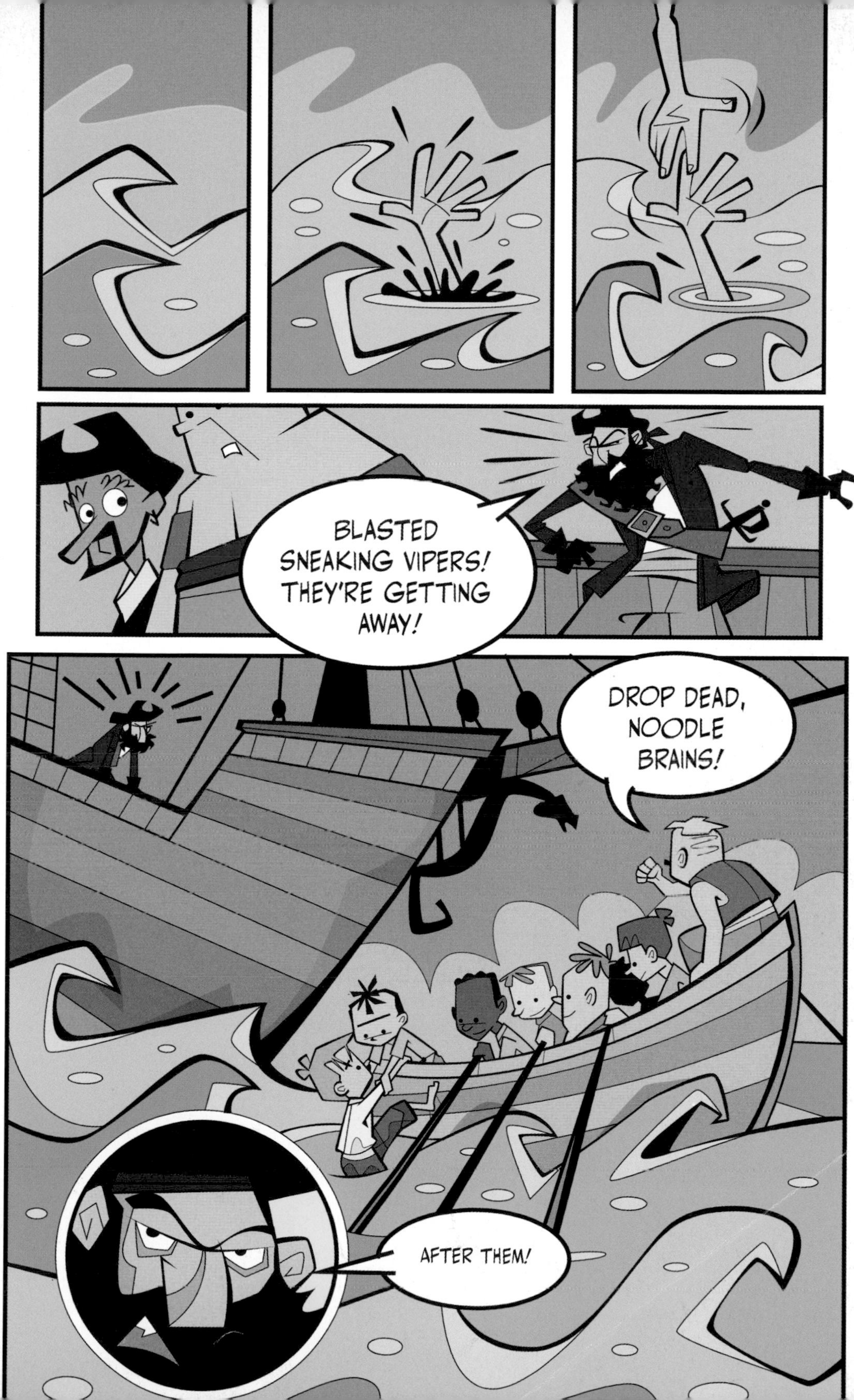
BLASTED SNEAKING VIPERS! THEY'RE GETTING AWAY!
DROP DEAD, NOODLE BRAINS!
AFTER THEM!

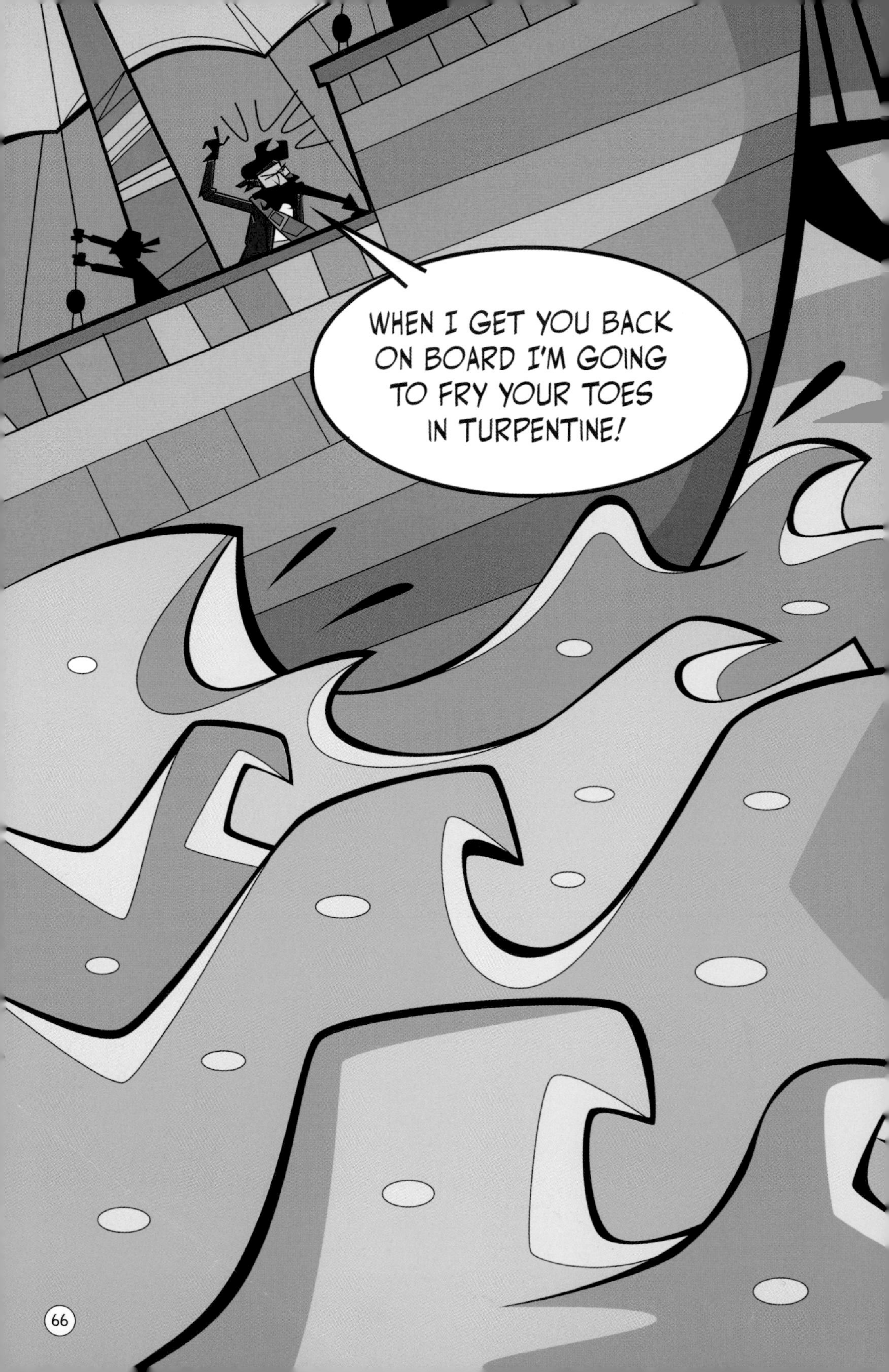
WHEN I GET YOU BACK ON BOARD I'M GOING TO FRY YOUR TOES IN TURPENTINE!

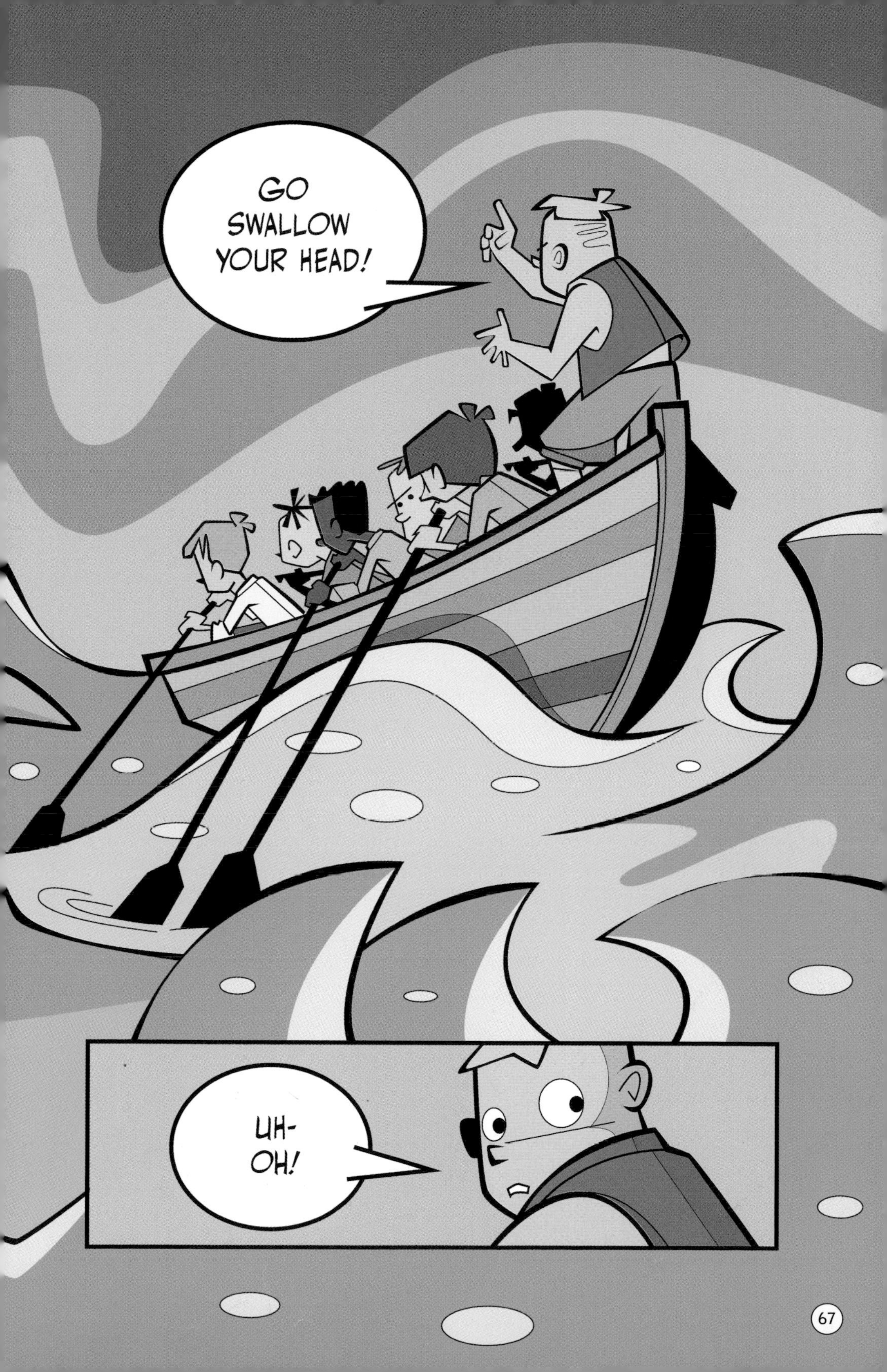
GO SWALLOW YOUR HEAD!
UH-OH!

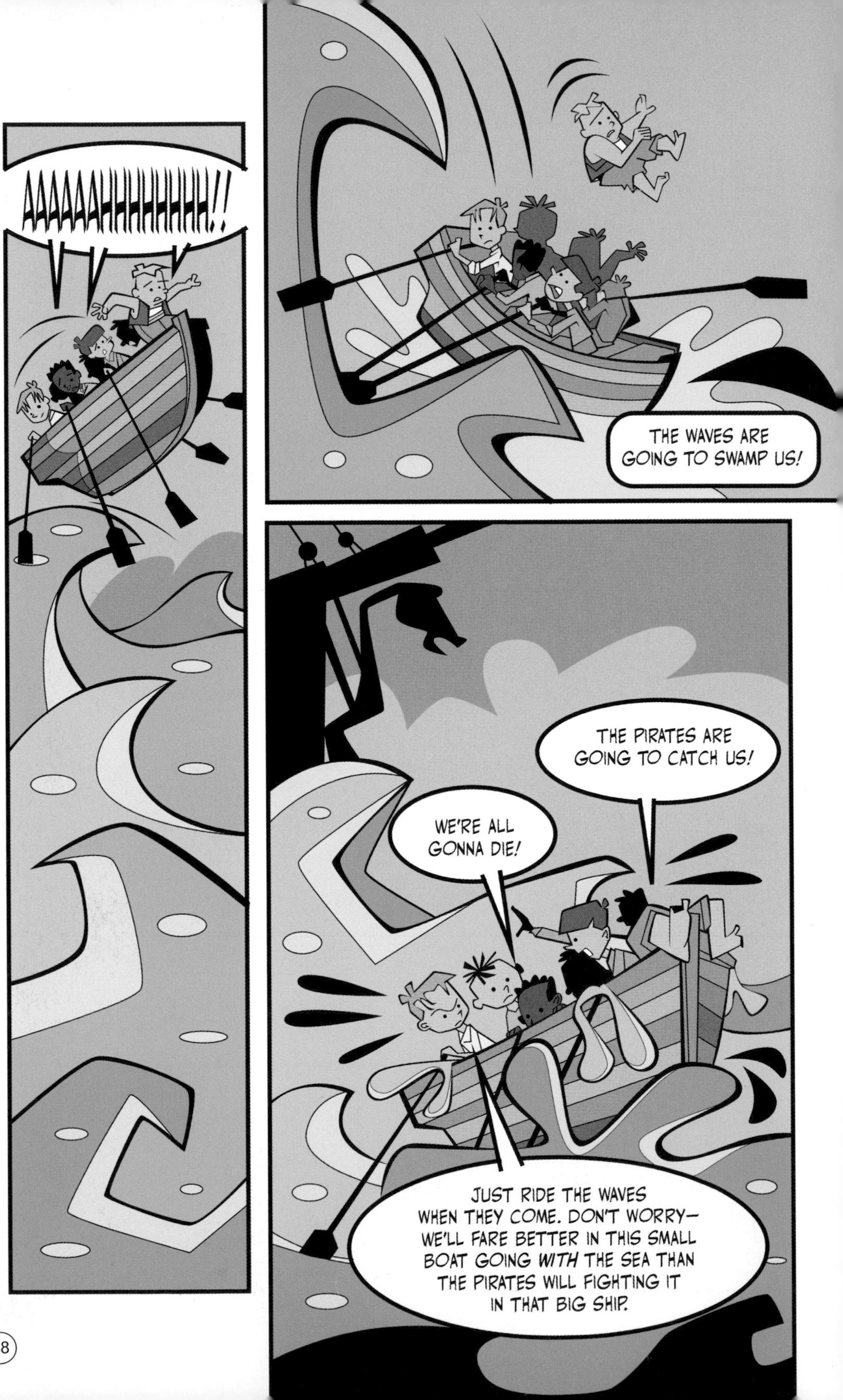
AAAAAAHHHHHHHH!!
THE WAVES ARE GOING TO SWAMP US!
THE PIRATES ARE GOING TO CATCH US!
WE'RE ALL GONNA DIE!
JUST RIDE THE WAVES WHEN THEY COME. DON'T WORRY—WE'LL FARE BETTER IN THIS SMALL BOAT GOING *WITH* THE SEA THAN THE PIRATES WILL FIGHTING IT IN THAT BIG SHIP.

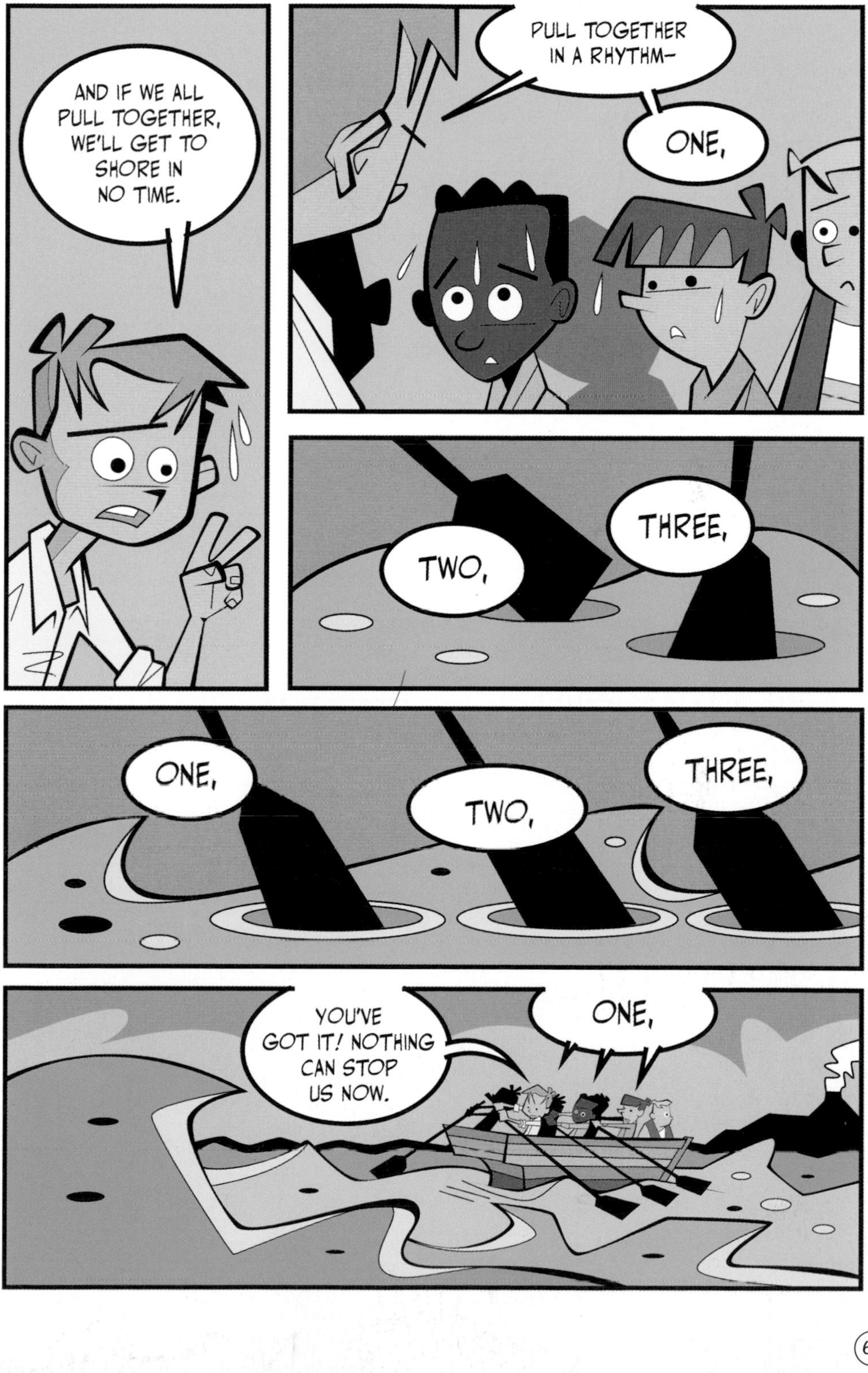
AND IF WE ALL PULL TOGETHER, WE'LL GET TO SHORE IN NO TIME.
PULL TOGETHER IN A RHYTHM-
ONE,
TWO,
THREE,
ONE,
TWO,
THREE,
YOU'VE GOT IT! NOTHING CAN STOP US NOW.
ONE,

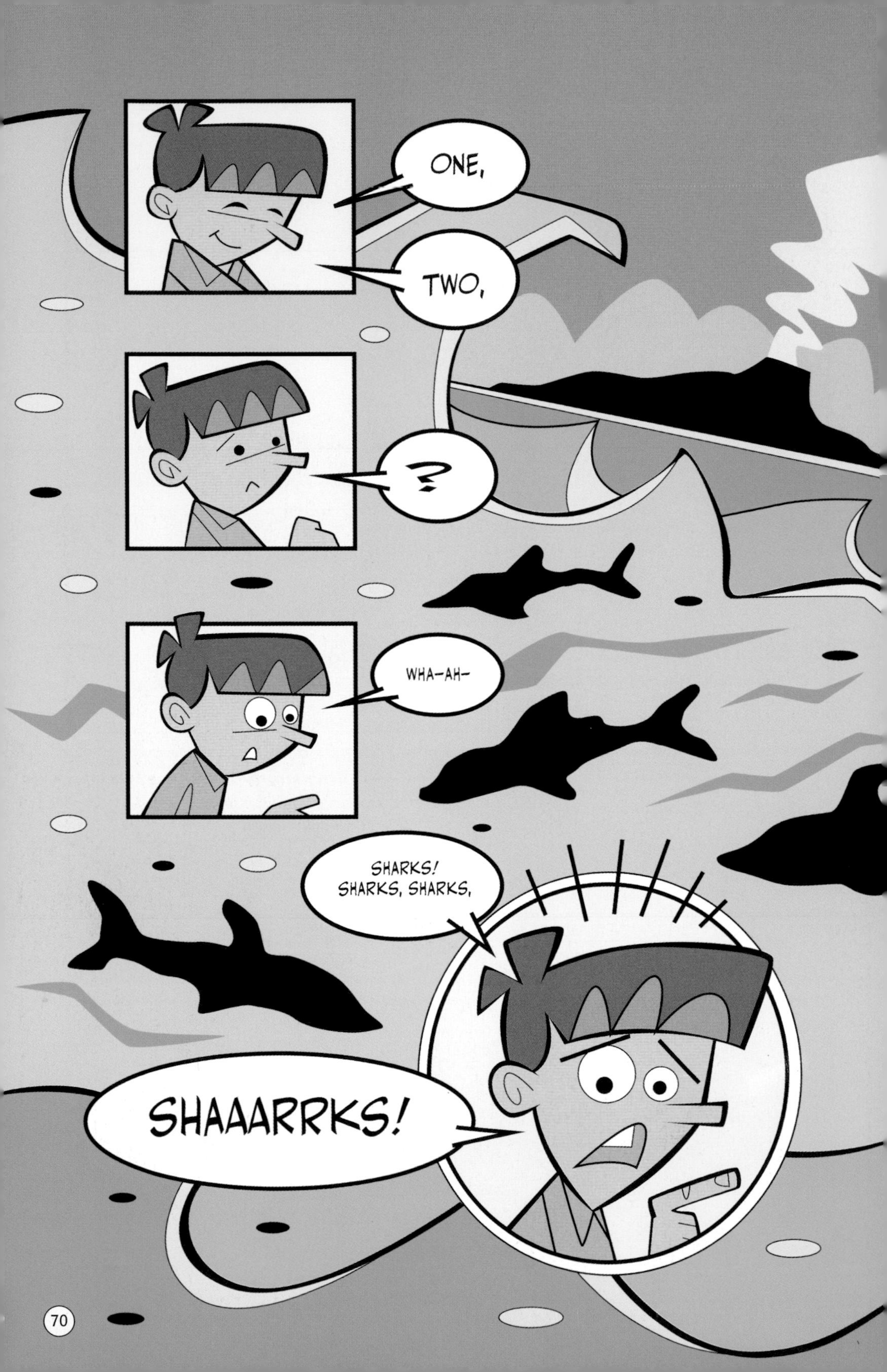
ONE,
TWO,
?
WHA-AH-
SHARKS! SHARKS, SHARKS,
SHAAARRKS!

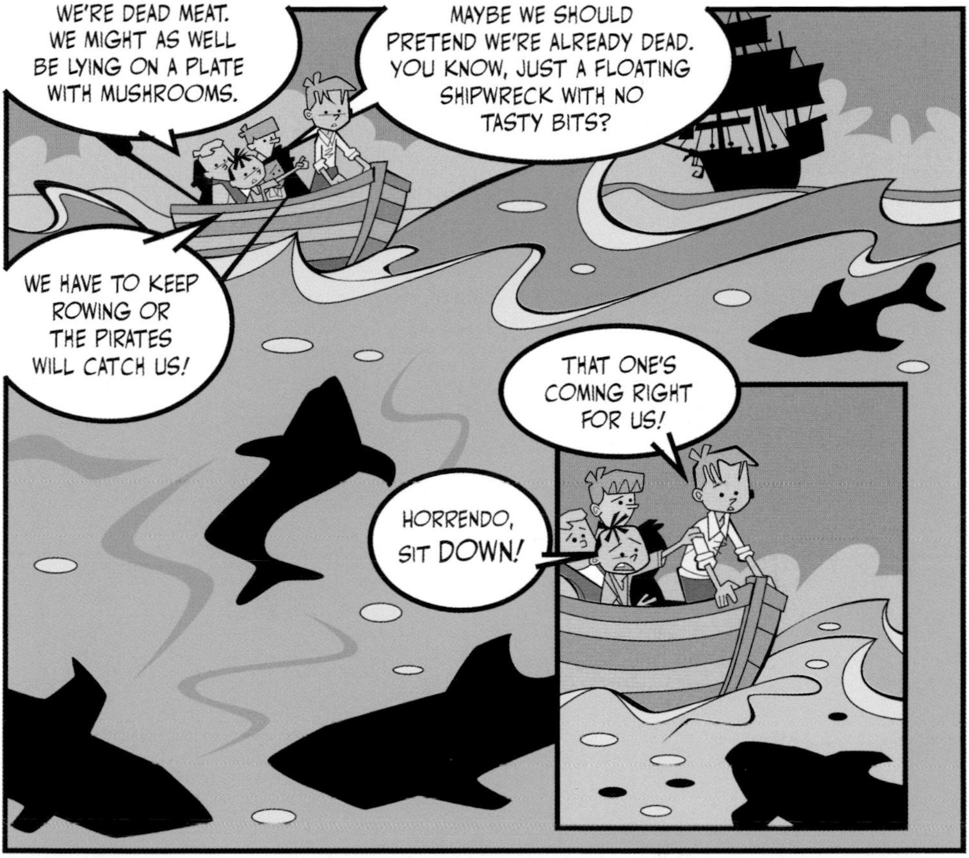
WE'RE DEAD MEAT. WE MIGHT AS WELL BE LYING ON A PLATE WITH MUSHROOMS.
MAYBE WE SHOULD PRETEND WE'RE ALREADY DEAD. YOU KNOW, JUST A FLOATING SHIPWRECK WITH NO TASTY BITS?
WE HAVE TO KEEP ROWING OR THE PIRATES WILL CATCH US!
THAT ONE'S COMING RIGHT FOR US!
HORRENDO, SIT DOWN!

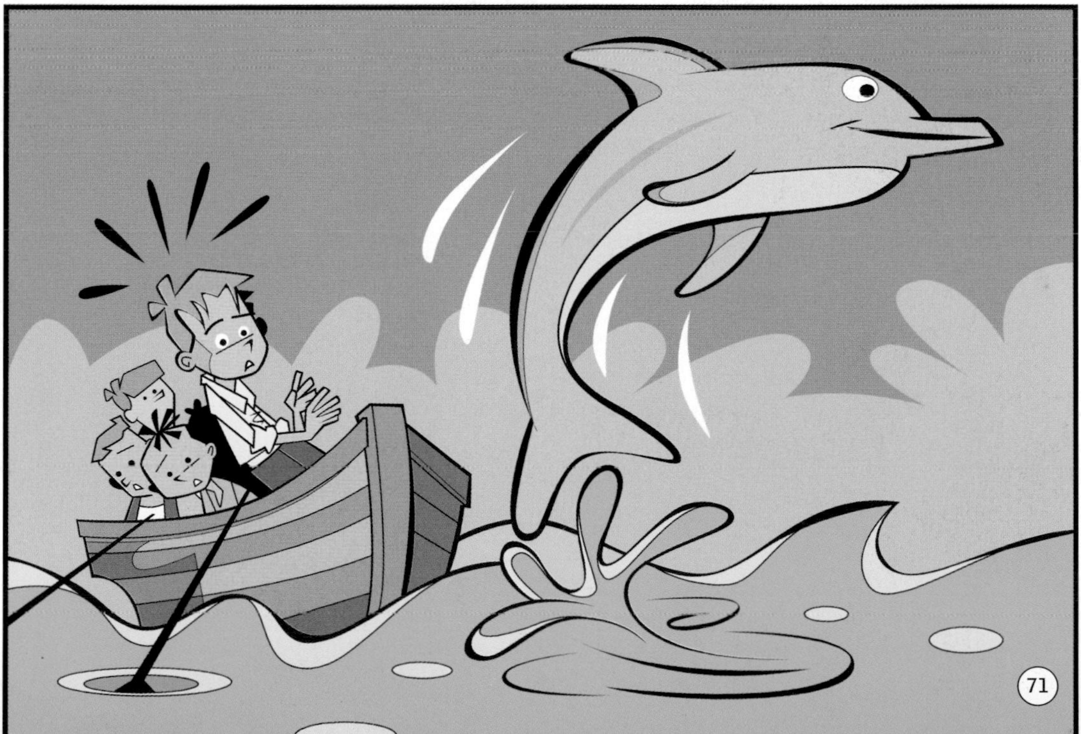

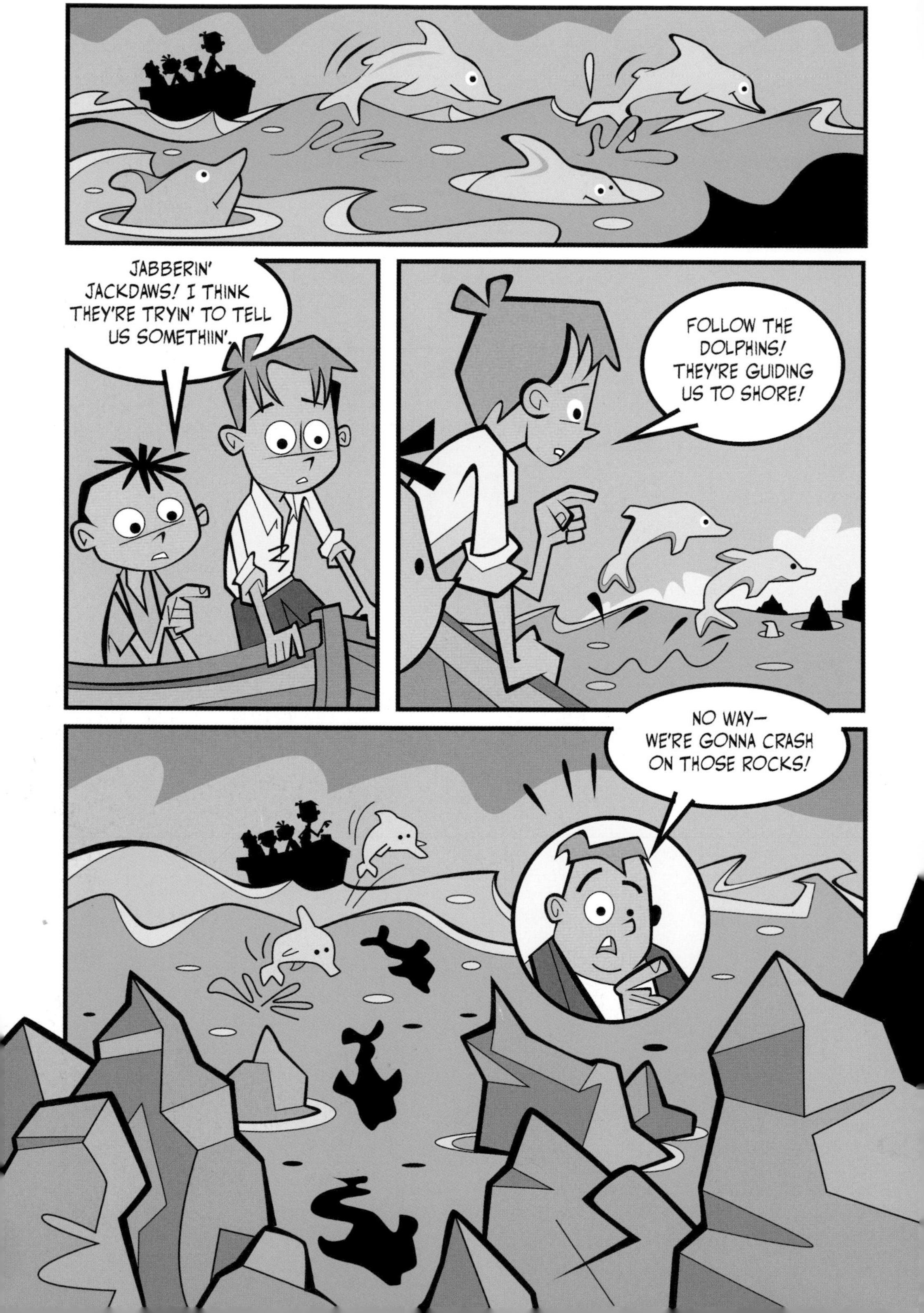
JABBERIN' JACKDAWS! I THINK THEY'RE TRYIN' TO TELL US SOMETHIIN'.
FOLLOW THE DOLPHINS! THEY'RE GUIDING US TO SHORE!
NO WAY— WE'RE GONNA CRASH ON THOSE ROCKS!

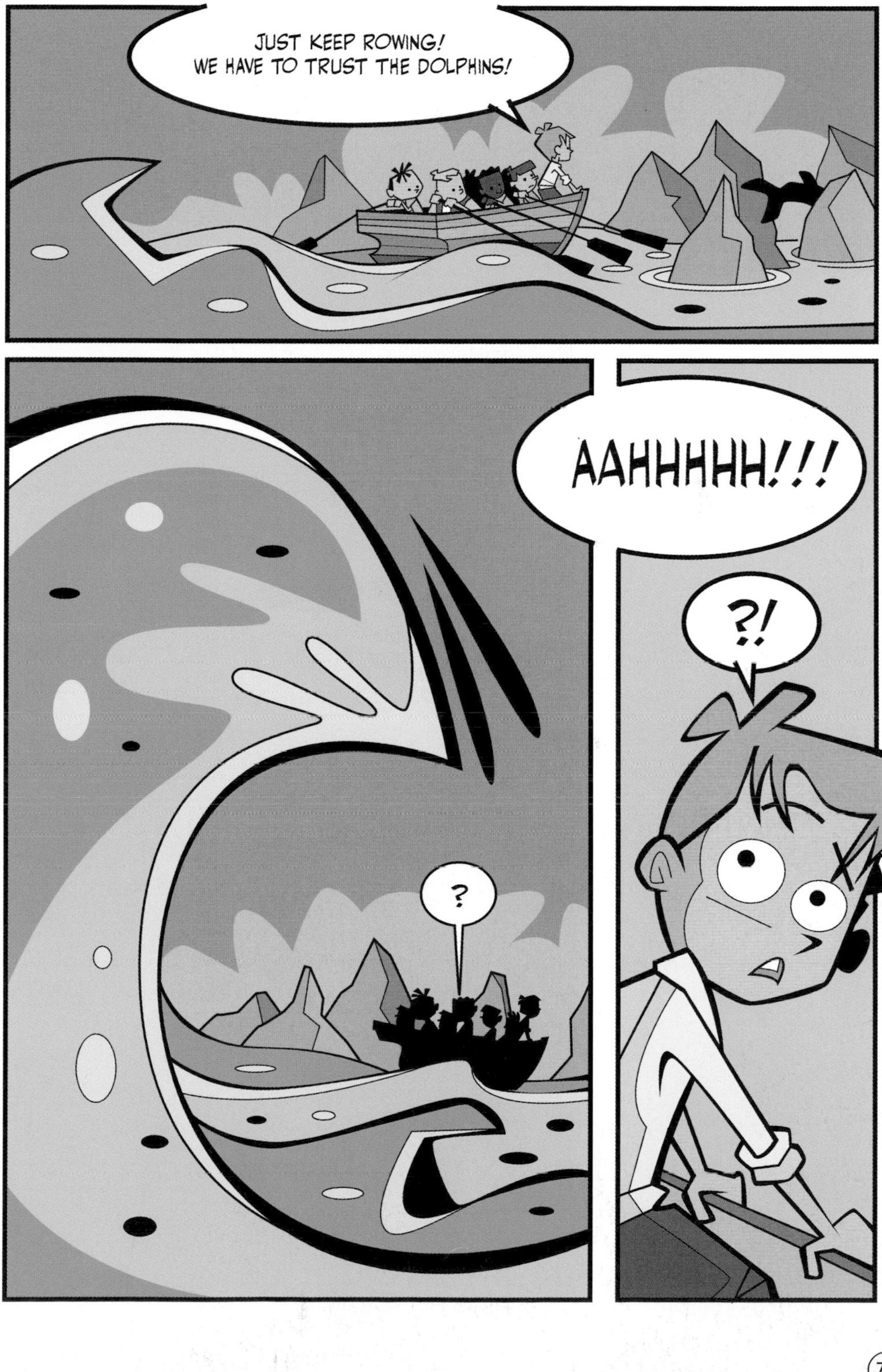
JUST KEEP ROWING!
WE HAVE TO TRUST THE DOLPHINS!
?
AAHHHHH!!!
?!

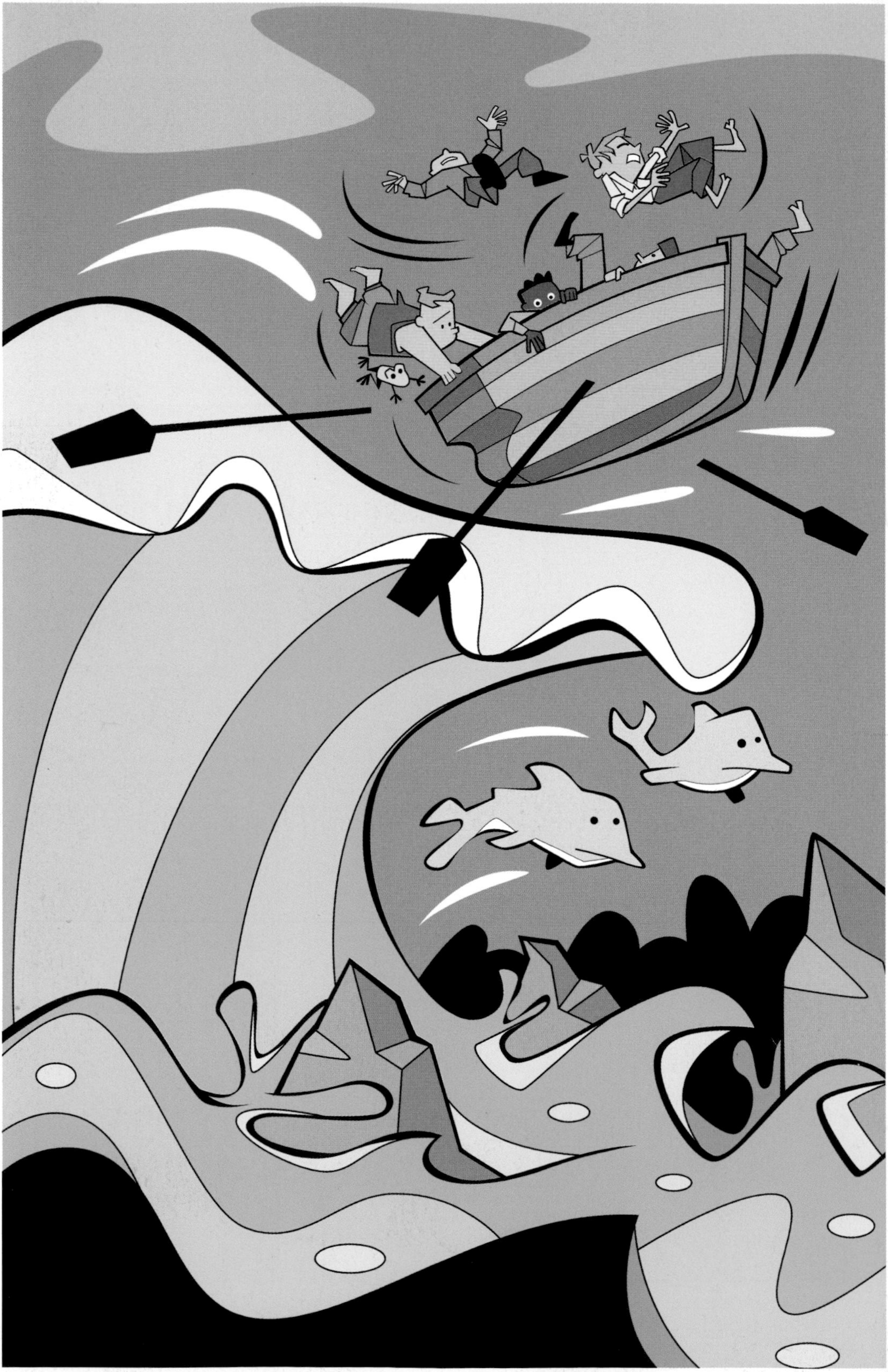

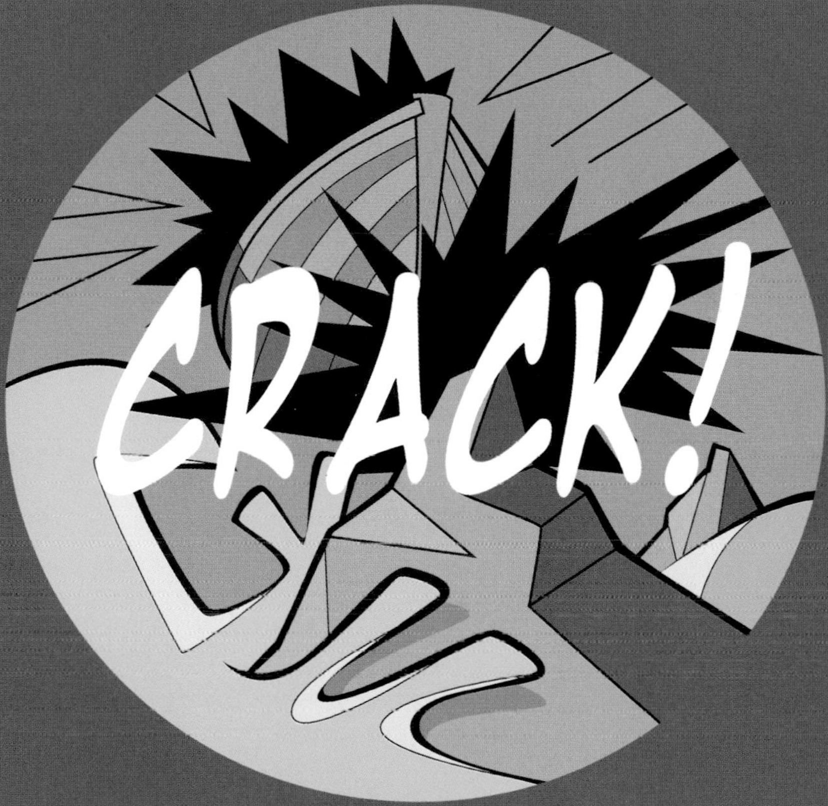
CRACK!

CHAPTER 7

PETRIFYING PEST

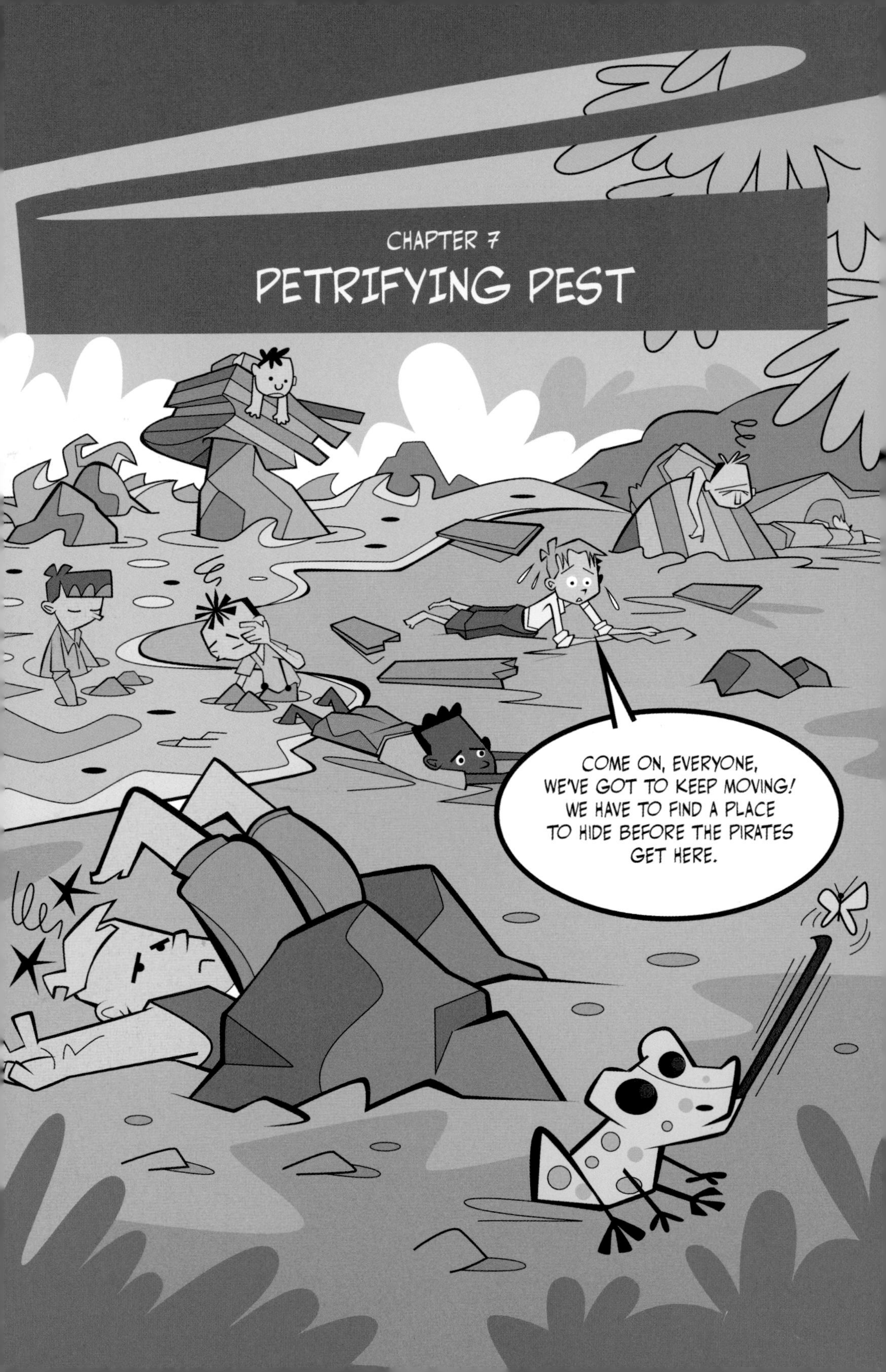
COME ON, EVERYONE, WE'VE GOT TO KEEP MOVING! WE HAVE TO FIND A PLACE TO HIDE BEFORE THE PIRATES GET HERE.

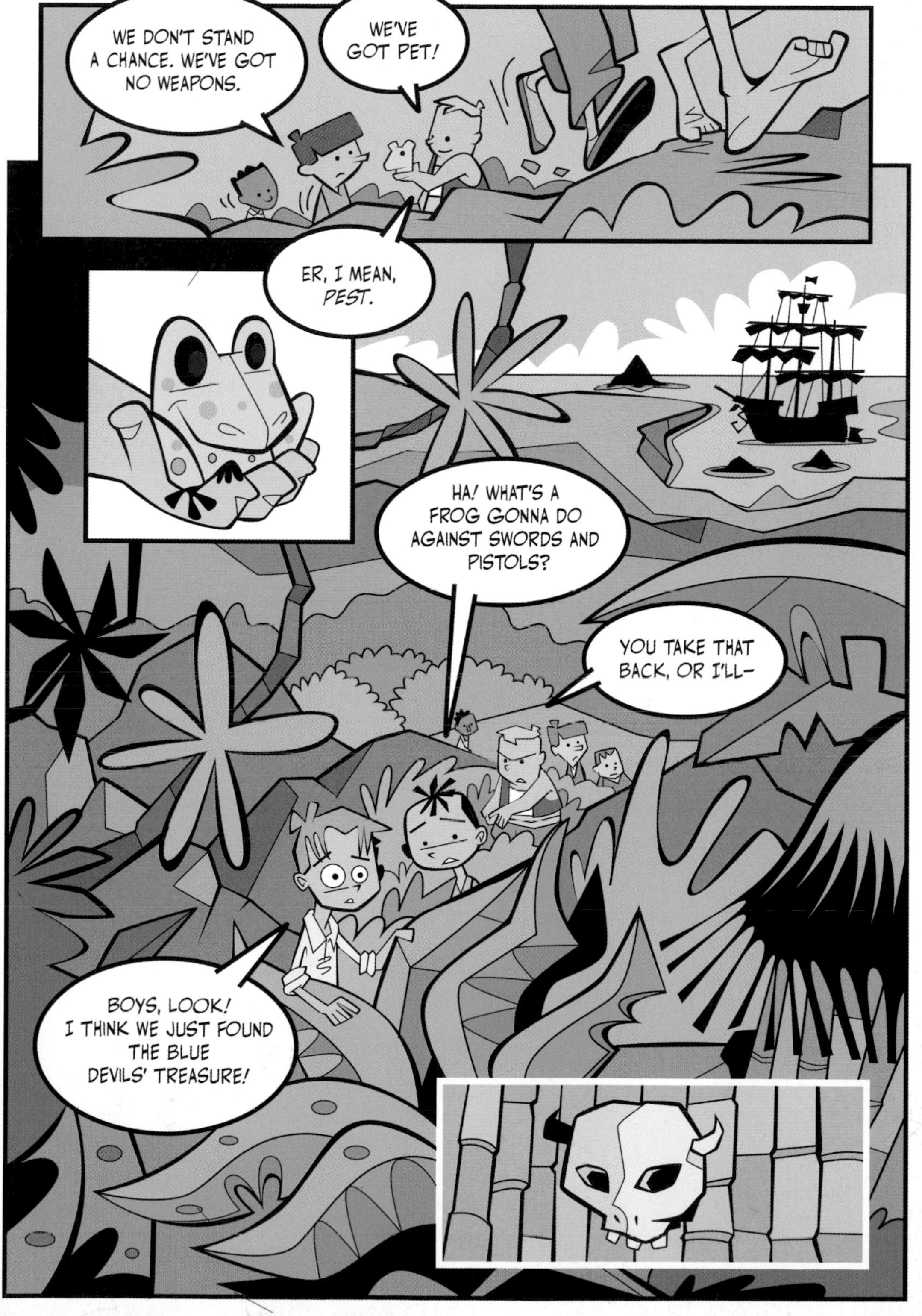
WE DON'T STAND A CHANCE. WE'VE GOT NO WEAPONS.
WE'VE GOT PET!
ER, I MEAN, PEST.
HA! WHAT'S A FROG GONNA DO AGAINST SWORDS AND PISTOLS?
YOU TAKE THAT BACK, OR I'LL—
BOYS, LOOK! I THINK WE JUST FOUND THE BLUE DEVILS' TREASURE!

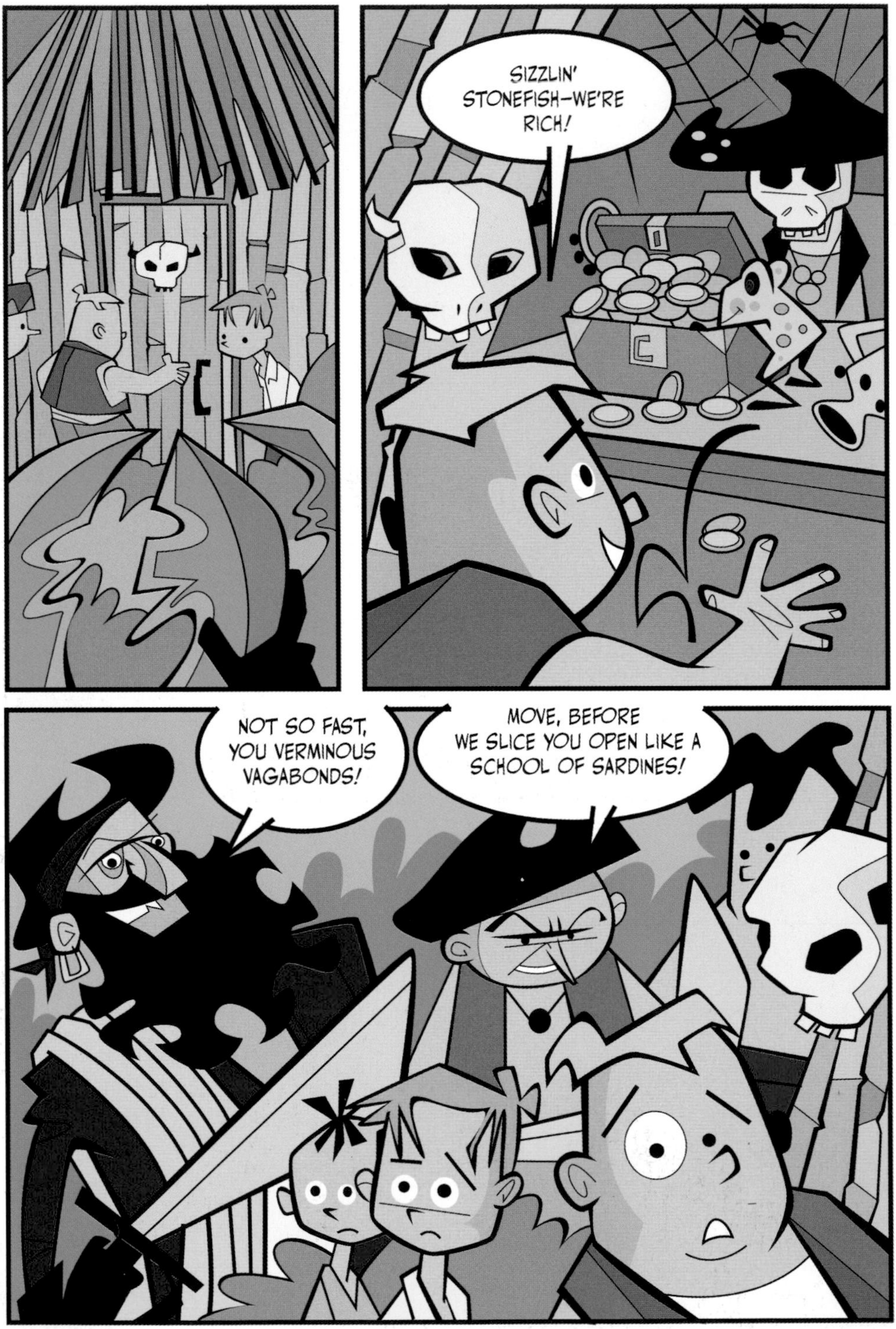
SIZZLIN' STONEFISH—WE'RE RICH!
NOT SO FAST, YOU VERMINOUS VAGABONDS!
MOVE, BEFORE WE SLICE YOU OPEN LIKE A SCHOOL OF SARDINES!

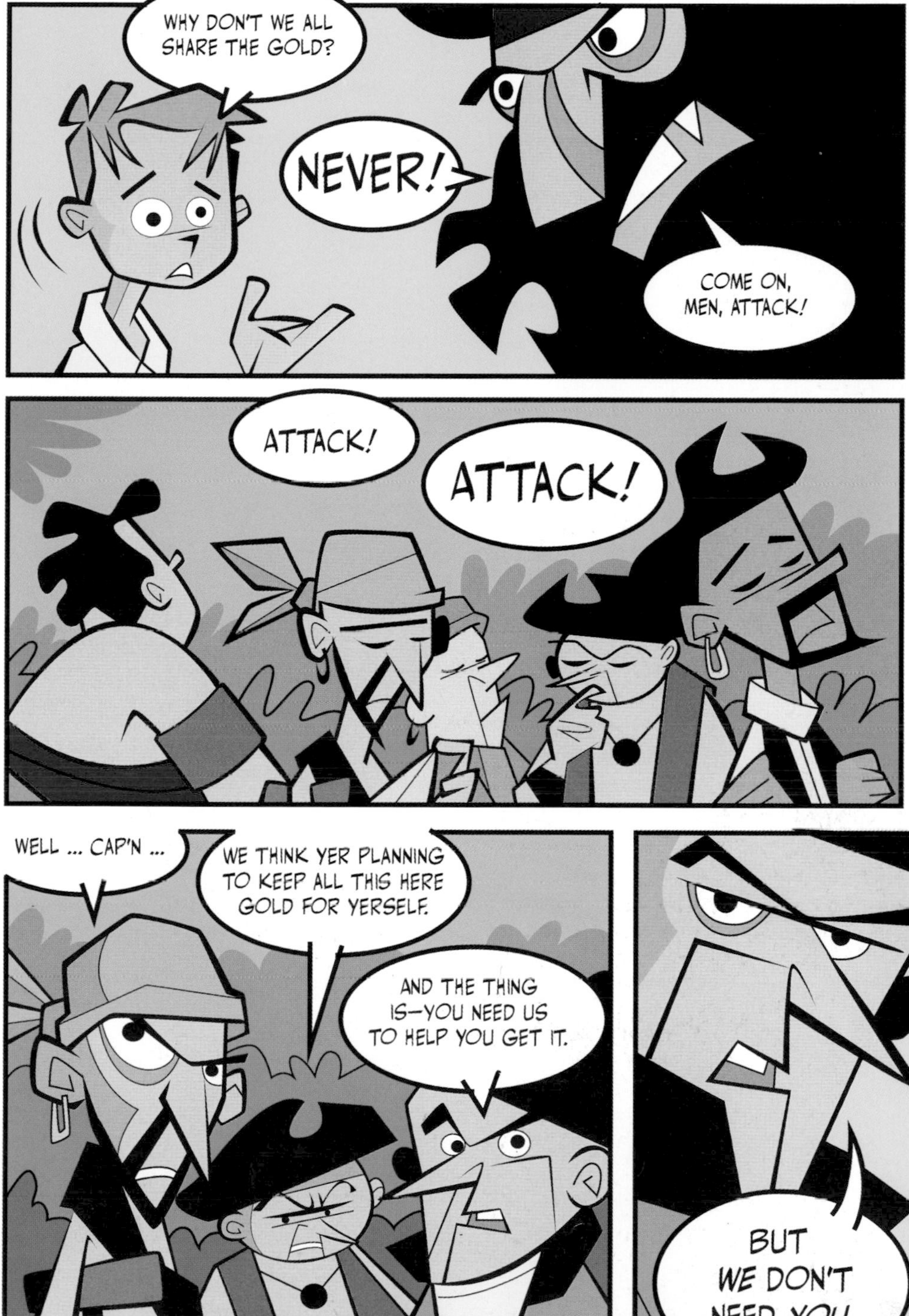
WHY DON'T WE ALL SHARE THE GOLD?
NEVER!
COME ON, MEN, ATTACK!
ATTACK!
ATTACK!
WELL ... CAP'N ...
WE THINK YER PLANNING TO KEEP ALL THIS HERE GOLD FOR YERSELF.
AND THE THING IS—YOU NEED US TO HELP YOU GET IT.
BUT WE DON'T NEED YOU.

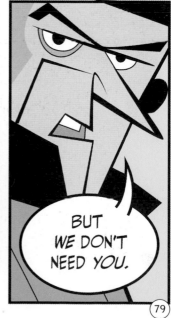

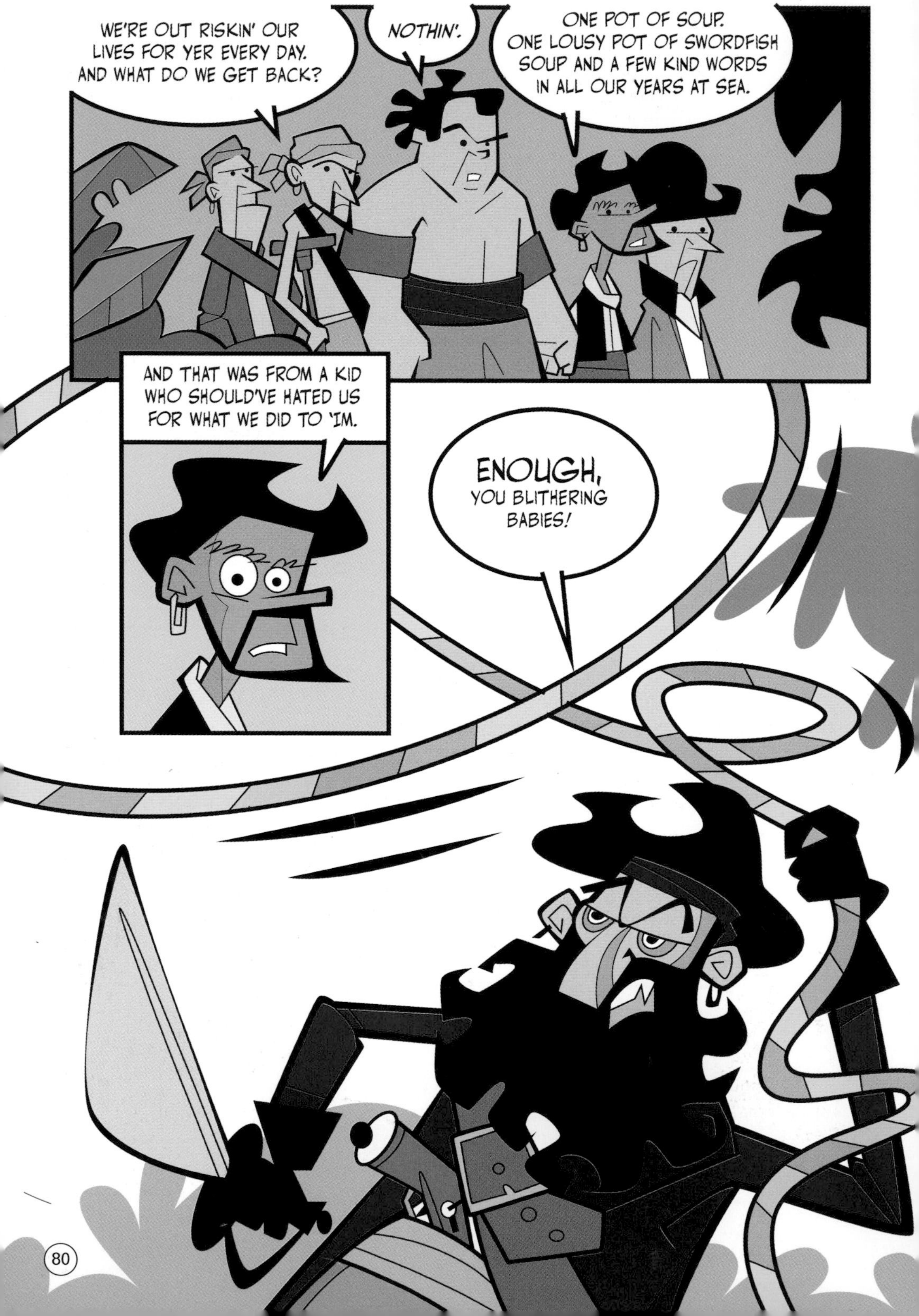
WE'RE OUT RISKIN' OUR LIVES FOR YER EVERY DAY. AND WHAT DO WE GET BACK?
NOTHIN'.
ONE POT OF SOUP. ONE LOUSY POT OF SWORDFISH SOUP AND A FEW KIND WORDS IN ALL OUR YEARS AT SEA.
AND THAT WAS FROM A KID WHO SHOULD'VE HATED US FOR WHAT WE DID TO 'IM.
ENOUGH, YOU BLITHERING BABIES!

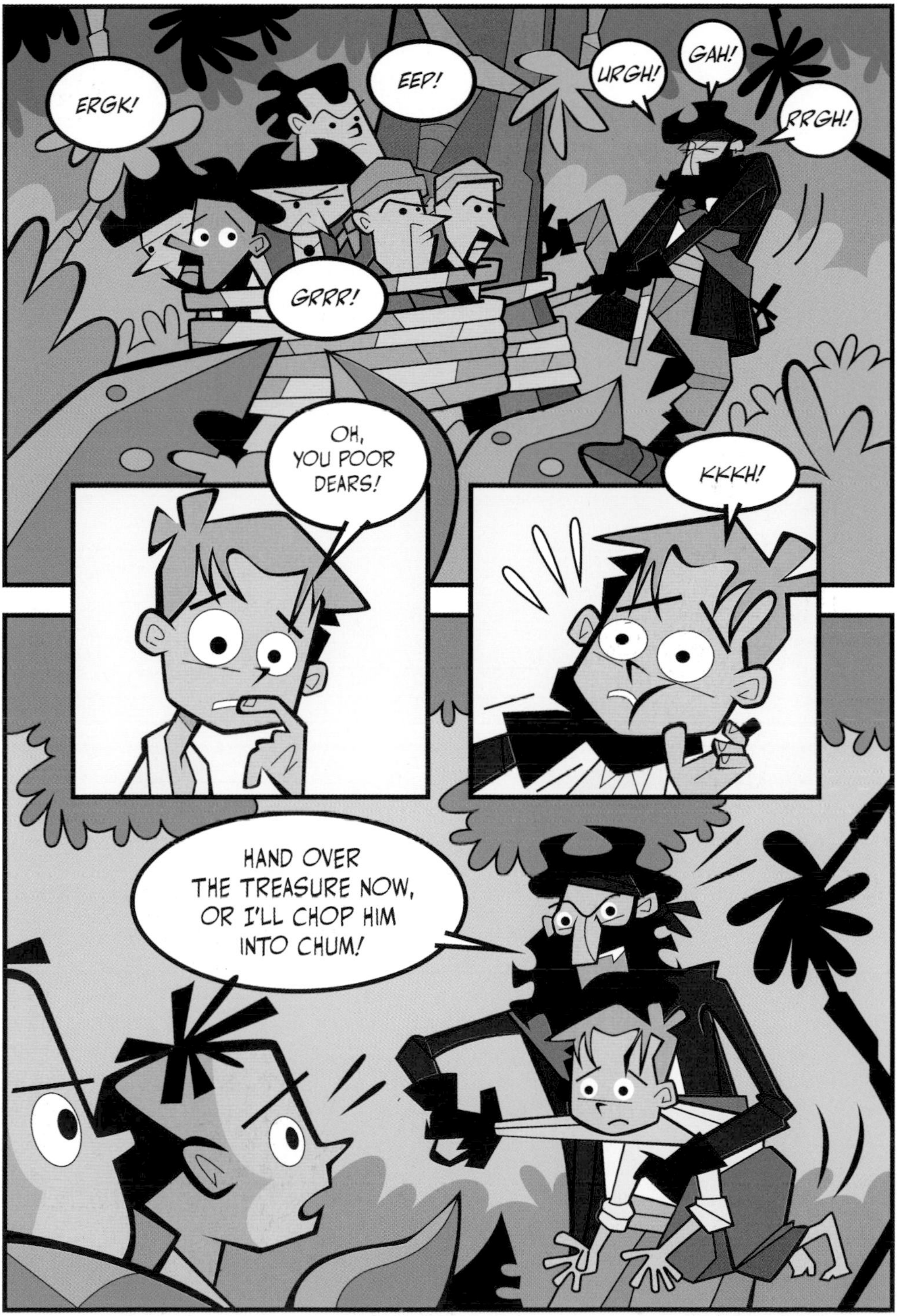
ERGK!
EEP!
URGH!
GAH!
RRGH!
GRRR!
OH, YOU POOR DEARS!
KKKH!
HAND OVER THE TREASURE NOW, OR I'LL CHOP HIM INTO CHUM!

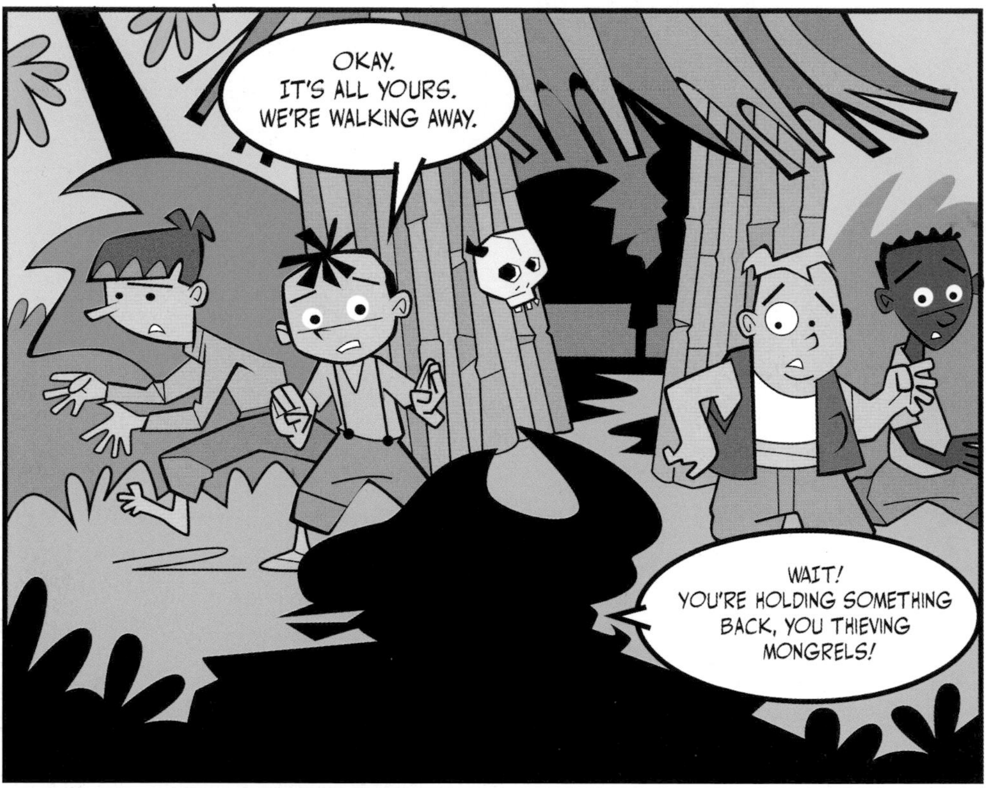
OKAY.
IT'S ALL YOURS.
WE'RE WALKING AWAY.
WAIT!
YOU'RE HOLDING SOMETHING
BACK, YOU THIEVING
MONGRELS!

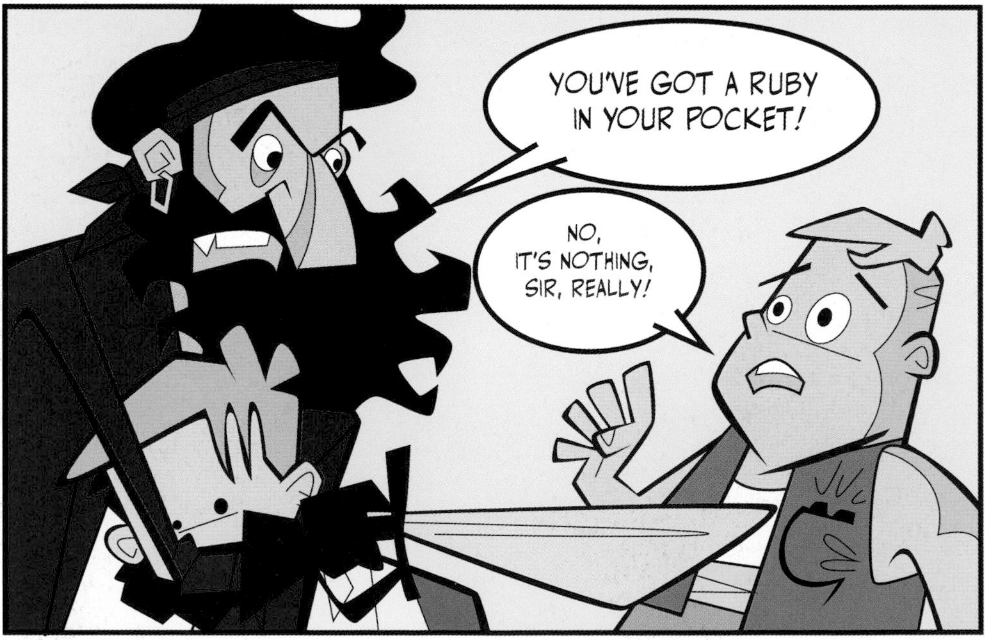
YOU'VE GOT A RUBY
IN YOUR POCKET!
NO,
IT'S NOTHING,
SIR, REALLY!

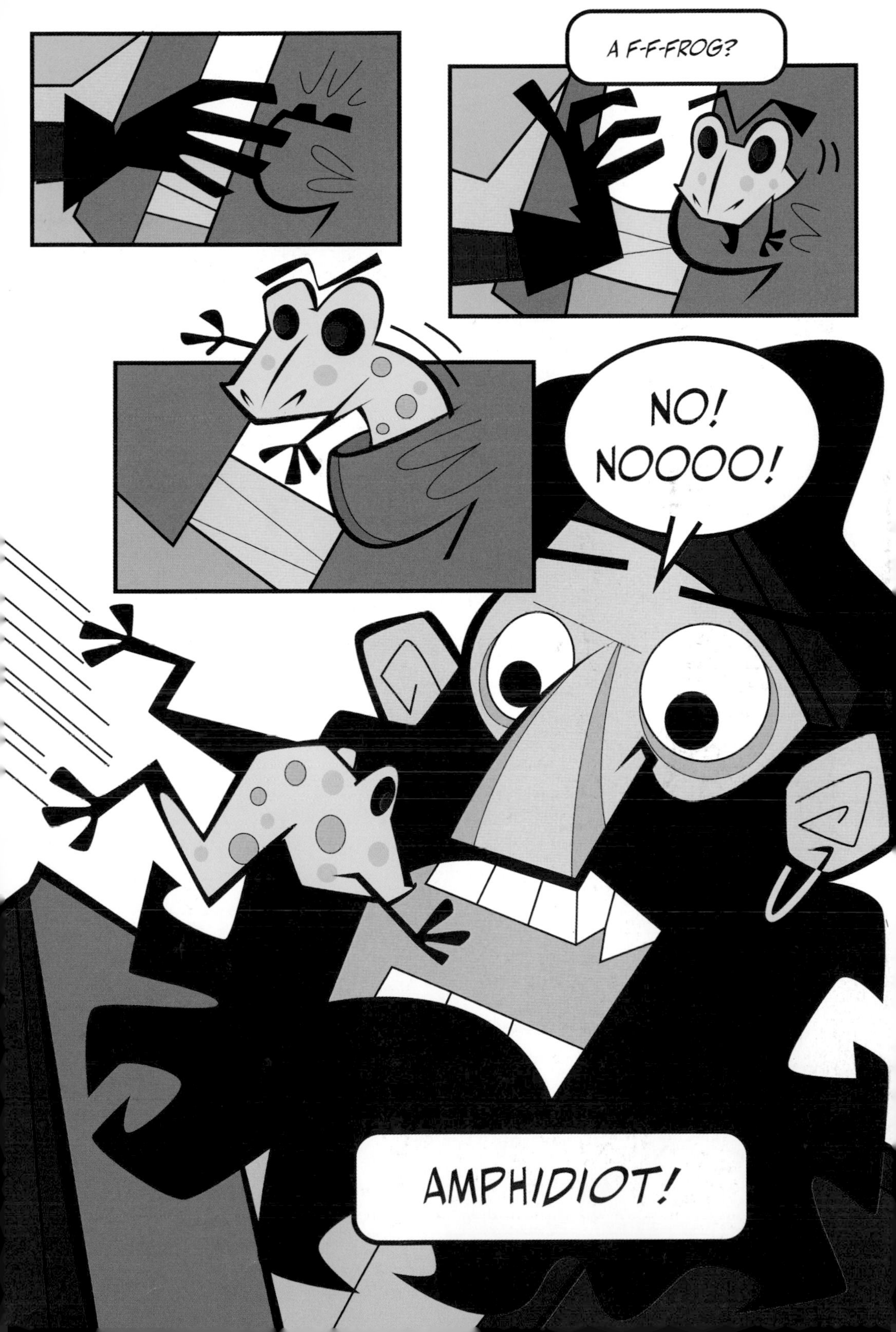
A F-F-FROG?
NO! NOOOO!
AMPHIDIOT!

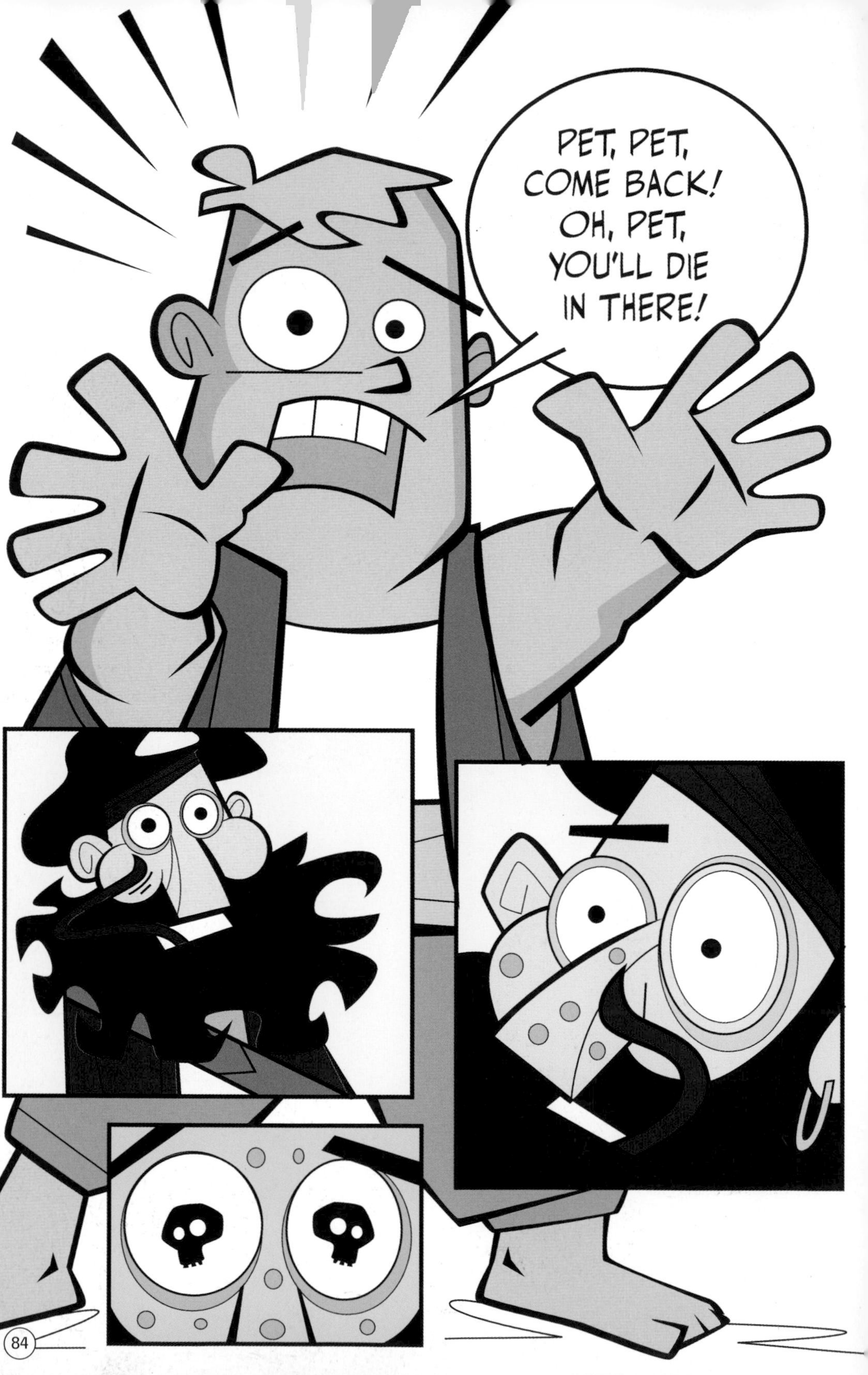
PET, PET, COME BACK! OH, PET, YOU'LL DIE IN THERE!

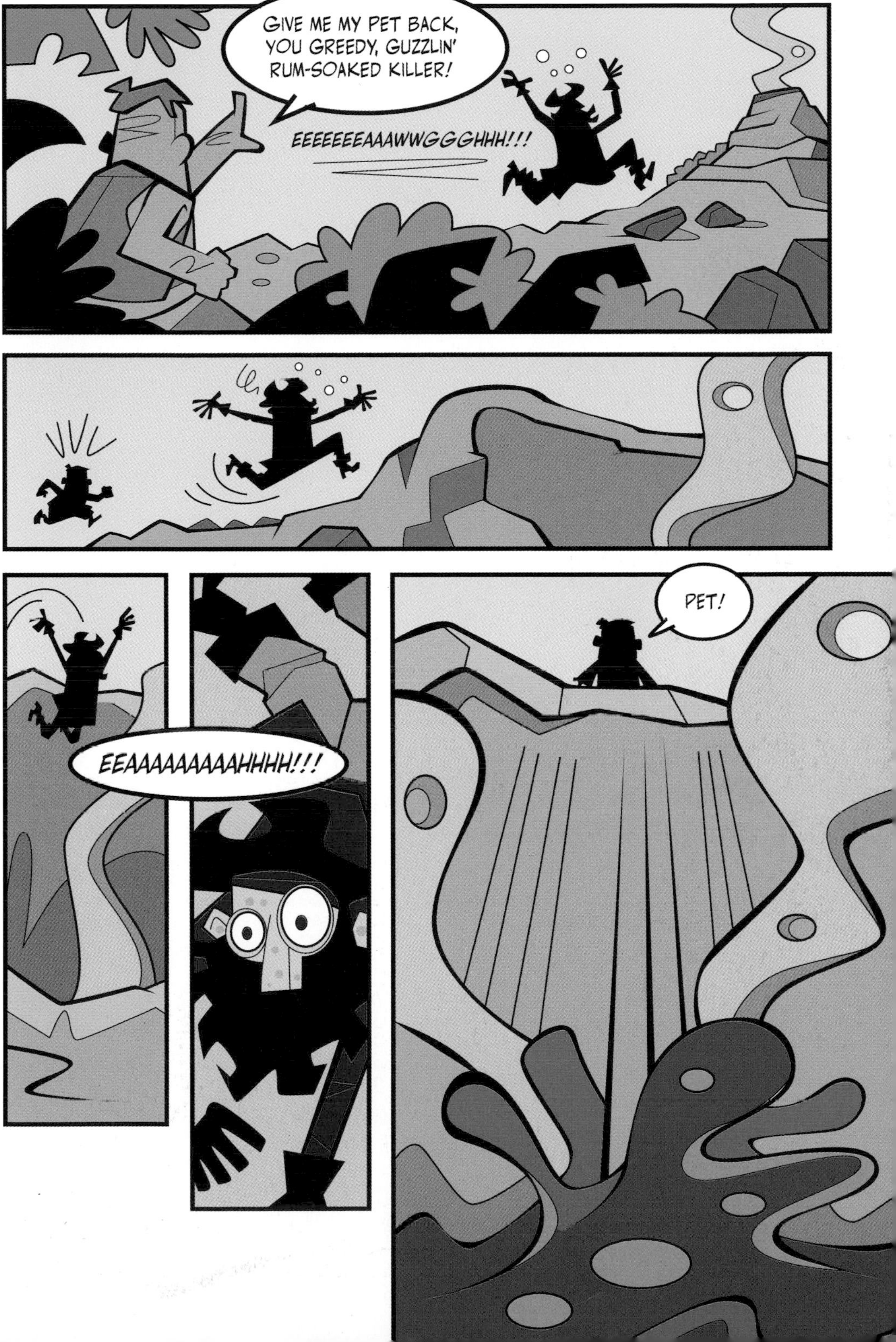
GIVE ME MY PET BACK, YOU GREEDY, GUZZLIN' RUM-SOAKED KILLER!
EEEEEEEAAAWWGGGHHH!!!
EEAAAAAAAAAAHHHH!!!
PET!

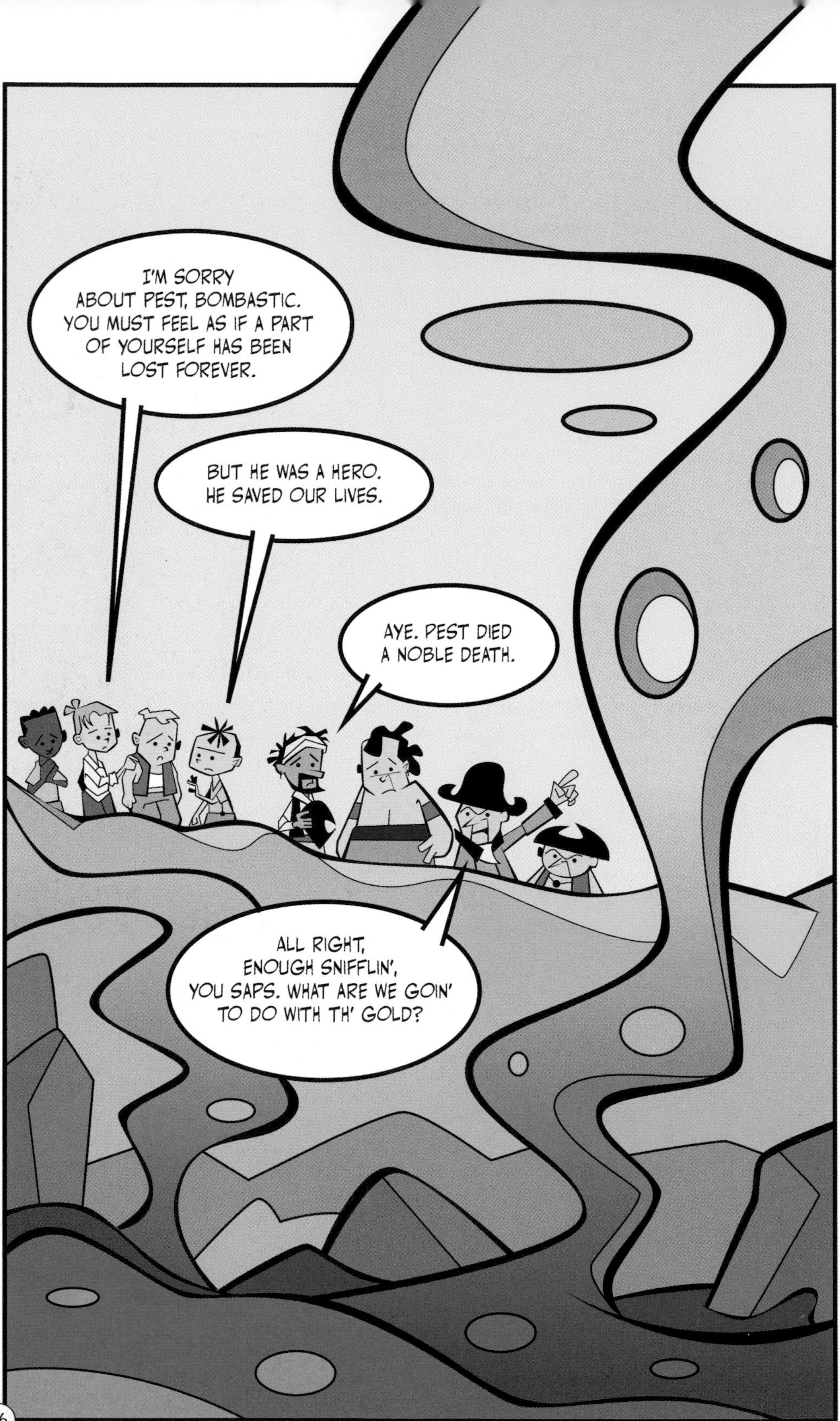
I'M SORRY ABOUT PEST, BOMBASTIC. YOU MUST FEEL AS IF A PART OF YOURSELF HAS BEEN LOST FOREVER.
BUT HE WAS A HERO. HE SAVED OUR LIVES.
AYE. PEST DIED A NOBLE DEATH.
ALL RIGHT, ENOUGH SNIFFLIN', YOU SAPS. WHAT ARE WE GOIN' TO DO WITH TH' GOLD?

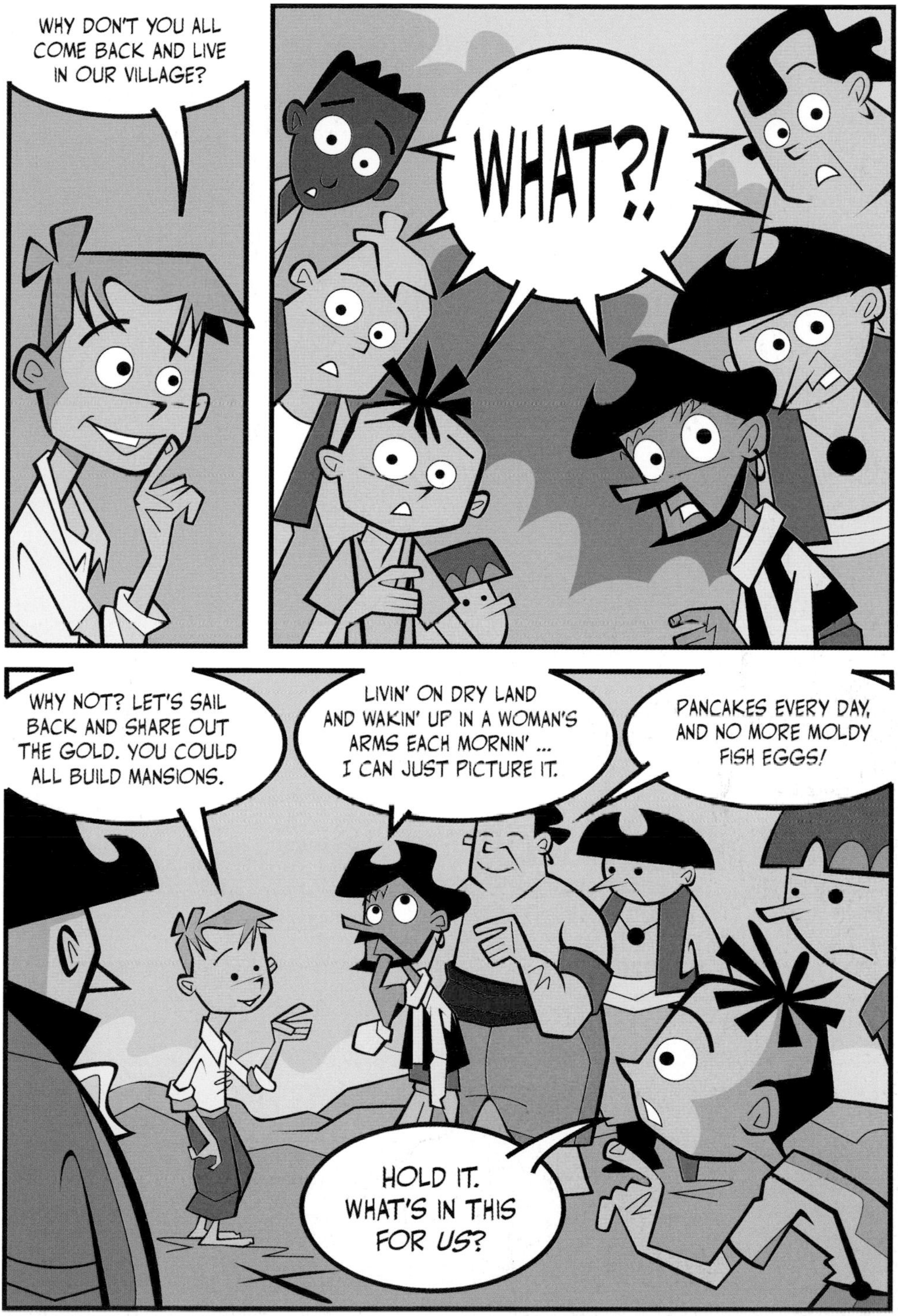
WHY DON'T YOU ALL COME BACK AND LIVE IN OUR VILLAGE?
WHAT?!
WHY NOT? LET'S SAIL BACK AND SHARE OUT THE GOLD. YOU COULD ALL BUILD MANSIONS.
LIVIN' ON DRY LAND AND WAKIN' UP IN A WOMAN'S ARMS EACH MORNIN' ... I CAN JUST PICTURE IT.
PANCAKES EVERY DAY, AND NO MORE MOLDY FISH EGGS!
HOLD IT. WHAT'S IN THIS FOR US?

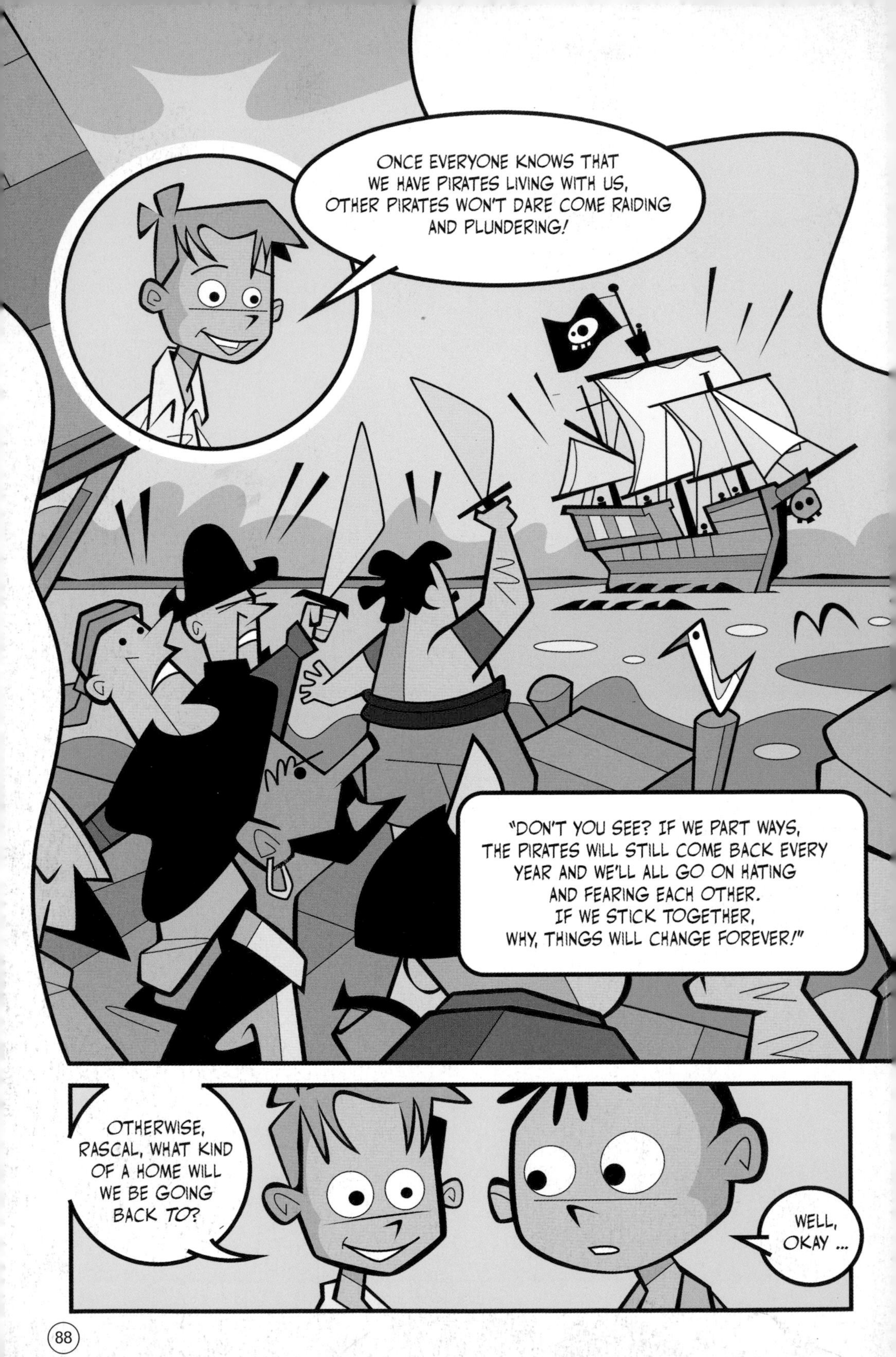
ONCE EVERYONE KNOWS THAT WE HAVE PIRATES LIVING WITH US, OTHER PIRATES WON'T DARE COME RAIDING AND PLUNDERING!
"DON'T YOU SEE? IF WE PART WAYS, THE PIRATES WILL STILL COME BACK EVERY YEAR AND WE'LL ALL GO ON HATING AND FEARING EACH OTHER. IF WE STICK TOGETHER, WHY, THINGS WILL CHANGE FOREVER!"
OTHERWISE, RASCAL, WHAT KIND OF A HOME WILL WE BE GOING BACK TO?
WELL, OKAY ...

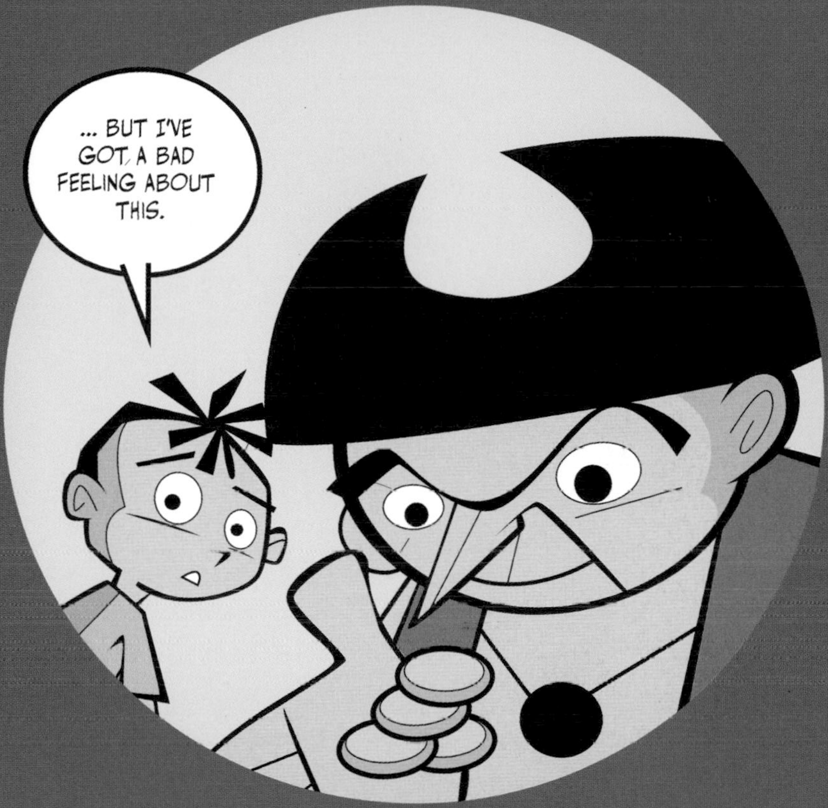
... BUT I'VE GOT A BAD FEELING ABOUT THIS.

CHAPTER 8

TAKING A LEAP OF FAITH (FROM A GREAT HEIGHT)

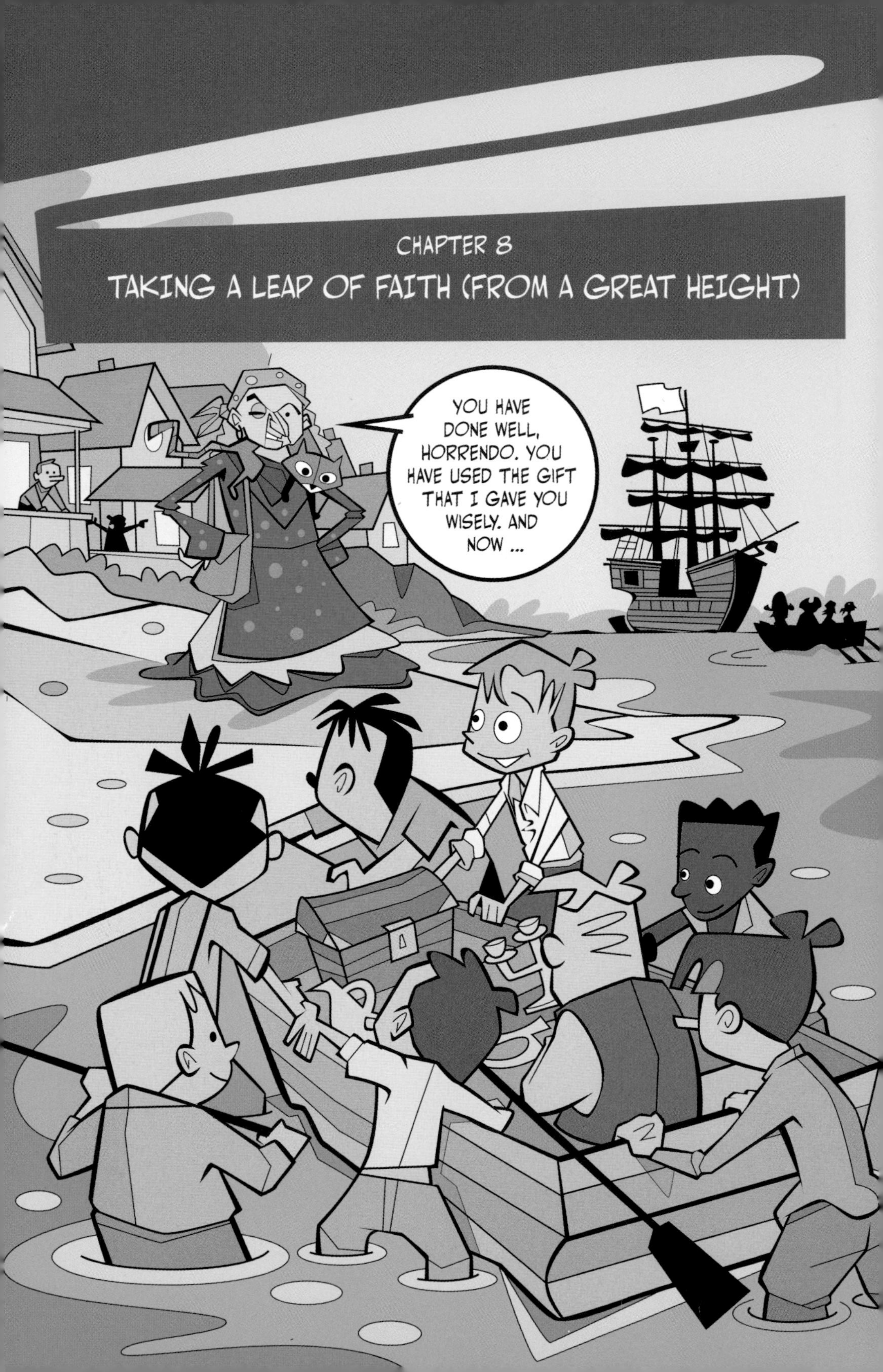
YOU HAVE DONE WELL, HORRENDO. YOU HAVE USED THE GIFT THAT I GAVE YOU WISELY. AND NOW ...

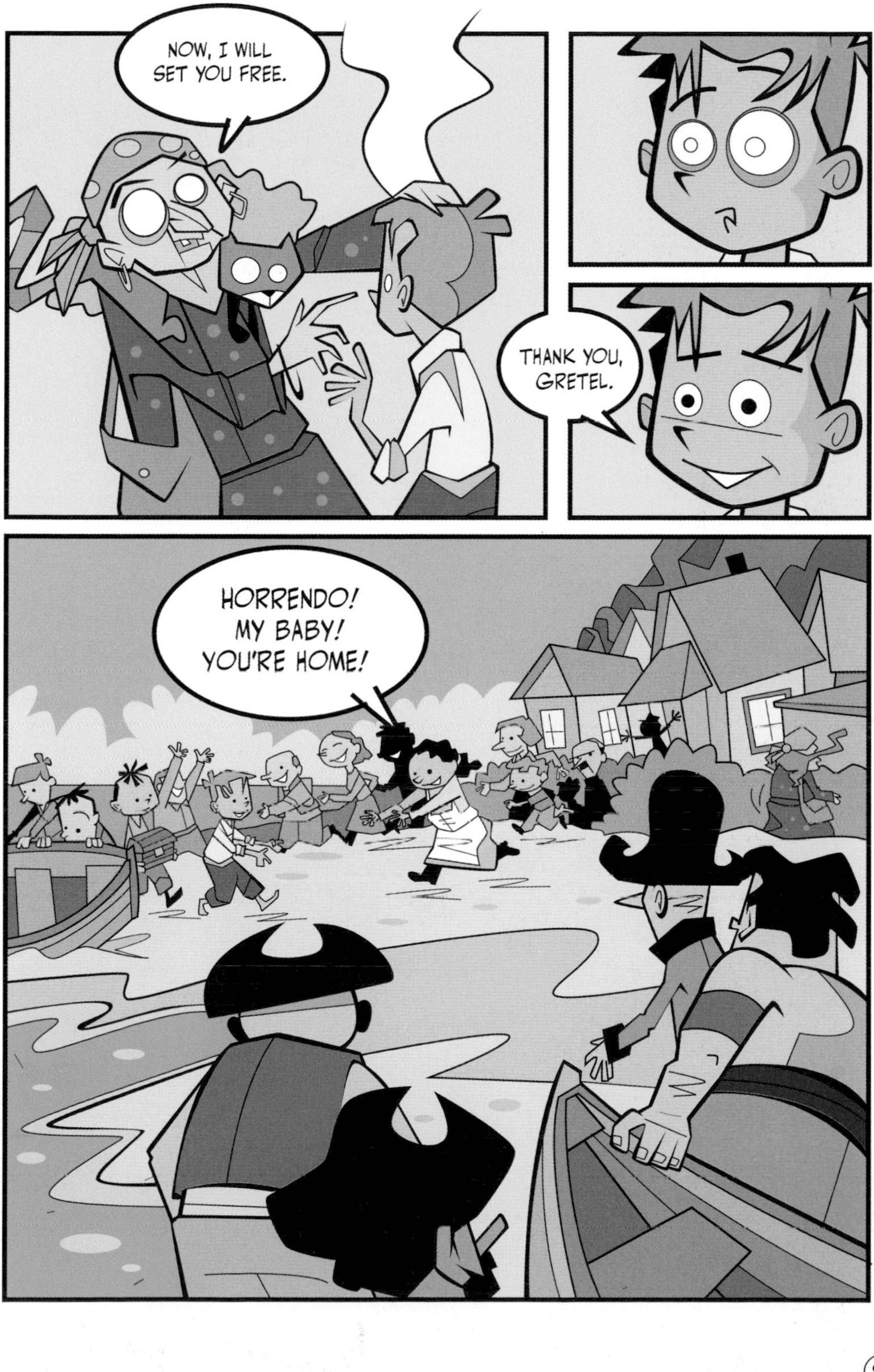
NOW, I WILL SET YOU FREE.
THANK YOU, GRETEL.
HORRENDO! MY BABY! YOU'RE HOME!

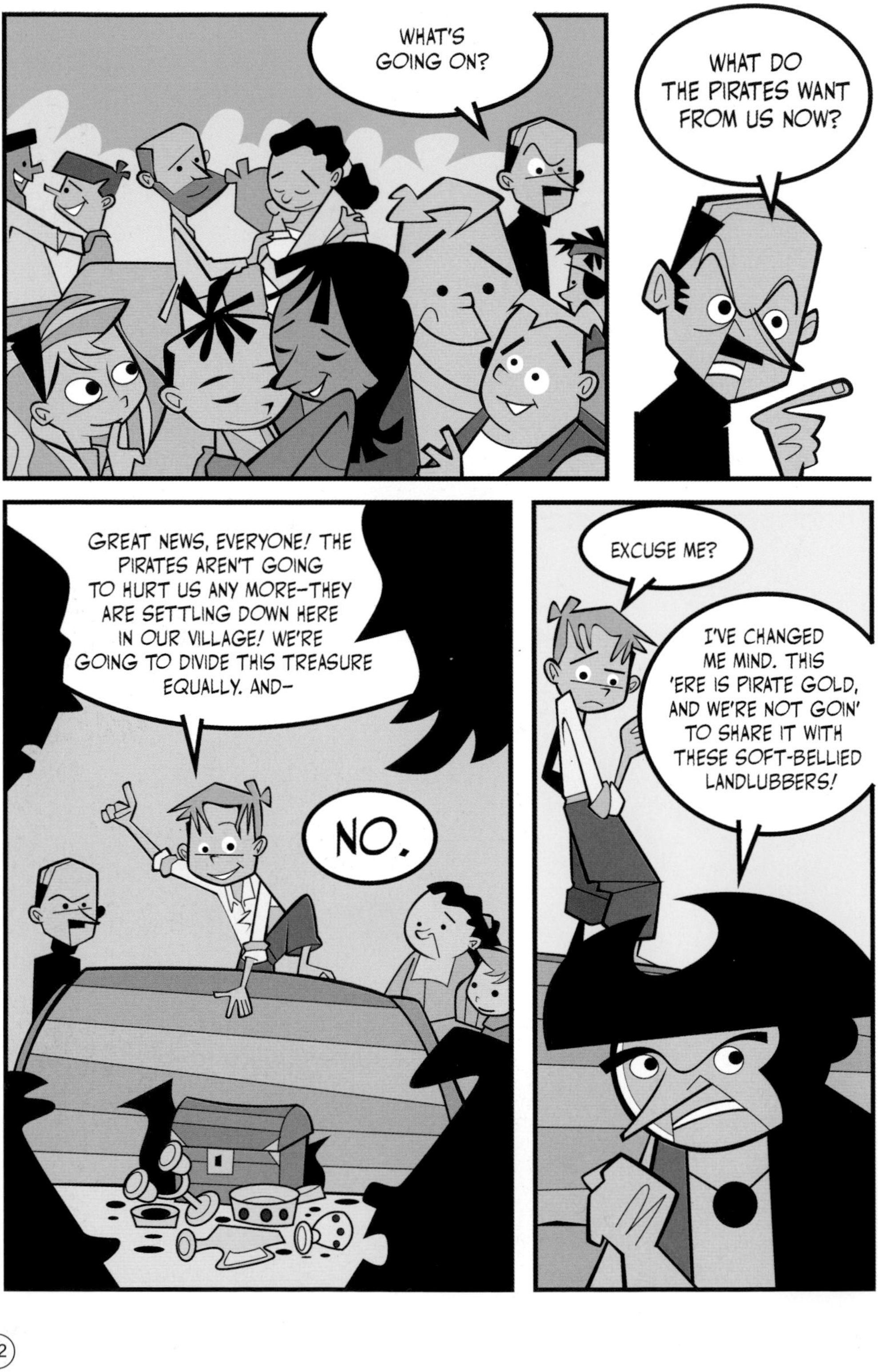
WHAT'S GOING ON?
WHAT DO THE PIRATES WANT FROM US NOW?
GREAT NEWS, EVERYONE! THE PIRATES AREN'T GOING TO HURT US ANY MORE–THEY ARE SETTLING DOWN HERE IN OUR VILLAGE! WE'RE GOING TO DIVIDE THIS TREASURE EQUALLY. AND–
NO.
EXCUSE ME?
I'VE CHANGED ME MIND. THIS 'ERE IS PIRATE GOLD, AND WE'RE NOT GOIN' TO SHARE IT WITH THESE SOFT-BELLIED LANDLUBBERS!

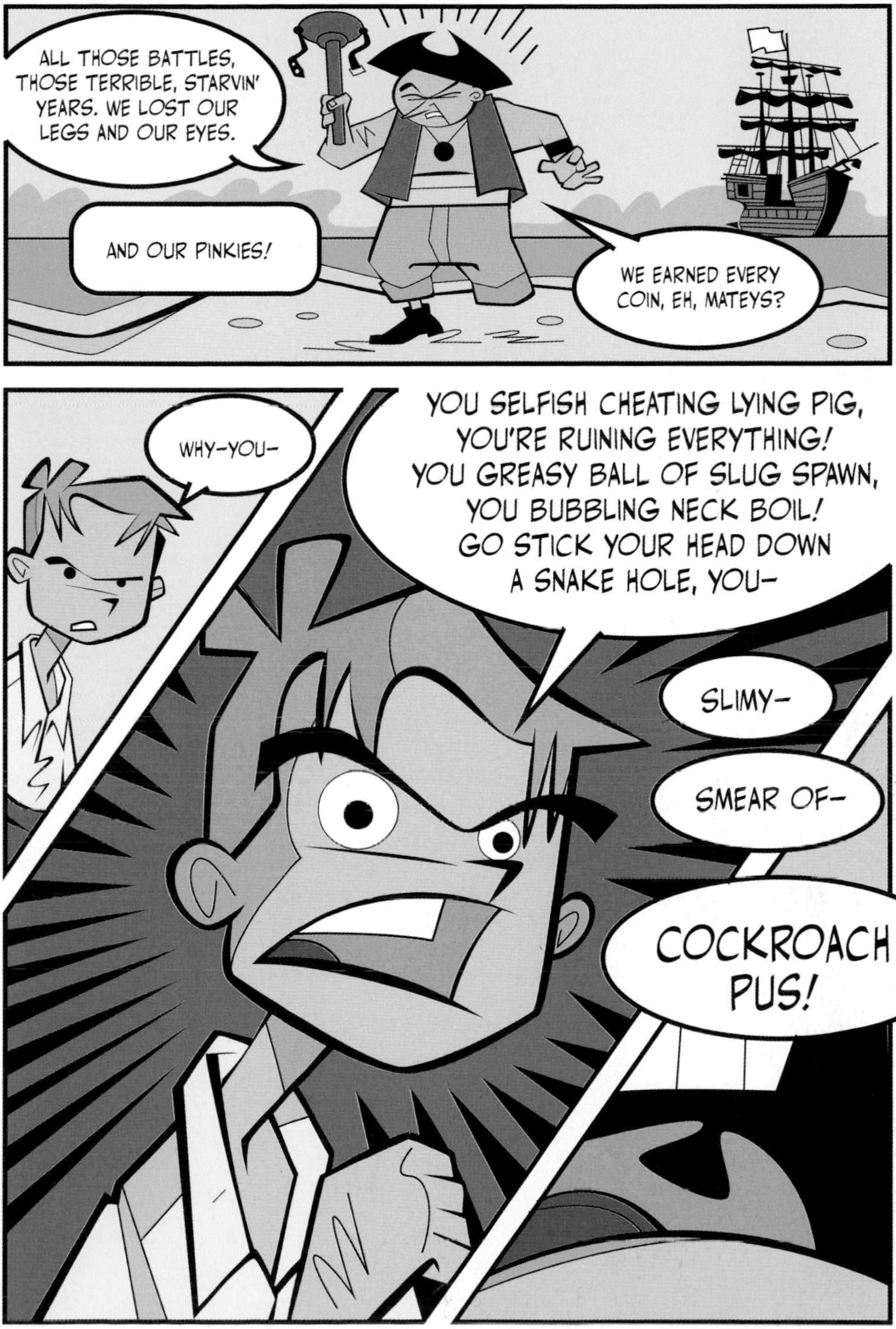
ALL THOSE BATTLES, THOSE TERRIBLE, STARVIN' YEARS. WE LOST OUR LEGS AND OUR EYES.
AND OUR PINKIES!
WE EARNED EVERY COIN, EH, MATEYS?
WHY-YOU-
YOU SELFISH CHEATING LYING PIG, YOU'RE RUINING EVERYTHING! YOU GREASY BALL OF SLUG SPAWN, YOU BUBBLING NECK BOIL! GO STICK YOUR HEAD DOWN A SNAKE HOLE, YOU-
SLIMY-
SMEAR OF-
COCKROACH PUS!

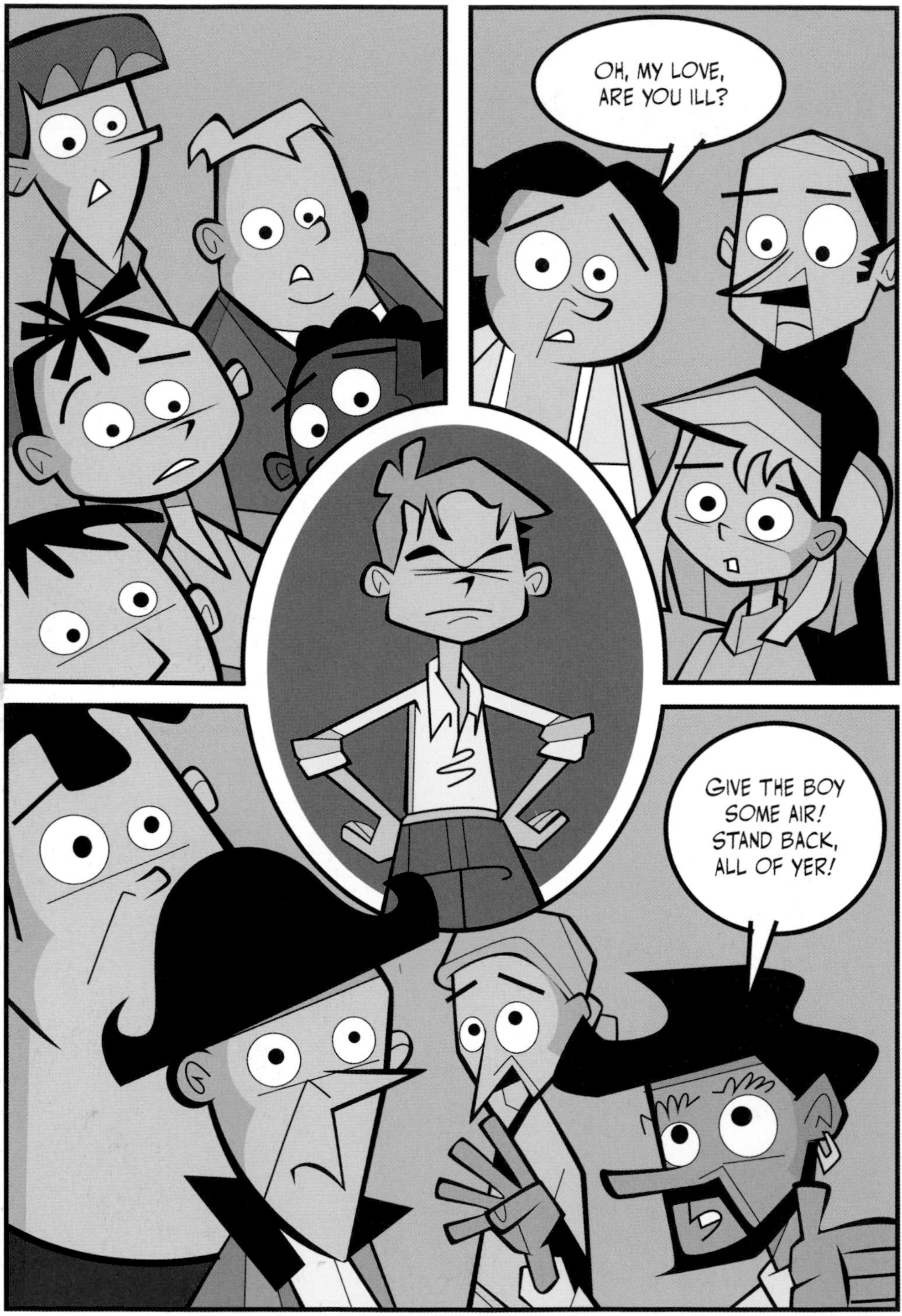
OH, MY LOVE, ARE YOU ILL?
GIVE THE BOY SOME AIR! STAND BACK, ALL OF YER!

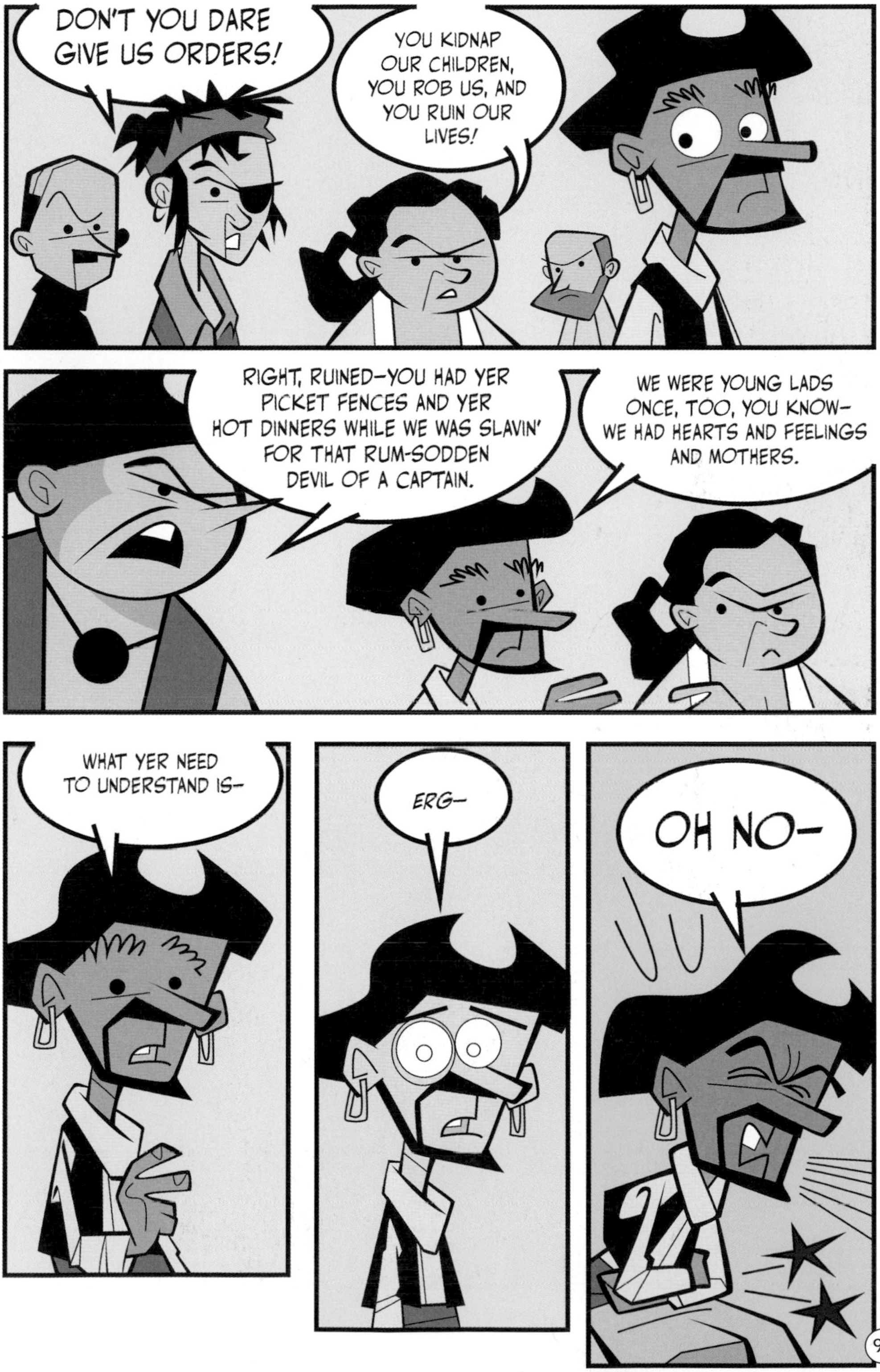

DON'T YOU DARE GIVE US ORDERS!
YOU KIDNAP OUR CHILDREN, YOU ROB US, AND YOU RUIN OUR LIVES!
RIGHT, RUINED—YOU HAD YER PICKET FENCES AND YER HOT DINNERS WHILE WE WAS SLAVIN' FOR THAT RUM-SODDEN DEVIL OF A CAPTAIN.
WE WERE YOUNG LADS ONCE, TOO, YOU KNOW—WE HAD HEARTS AND FEELINGS AND MOTHERS.
WHAT YER NEED TO UNDERSTAND IS—
ERG—
OH NO—

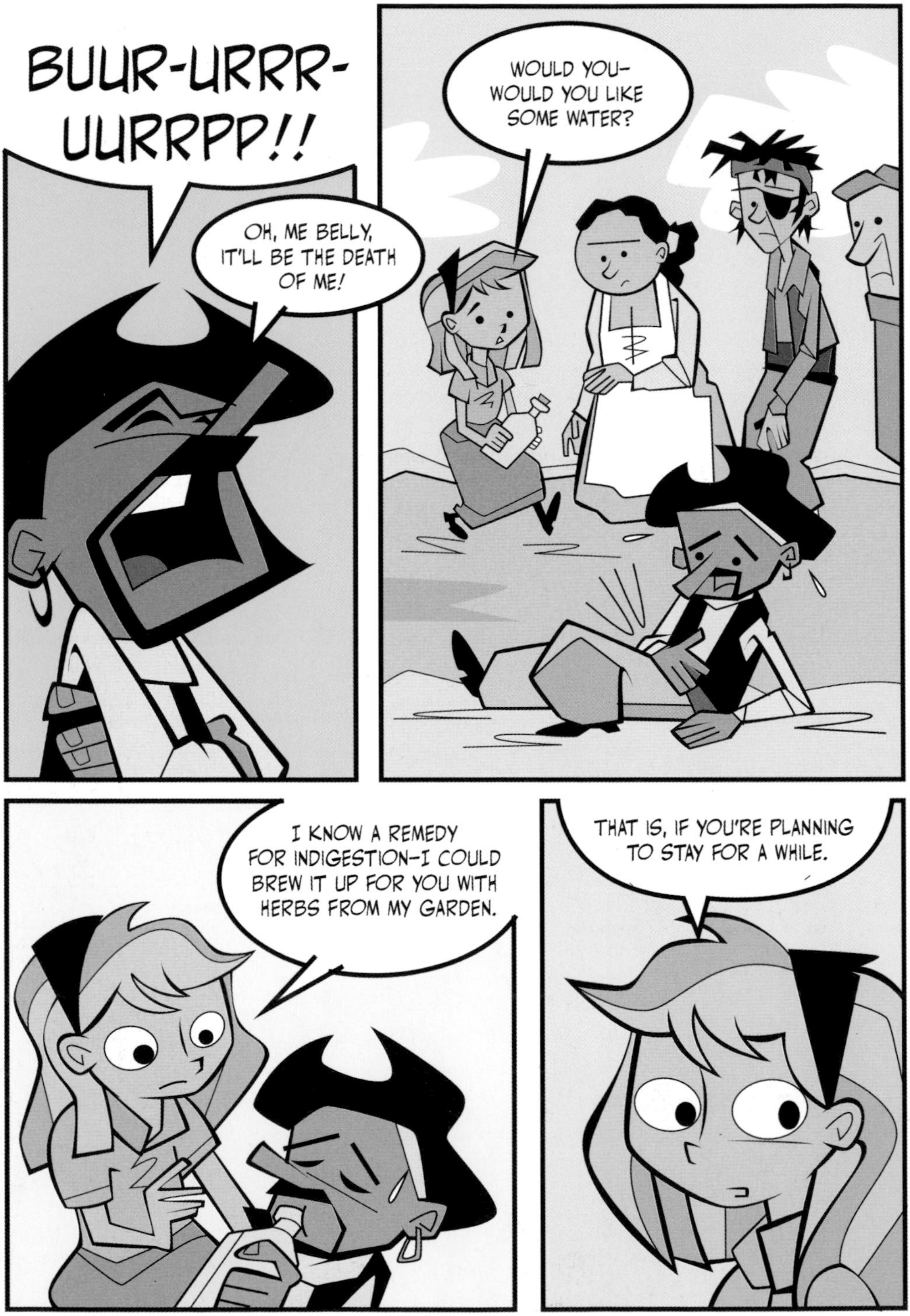
BUUR-URRR-UURRPP!!
OH, ME BELLY, IT'LL BE THE DEATH OF ME!
WOULD YOU— WOULD YOU LIKE SOME WATER?
I KNOW A REMEDY FOR INDIGESTION—I COULD BREW IT UP FOR YOU WITH HERBS FROM MY GARDEN.
THAT IS, IF YOU'RE PLANNING TO STAY FOR A WHILE.

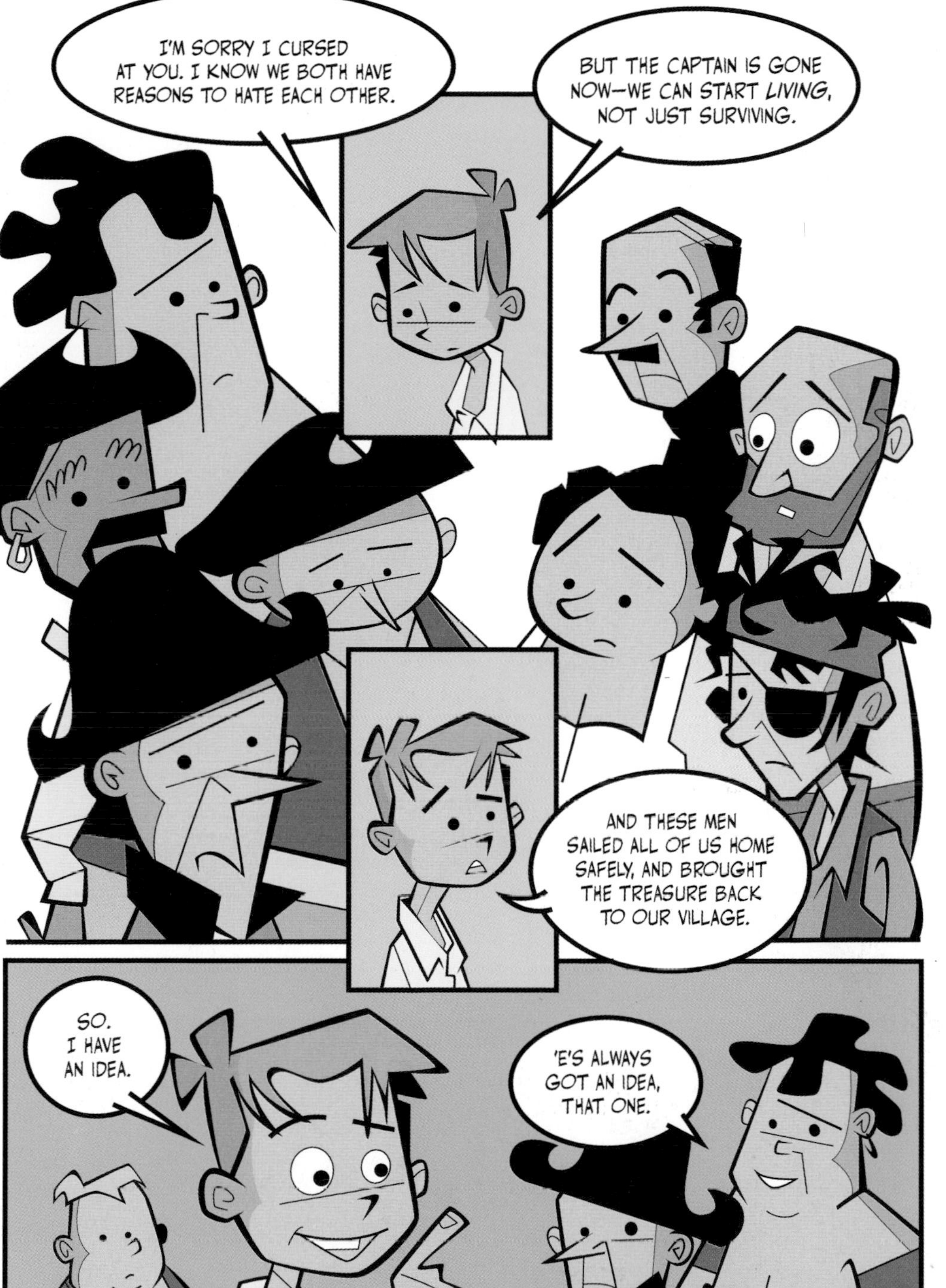
I'M SORRY I CURSED AT YOU. I KNOW WE BOTH HAVE REASONS TO HATE EACH OTHER.
BUT THE CAPTAIN IS GONE NOW—WE CAN START *LIVING*, NOT JUST SURVIVING.
AND THESE MEN SAILED ALL OF US HOME SAFELY, AND BROUGHT THE TREASURE BACK TO OUR VILLAGE.
SO. I HAVE AN IDEA.
'E'S ALWAYS GOT AN IDEA, THAT ONE.

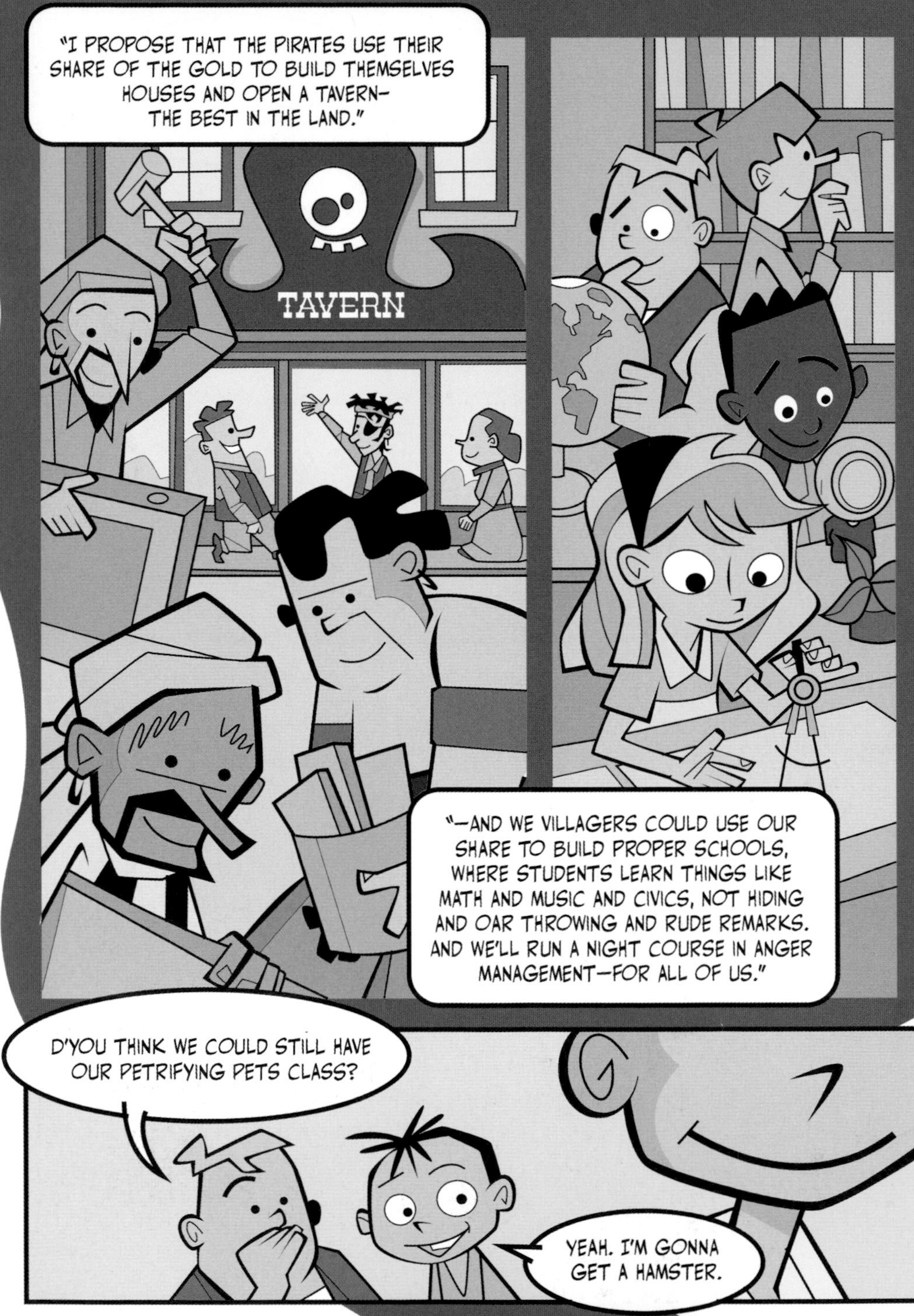
"I PROPOSE THAT THE PIRATES USE THEIR SHARE OF THE GOLD TO BUILD THEMSELVES HOUSES AND OPEN A TAVERN— THE BEST IN THE LAND."
TAVERN
"—AND WE VILLAGERS COULD USE OUR SHARE TO BUILD PROPER SCHOOLS, WHERE STUDENTS LEARN THINGS LIKE MATH AND MUSIC AND CIVICS, NOT HIDING AND OAR THROWING AND RUDE REMARKS. AND WE'LL RUN A NIGHT COURSE IN ANGER MANAGEMENT—FOR ALL OF US."
D'YOU THINK WE COULD STILL HAVE OUR PETRIFYING PETS CLASS?
YEAH. I'M GONNA GET A HAMSTER.

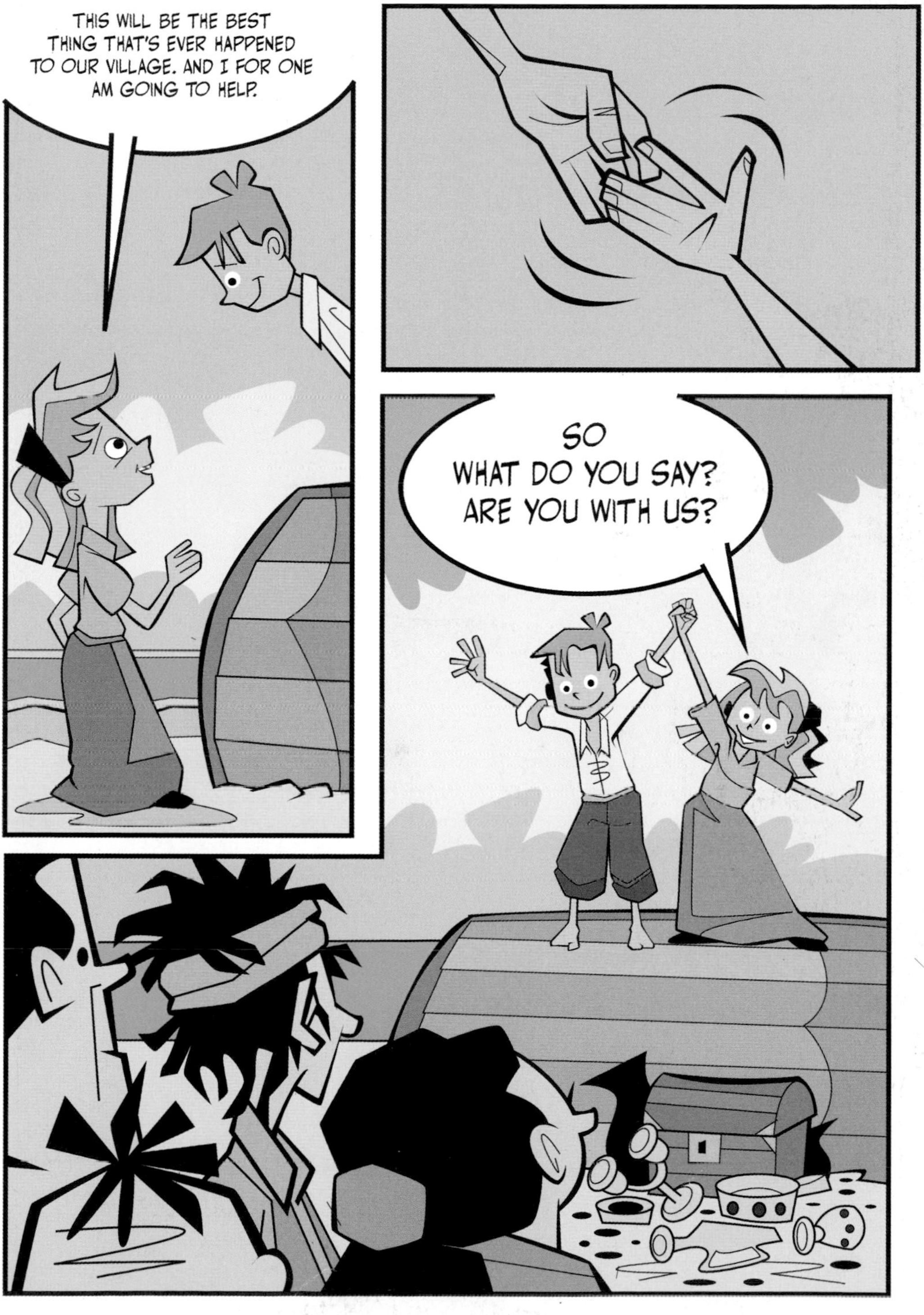
THIS WILL BE THE BEST THING THAT'S EVER HAPPENED TO OUR VILLAGE. AND I FOR ONE AM GOING TO HELP.
SO WHAT DO YOU SAY? ARE YOU WITH US?

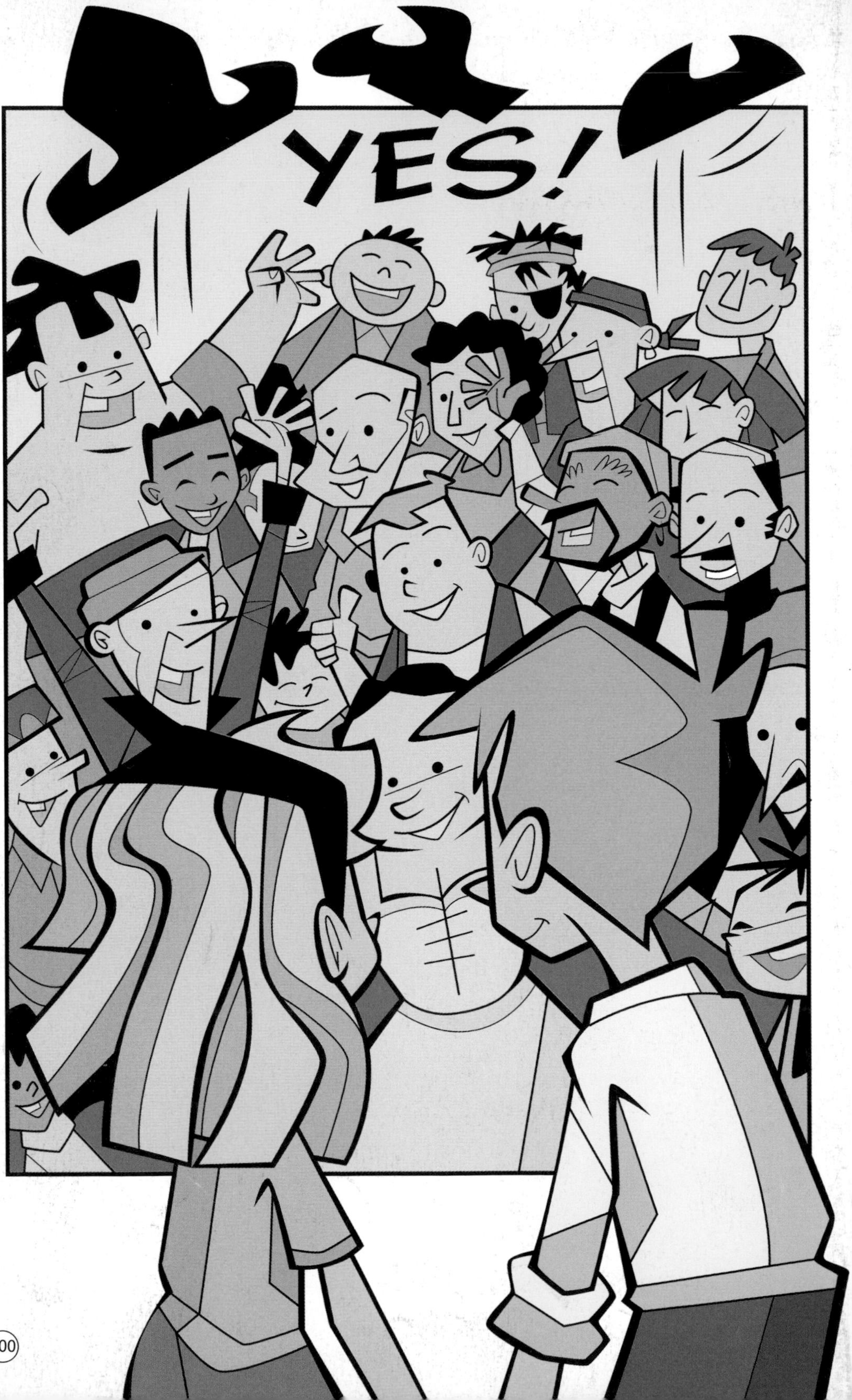
YES!

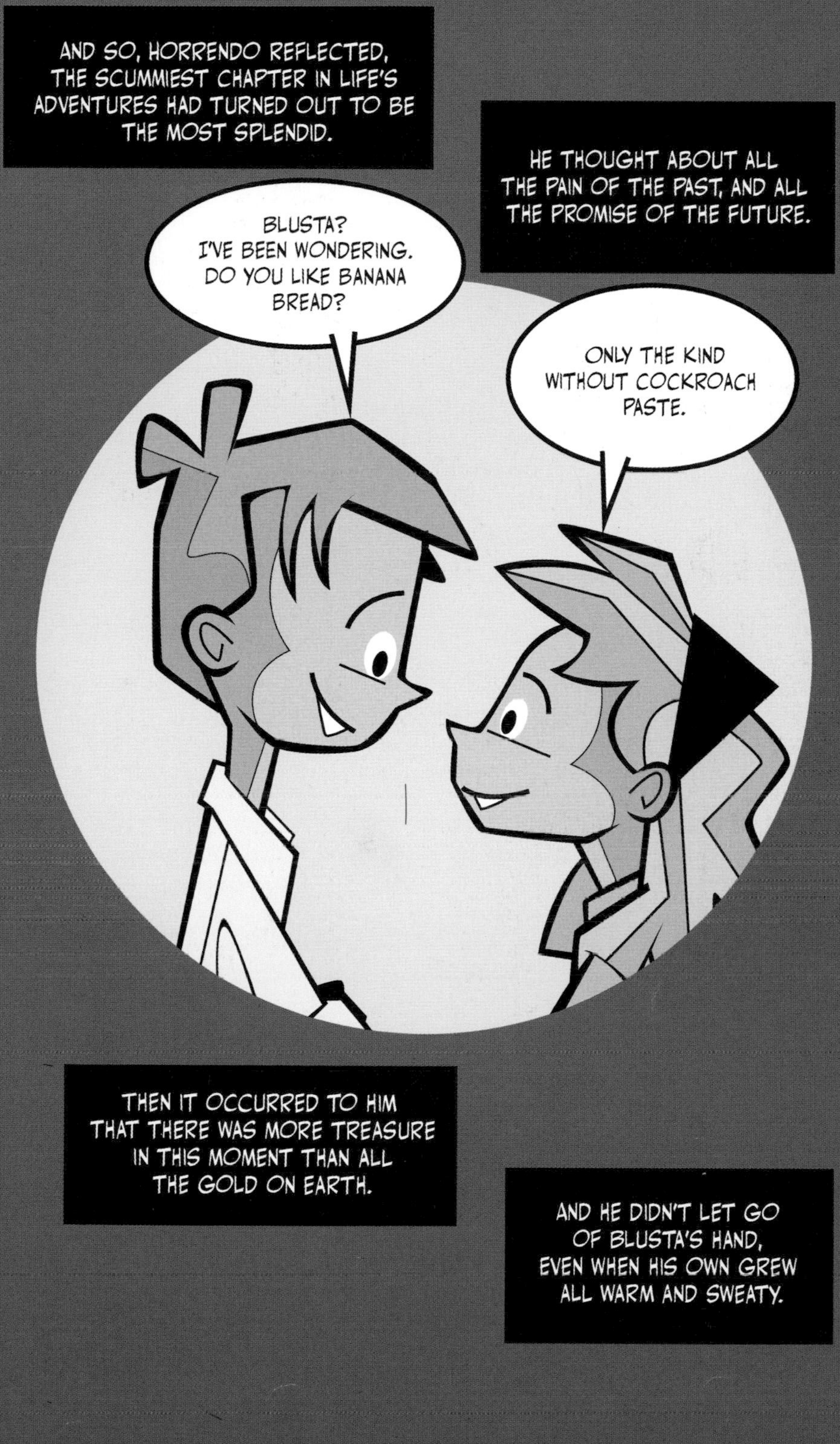
AND SO, HORRENDO REFLECTED, THE SCUMMIEST CHAPTER IN LIFE'S ADVENTURES HAD TURNED OUT TO BE THE MOST SPLENDID.
HE THOUGHT ABOUT ALL THE PAIN OF THE PAST, AND ALL THE PROMISE OF THE FUTURE.
BLUSTA? I'VE BEEN WONDERING. DO YOU LIKE BANANA BREAD?
ONLY THE KIND WITHOUT COCKROACH PASTE.
THEN IT OCCURRED TO HIM THAT THERE WAS MORE TREASURE IN THIS MOMENT THAN ALL THE GOLD ON EARTH.
AND HE DIDN'T LET GO OF BLUSTA'S HAND, EVEN WHEN HIS OWN GREW ALL WARM AND SWEATY.

ABOUT THE AUTHOR AND ILLUSTRATOR

Anna Fienberg is an Australian author who has written many popular and award-winning books for children of all ages, including the *Tashi* series. *Horrendo's Curse* was first published as a novel, and it was an Honour Book in the 2003 Australian Children's Book Council awards.

Rémy Simard is a cartoonist, commercial artist, and award-winning author and illustrator. His work has appeared in a wide variety of magazines, newspapers, and books, including two nonfiction books published by Annick Press, *Duped!* and *Robbers!* He lives in Montreal, Quebec.

ALSO ILLUSTRATED BY RÉMY SIMARD:

ROBBERS!
True Stories of the World's Most Notorious Thieves
by Andreas Schroeder
illustrated by Rémy Simard
paperback $12.95 • hardcover $21.95

"a fascinating and informative look at eight famous robbers and robberies around the world that will be enjoyed by many different readers. Highly recommended" —*CM Reviews*

DUPED!
True Stories of the World's Best Swindlers
by Andreas Schroeder
illustrated by Rémy Simard
paperback $12.95 • hardcover $21.95

"a fun lesson on how the masses can be made into fools." —*School Library Journal*
" it's hard to imagine a more kid-friendly piece of non-fiction." —*Booklist*